I0614897

For John Skipp

It's because of you that my stories ever had a chance to come to life on film. Thank you for believing in me, and just for being one bad ass motherfucker. I love you, man!

WET AND SCREAMING

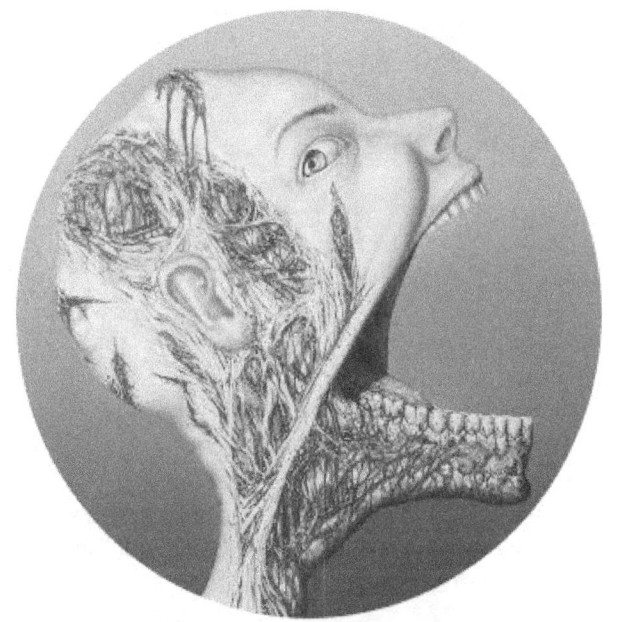

SHANE MCKENZIE

deadite
press

deadite press

DEADITE PRESS
P.O. BOX 10065
PORTLAND, OR 97296
www.DEADITEPRESS.com

AN ERASERHEAD PRESS COMPANY
www.ERASERHEADPRESS.com

ISBN: 978-1-62105-189-3

All stories copyright © 2015 Shane McKenzie

Cover art copyright © 2015 Suzzan Blac
www.SUZZANB.com

All rights reserved. No part of this book may be reproduced or
transmitted in any form or by any means, electronic or mechanical,
including photocopying, recording, or by any information storage and
retrieval system, without the written consent of the publisher, except
where permitted by law.

Printed in the USA.

Acknowledgements:

There are just too many people to thank. You all know who you are. I love each and every one of you.

We all come into the world wet and screaming, but only the lucky ones leave it that way.

CONTENTS

AN INTRODUCTION BY JEN AND SYLVIA SOSKA

Intimate.
Disgusting.
Grotesque.
Horrifying.

These are the words that go through the reader's mind as they are treated to a very revealing look into author Shane McKenzie's psyche in a series of deep and moving short stories. In many cases, you will be moved by how the material gets under your skin, but that is half the fun of these visceral and unique stories.

The fact remains that Shane has the inherent ability to take routine from the everyday and bring it into the fantastical and hilarious—from dead kittens at a Hoarder's home or how fucking hot Jessica Rabbit was/is/always will be. These stories are totally relatable but always manage to venture into a pitch black macabre dark satire.

How often do you read literature where a liposuction creature feeds on a horrendously obese man after the author explains his obsession with the gluttonous in a peek behind the curtain honest forward? That is the type of fantastic artist that Shane is. You get in on the inner thoughts that birthed these strange and disturbing tales.

Wet and Screaming reminds me of what it would be like to have a friend with a foul mouth and batshit crazy imagination make up Goosebump stories for adults. He brings these odd characters to life with rich, unrelenting, and very adult situations. You feel you know or have at least met these people in passing which makes the tortured tales just that more fascinating.

In today's media, where there is an onslaught of unoriginality in the horror genre, it is a breath of fresh air and extremely encouraging for fans of the genre to be able to still find such genuine passion for the medium and true artistic insanity. And we mean that as the highest compliment, Shane.

You are fucking nuts.

Please don't ever get better.

MY OBESSION WITH OBESITY

I'm not a chubby chaser. Not that there's anything wrong with that.

I'm thankful as hell they exist, because if not, I might not be married.

So, here's the thing. I didn't actually mean to write so much about eating and obese characters in my early fiction. It just sort of happened. Someone had to actually pull me aside and tell me that eating was in just about every single thing I was writing at the time.

I made up an excuse that I wrote about eating because every single person could relate to that. We all gotta eat, right? And that we are scared of monsters because of our fear of being eaten. I don't know how true that is, but it sounded like a good answer at the time.

I may have been full of shit with that answer. I don't think I was ready to admit I was using my writing to defeat old demons still fucking me in the brain with their forked phalluses. I needed to write about it. Writing about it was basically venting for me. Same with acne. I had a nasty acne problem growing up. And look at that...I've got a book called *Pus Junkies*.

I've struggled with my weight my whole life. I was the kid who went swimming with his shirt on. And when I actually took my shirt off in front of anyone, I would suck my gut in so hard I damn near passed out.

And I'll be honest, my family's got a history of weight problems. I spent a good deal of time at buffets, which was the inspiration for my novel *All You Can Eat*. As a kid, I never really thought about it. Didn't notice it, I guess. But once I was in school, the teasing started. Not just about my own chubbiness, but my family's also. And shit, man, that

13

hurt. I started feeling embarrassed of my family. Didn't want the other kids to see them pick me up from school, or see me in public with them. Which is ridiculous, but at the time, these were very real feelings I had.

I remember one time my uncle was supposed to substitute teach at my high school. And I asked him if he'd use a fake name. I mean…how fucked up is that? And I didn't just think it, I looked him in the eye and asked him to do that.

So, I have a lot of weird feelings about the obesity thing. And when I started writing stories, those feelings just sort of oozed out of me like hot grease.

I mention all of this because the following story is, you guessed it, about obesity. When I wrote it, I was already aware that I was doing too much of that, so I told myself this story would be my last one. So I went fucking nuts with it. It's a strange, twisted story about liposuction. And while writing it, I imagined all the fat getting sucked out of my head. Or eaten out…

I hope you enjoy my story "Fat Slob." I promise I won't write about eating or gluttony ever again.

Unless I think of something awesome.

FAT SLOB

"I'm not kidding, Sam. This…this has to stop. I can't take it anymore. I, I just can't."

Sam struggled to keep his body balanced on its right side as Beth ran the sponge over his soiled skin. The soap stung the bedsores on his hips, and he grimaced, hissed, lost his balance and rolled onto his back.

"Ow! Goddammit…" Beth's hand was pinned underneath him, and she yanked, slapped his stomach with her free hand. "Shit, Sam… Get the hell off me…!"

"I'm trying, okay?" He grabbed a handful of bed sheet, pulled, was able to lift his left side just enough for her to slip her hand away. The sores ignited with pain, and he tried to readjust his position to ease it some, but he couldn't manage it.

Beth stood above the bed, shaking her head and rubbing the back of her hand with gentle fingers. Sweat ran down her forehead and her eyes were half-closed, crosshatched with red veins.

It felt like someone held a lighter against his hips and lower back. A low moan oozed from his mouth and he continued to rock his body, but got nowhere. His stomach fat swayed like a water bed. "Beth…ah shit…please. Please help me. Lift me up so I can…*fuck! Fuck just help me!*"

She shook her head and stared at him, nose wrinkled and lips curled. Like he wasn't a human fucking being. Just some beached whale clinging to a shred of life while the sun baked him alive, dried him out.

"Beth. *Beth please!*"

"No. No more. This has to stop. I'm not kidding this time. I'm done. Finished." She picked up the sponge and tossed it into the plastic bucket full of brown-tinted water like beef broth. "I feel like I'm going crazy here, Sam. I won't let you drag me down with you…not anymore."

Sam rocked his body, whimpered as the pain burned his skin. "Okay…okay, I get it. Just please…please help me."

She sighed, tears rolling from her eyes as she shoved him with all of her strength. Her nails dug into the rolls of fat on his side, but that pain was nothing compared to the agony of the bedsores. A frustrated growl seeped from between her teeth, and just then, Sam felt something shift under him, a roll of fat maybe unfolding, and relief swept over him. Beth let go, wept into her forearms as if her hands were too filthy after coming into contact with his repulsive body.

"Beth…I…" Sweat coated every inch of him, rolling down his body and turning the spaces between his overlapping fat into salty rivers and lakes. He panted, still recovering from the exertion of moving his massive body. His tongue felt swollen, wouldn't allow the space in his mouth to breathe and speak at the same time.

"Save it. Really, I don't need to hear it." The tears poured now. "All of this," she said, waving her hands over his bed and sweating rolls of flesh, "all of this destroyed us. Not the car accident, not the bankruptcy. It's you, Sam. And your fucking selfishness. I admit I may have enabled you through the past few years…but this is just…it's just too much."

Sam's heart twisted in his chest, and he fought to sit up, to face his wife with some form of dignity, but he couldn't do it. His bulbous belly made it impossible to bend that way, so he gave up, his skin burning red, the sweat sizzling on top. He relaxed his body and sunk back down into the damp mattress. "My selfishness? It's because of those things… *because* of them I'm this way. *You know that better than anybody!*"

She ran her fingers through her hairline, sighed, leaned her head back and stared at the ceiling. The television played in the background—muffled studio audience laughter bursting from the speakers every few seconds.

"And me? What about me? You think Lily's accident didn't hurt me? Didn't fucking *kill* me?" She paced in front of the bed, and though the rest of her body moved, her eyes stayed pinned to Sam. "And that was our restaurant, Sam. Us. Me and you, remember? When it went under, I felt it just as fucking hard as you. And look at me. *Look at me!*"

Sam's eyes moved from his glistening stomach to his wife's eyes. It was like staring into the sun.

"I didn't just give up. I wanted to, believe me, I wanted to. But I stayed strong. For our family, or what's left of it. *For you!* And you..." The ferocity tightening her face sunk, and she collapsed on the end of the bed. Far enough away that Sam couldn't reach her. "And you just let yourself go, threw in the towel. What about me? Did you forget about your wife? You're a fucking coward."

Sam tried to hold back his tears, but there were too many of them, and they sliced clean trails down his grimy cheeks. He sniffled, cleared his throat. "I can admit it. You're stronger than me. I didn't mean for this to happen... You think I fucking asked for this? *For this?*" He slapped himself on the stomach, watched the hairy, filthy flesh jiggle endlessly. "I'm just so...I'm broken, Beth. Fucking broken, used up."

"You're such an asshole."

She stood back up from the bed and disappeared into the closet. Scraping sounds like she was sharpening knives in there, some pounding and frustrated cussing. After what felt like a year, she strolled back into the room, bag packed.

"You say you didn't mean for this to happen? You didn't mean to get so fucking fat that you can't even roll yourself over? You're disgusting! I can hardly look at you anymore. And you for damn sure meant for it to happen. I sure as shit didn't shovel all that junk down your throat. I didn't chain you to the bed and force you to watch TV all fucking day. So fuck you, Sam. I'm gone."

She stomped toward the bedroom door.

"Beth, wait. Please don't leave. I swear to God, if you leave, I'll kill myself! I'll kill myself *tonight!*"

She stopped midstride, blew another heavy sigh into the thick air of the bedroom. Her claw-like hand, pink from the scald of the hot water in the bucket, shook as it reached out, clamped shut over the corner of a stainless steel picture frame on the dresser.

She turned and faced Sam, wiped her eyes with the back of her wrist. "You see this man? This one, the one in the picture here? That's who I love, Sam. Not this fucking hog in front of me." She tapped her nail hard against the glass. "This man. I miss him so bad. I love him. I'd do anything for him."

Sam glared at the photo, him and his wife, their faces full of teeth as they smiled, Lily between them smiling equally as wide. That was the year she turned sixteen, the year she got her license—the last year of her life. In the background was their diner, *his* diner.

"I'm right here. Please don't leave me. I'll change, I'll do my best to change. Okay? I need your help, baby."

Her head shook slowly, and she frisbeed the frame at him. It struck him in the side, and he yelped, his body jiggling from the impact.

"I'm going to my sister's. If you—"

"Your sister's? That fucking devil worsh—"

"Don't you dare say it. You of all fucking people have no right to judge anybody. You understand me?" Her voice quivered and her pointing finger shook. "Unless the man in that photo comes back, you won't ever see me again."

She turned and swiftly stomped away.

"Beth! *Beth!* Please don't leave me! *I swear to god I'll be dead when you get back! Beth!*" With every scrap of energy he could muster, with every drop of will he had, he rocked his body, left to right, the mattress squeaking and threatening to disintegrate beneath the weight of him.

The door slammed, rattling the walls.

"No! No, come back!" No matter how hard he rocked, he wasn't going anywhere, and frustration coursed through him like flesh eating bacteria. "Fuck...*fuck! Fffuuuck!*" Meaty fists slammed into the mattress, padded knuckles cracked against the wall above his head. The bedsores throbbed with agony, but he didn't care anymore. Nothing mattered if Beth was gone.

She's right. I'm worthless. A fat fucking slob...and I don't deserve her. I don't deserve to live.

Sam reached under his head and yanked the pillow out, held it above his face with both hands. The pillow felt like damp bread, soaked completely through with sweat and filth. It shook in his hands, then he slammed it to his face, held it there, pressed harder as the air in his lungs ran out. Feet kicking, springs squeaking, studio audience laughing.

He pulled the pillow away from his face and threw it across the room.

You're a fucking coward.

Sam grabbed handfuls of his hair and wept. The photo of the family he used to have, the man he used to be, bit into his side. He clutched it, held it against his forehead, and sobbed.

***

A knock at the door.

Sam didn't even realize he'd fallen asleep until the knock shattered his dream like a plate against the wall. But it wasn't the knock of a person, not the universal three rhythmic knuckle-raps.

Just one loud knock.

Crack!

Sam flinched, then winced at the pain in his hips. Some made-for-TV movie played on the screen, but without the pillow to prop his head, he couldn't see which one.

He held his breath as he waited for another knock—it didn't come. But there was another sound.

Scraaape.

Back and forth over the door, almost as if someone was writing their name into the wood with their fingernail. He was quickly reminded of how Lily used to do that with her sparklers on Fourth of July and New Year's, waving them around the air like magic wands.

"Beth? Beth, is that you?" He could tell it was coming from the front door, but it might as well have been in Alaska. All he could do was stretch his neck and stare out the bedroom

19

doorway. The living room sat empty on the other side. The television threw splashes of vibrating color onto the walls, deepening the shadows of everything else in the room.

The pulsating sores called his attention, and he whimpered lightly. Some kind of gun fight ensued from the television, and Sam swiped his hand over the damp bed sheets until he found the remote, then cut off the TV.

Glass broke from somewhere in the house. He clenched his teeth, pushed with all his might to sit up, but fell back unsuccessfully. "Hello? Wh-who's there?"

With the TV powered off, the throbbing of his pulse was like a deep bass. The glass sounded like it came from the kitchen window, but he couldn't be sure. He tried to swallow, but his throat had dried up, all the moisture in his body now oozing through his pores and soaking his jaundiced Fruit of the Loom shirt and swim trunks.

"Whoever's out there, I already called the fucking cops! And I got a gun in here." His eyes stayed glued to the doorway, his head turned and held painfully to the left. "You get the fuck out now before I put a bullet in your ass!"

A flutter of shadow. On the floor, just outside the door. The shadow grew larger, darker as he watched it, as if whoever was casting it were stepping closer and closer to his bedroom.

Sam's breaths came in ragged gasps, and he struggled with his bulk to sit up, at least give himself a chance before whoever this was did whatever it was they came into his home to do. Perspiration gleamed over his skin like pork grease. Each mucus-coated breath rattled out of his throat, and he whimpered as his weight refused to comply.

Without the television, the room was too dark to see the features of the intruder. But from the size of the figure now standing motionless in his doorway, facing him, he knew it was a child. A young child—a toddler. Sam thought for sure he was dreaming, could think of no feasible way or reason an infant would break into his home through a window.

The kid sounded sick, a bad cold maybe. A low rasping sound emitted from the darkness, along with a sort of wet choking. Something pitter pattered onto the laminate flooring, followed closely by a slight sizzling noise.

"Who are you? Are you in…some kind of trouble?" Sam figured if somehow this was real, and he was awake, then whoever this kid was, his parents were probably looking for him. But Sam was useless to the child, could do nothing more than stare.

The kid, a boy from the outline of him, only stood, gawking, breathing. That dripping sound continued, and Sam wondered if the kid might be hurt, bleeding maybe.

"Where are your parents? How did you…?" The words trailed off, turned into a whispered gasp as the boy stepped forward. Just enough moonlight seeped in through the blinds to illuminate the boy's face, and Sam bucked in the bed, begged his body to supply him with the adrenaline he needed to get to his feet, run for his life.

The boy—the thing—took slow steps toward the bed. Two purple tongues writhed from the center of a circular maw that took up most of its face, lined with serrated, pointy teeth. A milky substance coated its jaws, its tongues, and globs of it splashed onto the floor. Wisps of white smoke drifted up as it sizzled. Its eyes, two tiny black pinpoints, sat above the massive mouth.

"No…get away from me. Don't you…*don't you come near me!*" Sam did everything he could to tilt his body away from the creature, but all he could do was thrash in place as the thing crept closer and closer.

Its skin was the color and consistency of chicken fat, with purple veins webbing the flesh like shattered glass. It reached out with tiny clawed hands, pink and fuzzy like a rat's, that soggy choking sound splattering from its mouth. The tiny fingers gripped the mattress, acidic saliva burning holes into the sheets as the creature lifted itself onto the bed.

The wooden bed frame creaked and the mattress springs squealed—the bed felt like it would crumble in on itself at any moment. Sam flapped his arms, kicked his legs, rolled his head, but could only scream as the thing crawled onto his stomach.

The saliva oozed from its mouth, each dot that hit Sam's skin like a cigarette being put out on his flesh. The fat engulfing and weighing down his body shook as he fought.

The thing made a sound, almost as if trying to talk, though its hellish mouth made it impossible to form words. The sound was high-pitched, a sort of coo-like gurgle, then its tongues slid across Sam's gut, burning like wet flat irons. Sam's skin hissed, popped. The air smelled of bacon.

"Aaannngh! No...no God...!"

The tongues slithered across his belly in a circular motion. Oozing globs of mucus poured into the center of the searing circle like liquid magma. With his fingers and toes spread wide, his teeth bared and his eyes squeezed shut, Sam's body thrashed. The sound of his flesh crackling and spitting as it was cooked, along with the smell and savory flavor, assaulted Sam's senses. He choked on his own saliva as he tried to scream, his eyes now wide open and swollen, but the pain soaked up his bellow like a sponge.

The creature sat up, its claws digging into Sam's stomach as it clutched a fat roll. It sucked in its tongues like two tape measures, the eel-like ropes disappearing into its throat. It made another choking sound, sputtering and baritone, then lowered its face into the agonizing patch its tongues and mucus had cooked.

The veins in Sam's neck and face bulged, muscles tightened as the pinching, tearing pain brought him to tears. He felt every bite, every tooth as the creature fed on the yellow and pink fat inside of him, its head rolling as it ate and slurped. Blood rushed from the basketball-sized crater on Sam's belly, rolled over his sides and mixed with the sweat soaked into the sheets. Dollops of warm fat slapped the mattress, the wall, Sam's face.

He reached forward, tried to grip the creature with clawed fingers. Its skin was slimy like a jellyfish, and Sam couldn't get a hold of it. Every second, the thing plunged deeper into him, feasted on blubber like a cookie-cutter shark. Its little pink digits gripped the edges of the wound as it smashed its face in deeper.

22

Sam roared with agony, gave up on trying to pry the thing off and just wept, wishing for death to hurry up and claim him. The thing gurgled from within him, gorging itself on an avalanche of lard.

Sam, with eyes flittering, lifted his head just enough to catch another look at the thing consuming him. It had its head nearly submerged in fat, but its beady black eyes were aimed right at Sam, unblinking, glistening with moisture.

No words would come, though Sam tried to form them. He gave one final gasp before the blackness came.

***

Sam's eyes slid open, thick with crust. He smacked his mouth, reached up and wiped the morning goop from his lips. His brain tickled as if it was injected with static, and he couldn't get his thoughts together as the grogginess slowly dissolved.

Beth.

She left me. And I can't blame her.

Sam sat up, leaned his head against the wall. Then he paused, blinked, shook his head and let out a small titter.

I sat up! I fucking sat up!

And then the rest of the night's events slithered into his memory, and he shrieked, searched the room for the tiny fat-eating creature.

Nobody there. He ran his hands over his stomach, and though there was some soreness, the gaping hole the thing had carved from his belly was gone. The flesh on his belly seemed smoother, almost like scar tissue, and hairless.

Something poked him on the left love handle, and he reached down, was actually able to turn his body, and picked up the picture frame. He scooted back, sat up further, and though he still couldn't lift himself all the way up, he got far enough to lean the back of his head on the wall. The bedsores were still there, but after the excruciating pinching and burning of being eaten alive, they seemed slightly less intense. But just slightly. He winced, hissed, pursed his lips and adjusted himself.

Lily's smile beamed out at him from behind the thin plate of glass, and he ran his finger over her face, sniffled, clenched his teeth.

I'm sixteen, Daddy. All my friends are getting their license, why not me?

Sir, there's been an accident.

The glass cracked as Sam squeezed the frame, nearly broke it in half. The smile on Beth's face was now a broken, misshapen grimace, and he thought it wasn't too different a look that she'd given him before storming out of the house.

He threw the frame across the room. His thoughts roared back to the small creature that had burrowed into him.

What in the flying fuck was that thing?

Punishment.

It's punishment for letting my family down. For allowing my daughter to...my wife...

He ran his palm over the smooth, pink skin of his belly. His toes poked up over the fat mound of his midsection like mountains in the distance. Sam couldn't remember the last time he'd actually seen them. Pale, devoid of color, layered with dead skin. The nails long, sallow, as thick as lemon cookies.

The memory of the pain was fresh in his mind—the way the creature fried his flesh with its saliva, its dual tongues basting and spreading the acidic marinade just before biting into him, cutting out a hole, and sucking, sucking, sucking at the fat inside. The creamy center. With his head resting against the wall, with his bloodless toes wiggling on the other side of the bed, he was almost thankful.

He tried to turn himself, maybe get his feet on the ground, but he couldn't quite do it. *Jesus Christ*, he thought. *How the fuck did it come to this?*

Movement. The sting of the bedsores intensified for a moment as something slithered against them. Sam rocked himself to the side just a bit, tried to stretch his hand toward the sensation, but couldn't reach.

Then he felt the claws gripping him as the creature

crawled out from under the warmth of his back, scuttled over the mound of his body, and settled on his belly. The sunlight cutting lines through the dusty air splashed over the creature, its skin translucent, wet. The thing looked fatter, juicier, and its tongues darted out from the crater of its mouth, dripped burning dots over Sam's skin.

"No! No…don't. *Ungh. Please stop!*"

The creature coughed, chortled, then scurried in the other direction, toward the hanging jowls of Sam's lower belly. Its tiny pink feet kicked. Its spinal cord pressed tight against the skin of its back, looked on the verge of breaking through.

Sam leaned his head back, took long, deep breaths as the tongues slid over his bulbous flab again. The burning was back, more intense on the sensitive flesh of his underbelly. His legs got to kicking, arms flailing. A shriek rocketed from his throat, tore the flesh of his esophagus as it roared out. That salty pork scent filled the room again, and Sam was disgusted by how it made his mouth water.

Sucking. Moaning. Chewing.

Though he knew it was useless, his hands reached out, hoped to grab hold of the creature and smash it against the wall, make this hell stop. But his fingers tickled air and nothing else. The thing slurped, choked, slurped. Sam banged the back of his head against the wall repeatedly as he sobbed and bucked. Blood poured over his groin, his thighs, warm and sticky.

The creature tunneled into him, burrowed deeper into the cave of his stomach, flooded with jiggling fat. Its tiny pink feet wiggled in the air, its head and upper torso already submerged.

Sam gasped, his body spasming as the thing pushed deeper. His head slammed into the wall again, hard, causing bits of sheet rock to rain down on him. Breaths refused to come, no matter how hard he sucked for air. Hooked fingers dug into the mattress. Sweat and blood and liquid fat poured out of him.

Unconsciousness tried to sweep him away again, rescue him into some faraway dreamland where he was still a chef at his own diner, where Lily still sat at the counter and sipped Cherry Pepsi, munching on French fries covered in country gravy. Where he was happy.

But the pain kept him in that room, on that saturated mattress. Tears ran down the sides of his face, got soaked up by his sweaty hair. He could only whimper, suck in oxygen when the pain allowed it.

I deserve this. I deserve worse.

He watched as his stomach deflated, and suddenly, he could see his feet, his shins. Loose, stretch-marked skin hung from the gaping hole. Electric, crackling anguish coursed through him, and he stared at the ceiling, chewed on his tongue for what seemed like a lifetime as the creature had its fill.

Then it emerged. Climbed out of his stomach cavity and shook off like a wet dog, spraying blood and fat all over.

Sam panted, his chest rattling as the labored breaths pushed in and out of him. He stared at the thing standing on his chest. Its face was coated with grease and blood, and it coughed, made a sound like a diseased cat coughing up a soggy hairball.

"Enough...please." Sam's tongue slid across his lips, but there was no moisture to dampen them. Just a dried out hunk of pink flesh scraping over chapped skin. "Please, please stop. I've had e-enough..."

The thing stood staring at him for another few seconds, then it turned back to the hole it had just created. Crawled on all fours, its now swollen body shaking as it moved. And it went straight for the excess skin and tissue hanging down from Sam's torso.

Sam turned his head, slammed his eyes shut. A hoarse cry exploded from his mouth as the creature's teeth tore into the loose flesh, biting chunks away bit by bit. He couldn't stop himself from weeping, and his body shook, convulsed as he was eaten.

The creature worked its way around the belly hole, biting and tearing and ripping and swallowing.

Jesus Christ, just kill me. Just fucking kill me already!

But the torture continued, death refusing to show its grinning face. When the burning returned, the sizzling of cooking flesh, Sam's eyes popped open. He hissed, whined, stared toward the pain.

The creature licked the wounds with its elongated purple tongues, twirling them over the hole and ragged, torn skin. Smoke and the smell of barbeque filled the air, and through the horror, Sam couldn't help but watch in awe as the wounds were cauterized by the saliva. The flesh was welded back together, the flesh pink and smooth where the wound once was.

Steam floated around the room, and Sam was so exhausted, he did nothing to stop the creature from squeezing itself back under him. It wiggled beneath his body, as if trying to get comfortable, then went still.

Racking sobs still sputtered from his mouth as sleep finally came to claim him.

He went willingly.

***

Knock knock knock

Sam's left eyelid unpeeled itself from the sticky orb beneath. Still on the bed, still in the bedroom.

Knock knock knock

He reached up and massaged his forehead, ran his fingers through his hair. A hot tingling swept over his body.

Beth? She's come home!

He sat up, all the way up. Shaking fingers ran over his smooth stomach. His back ached, his legs throbbed, but he could sit up.

Knock knock knock

"Hold on a minute! I'm…I'm coming!"

With his hands behind him and supporting him, he swung his swollen legs over the edge of the bed, set his feet on the cold floor. God it felt good to feel the floor under his feet. He turned to check for the creature, and it lay on the sunken mattress, curled into a ball. It turned its head at him, its movements slow and lazy. A viscous slime coated its gelatinous body. It laid its head down, readjusted its position, and slept.

Sam cupped his hands over his mouth. "Don't leave! I'm coming!"

Maybe she just forgot her key at her sister's house, Sam thought.

Her sister. He shuddered at the thought of that woman. Into some sick shit, crazy shit. Sam had refused to allow Lily to get anywhere near her, forbade her from spending any time with her aunt.

Knock knock knock

The knocking was harder, frustrated. Sam took a breath, rocked himself forward, but the moment his weight was on his legs, they crumbled beneath him, his face bouncing off the laminate panels. The taste of blood filled his mouth, and he clawed at the floor, pulling himself forward, determined to let his wife inside.

A wheelchair sat in the corner, where Beth had left it. An accident at the diner, Beth standing on the countertop to clean the cobwebs from the upper corner. Sam would never forget the sound of her leg snapping, the way she screamed. Lily had been hysterical, hands over her ears, head shaking as her mother hollered.

Sam climbed the metal of the chair, growled as he pulled himself up. By the time he had his posterior in the leather seat, he was so out of breath he had to sit there for a minute to catch it. Another series of the knocks at the door fueled him with a surge of energy, and he wheeled himself across the house.

He took a moment to comb his hair with his fingers, wiped the beads of sweat from his brow, sighed, then opened the door.

The brightness of the sun was like a shotgun blast to the eyes. The person standing on his front porch had the shape of a woman, but he could tell right away it wasn't Beth. She stepped forward, leaned down, and smiled into his face.

"Hello, sir. I'd like to talk to you about your soul."

"What?" Images of the creature gorging itself on his fat splattered into his mind. *My soul? Is that thing...is it after my...?*

The woman handed him a pamphlet, a picture of a cross on the front of it. "How is your relationship with Jesus Christ?"

Sam chuckled, tossed the pamphlet back at the woman. "Take your Jesus and the both of you get the fuck off my property."

The woman's jaw worked up and down as if chewing a wad of invisible bubble gum, and before she had a chance to say a word, Sam slammed the door. There was some muffled mumbling on the other side, then it grew fainter until finally disappearing.

Sam struggled to turn the chair back around, had to catch his breath and wipe away another sheet of sweat. Hanging from the wall just to his right was a long mirror, the mirror Beth always used for those last minute adjustments to hair or makeup before heading out the door. Sam furrowed his brow as he and his reflection had a staring contest.

His stomach, what used to be an endless mountain of jiggling, dimpled flesh, was reduced to a flat, proportionate lower torso. He ran his fingers across it, could actually feel muscle beneath the skin. But the rest of him hadn't changed. His face, chest, arms, and legs all still bulged with obesity.

Sam reached up, grabbed a handful of chins, squeezed.

I look ridiculous. A fucking circus freak.

A series of clicks made him swing his head toward the bedroom door.

It's not finished yet.

The creature, plump and slow, trudged down the hall toward him. Its tongues whipped the air, splashing the walls with hissing liquid.

Sam clawed at the wheels, trying to turn the chair back around, get that front door open again.

Why the fuck didn't I escape when I had the chance?

He struggled to turn himself around, all the while the creature picking up speed. In the next instant, it collided with the back of his head, latched onto the spongy skin. It bent down, lapped at the bulge of fat under his chin. They crashed to the ground together in a knot of fat and wet flesh.

Sam willed his legs to work, to lift him up and help him escape this endless nightmare. But they just lay there, limp and useless and layered in blubber.

And the creature fed.

***

Sam spooned sugar into his coffee cup, strolled toward the table sipping lightly at the scalding liquid. The creature lay in a blubbery heap in the middle of the living room.

A rattle at the door.

Sam stood, left his coffee at the table as he rushed toward the front hallway. He couldn't keep the smile from opening his face as Beth stepped inside, her back to him.

She stared at the door for a moment, hand still on the knob.

"Beth, you…you're back."

She flinched, looked to the ceiling and sighed before turning to face him. Her jaw went unhinged, eyes squinted. "My God…it actually… Jesus Christ, Sam, is that you?"

Sam rubbed the back of his head, shrugged. "I don't even know how to explain this. It's…ah shit." He chuckled, turned his head toward the sleeping thing on the carpet.

Beth looked over his shoulder, wrinkled her nose. "Bleck, that thing's nasty." And then she stepped into him, wrapped her arms around him, nuzzled him. "God, how long's it been since I could wrap my arms all the way around you? You feel *so* good."

Jesus, she's handling this well.

Sam hadn't been able to stop looking at himself in the mirror since the creature had finished its liposuction job on him. His skin was smooth, and besides a little pinkness and some tenderness, he was unscathed.

Beth ran her hand over his chest, stomach, face. "Can I…can I see?"

Sam lifted his shirt. Beth's fingertips ran over his skin, sending tingles over the surface of his flesh. A wide smile pulled her mouth, and she leaned in and kissed him, hard and passionate. When she pulled her face away, it was wet with tears.

"Oh God, Sam. I've missed you so much."

He reached out, grabbed her face with both palms. "I'm sorry, baby. You don't deserve the way I've treated you."

They held each other for a few minutes, kissing and squeezing. Beth pulled away, looked into the living room again.

"It's disgusting…"

Sam nodded, then scrunched his forehead. "Why don't you seem at all surprised by any of this? I thought I'd lost my mind. Thought I was hallucinating. But you…I don't know, it's like you expected this shit."

She pursed her lips, trudged past Sam into the living room. The toe of her shoe nudged the creature, and it coughed, sputtered, but could barely lift its head. The blue veins covering its body bulged thick, throbbed rhythmically.

"Sam…please don't hate me. You have to understand. I, I just wanted my husband back. I couldn't watch you kill yourself anymore and…and—"

"What the hell are you talking about?"

She sat on the couch, eyes pinned to the moaning creature. Sam stayed standing in front of her, his eyes jumping from her pinched face to the chubby pile of inflating and deflating lard. The memories of his pain rode his flesh, and he shuddered, crossed his arms.

"It was my sister. I asked her to do it, and she did. She only wanted to help—"

"Your sister? And she did what exactly?" Sam already knew the answer to that question, though it still didn't make any sense. *I should have fucking known that bitch did this to me.*

"I told her how depressed you'd become, how you couldn't even roll over in bed without my help anymore. She told me about…about a way to help you. And Sam, it worked."

"It worked? Do you know what that little fucking thing did to me? Three days, Beth. *Three fucking days!* It ate me alive. Cut me right the fuck open and chewed the fat right out of me." He collapsed to his backside, cringed as he stared at the creature beside him.

"I'm sorry. But I didn't know what else to do."

Sam shook his head, wiped his eyes. Hell yes he was pissed at her, pissed that she would allow her sister to get involved, but at the same time, she was right. It *had* worked. He was a new man, even slimmer than he used to be when Lily was alive.

"Well, it's over now. The thing can't even move. It was hell, but—"

"No. It's not over. That's why I'm here."

His stomach sank and he glared at his wife with hard eyes. "What the hell are you talking about?"

She reached into her purse, pulled out a red envelope. Her finger traced the envelope's border, upper teeth clamped over her bottom lip. "Here. She told me to give this to you. Said I couldn't read it."

Sam hesitated, then reached out and plucked it from her grasp. Then she stood from the couch and started down the hallway.

"Wait a minute. Just…just hold on. This is insane. I don't know how much more of this I can take."

She turned back toward him, leaned down and kissed him. "All I know is that I was supposed to give you that, and that I shouldn't come back for another three days at least."

"Three days? You just fucking got here!"

"Something to do with a ritual. You have to complete it, or all of this was for nothing. Do whatever that letter says. Promise you will."

Hot rage roared through his bloodstream, but he looked into his wife's soft, hazel eyes and could only nod. "I promise."

"Good. I'll be back, baby, and then our lives can start again. Fresh." She hurried down the hall, and once she reached the front door, she turned back one more time. "I love you, Sam." And then she was gone.

Sam could only clutch the envelope, terrified of what it would say. *What else do you want from me, you crazy fucking bitch?*

The creature choked, spat wads of thick, yogurt-like substance onto the carpet. Slime coated its skin like a dead fish. Had a smell like earthworms in wet soil.

Sam licked his lips, and with shaking hands, tore the envelope open. Only a single sheet of paper inside.

He opened it, stared at the two words scribbled in bleeding black ink. A squeaky giggle tickled its way out of his throat.

Eat it.

Beth's kiss still burned on his lips, her smile chiseled into his eyes. It felt so good to have her wrap her arms around him, tell him she loved him. He knew he couldn't let her down.

Family pictures stared out of hung frames on the living room walls. Lily at all stages of life urged him on, pleaded with him to finish this thing.

The creature rolled over, its belly bulging, tongues hanging uselessly on either side of its head. The milky fluid sputtered from its fang-lined mouth, but had lost its acidic properties. It splattered harmlessly to the carpet as the thing took rattling, phlegmy breaths.

Eat it.

Three days, he thought. Beth said she'd be back in three days. During the whole ordeal, Sam hadn't eaten a thing. Getting the fat scooped out of him and the excess skin bitten off little by little had taken away his appetite.

His stomach growled.

He hurried into the kitchen, pulled the butcher knife from the wooden block, and trotted back into the living room. The creature's black, beady eyes bore into him, but Sam only smiled.

He glanced at his audience of photographs. "Don't worry, girls. I won't let you down again."

The creature writhed and choked as the cutting began.

ARE YOU MOVING IT?

So I saw this movie called *Witchboard*. On HBO, I think, late at night when I was about ten. Two things intrigued me about that movie: the red-headed lady who steps out of the shower (not to be vulgar, but I think that might've been the first bush I'd ever seen) and the Ouija board itself.

My brother and I begged our mom for one. The board in the movie was super fancy, looked like it came straight from a witch's lair or something. I had no idea where to even begin looking for something like that. I think we were at K-Mart. I was looking at board games...and holy shit. Wedged between Mouse Trap and Operation was a Ouija board. I was convinced some supernatural power had set it there for me to find. A spirit so desperate for conversation, it reached out to a chubby Korean kid who hadn't even discovered the joy of his own penis yet. Never mind that Parker Brothers made the damn thing. There was magic afoot, and nobody could convince me otherwise!

After begging and getting my little brother to turn on the tears and promising my mom I'd be good and do all the chores in the universe, she caved and bought it for us.

We played with that damn thing every single night. I think I asked my brother every other minute if he was moving it. He swore he wasn't.

Here's the thing. Let's say I was right. It was a real spirit. It went through the trouble of putting that Ouija board where I could find it at K-Mart. And if the movie Ghost is any indication, it's hard to learn how to move objects in the real world. So this poor spirit went through ghost training (imagine a Rocky-esque montage sequence please). The board was placed. I found it. Convinced my mother to buy it.

And I asked that poor spirit the stupidest fucking

questions. I think "What kind of cheese does my fart most smell like" might have been one of them. It attempted to spell Limburger. It spelled it wrong. I'll get back to that in a second.

So, I was so blown away by this Ouija board that I started inviting friends over to try it. We'd sit around that thing for hours. Laughing until we damn near pissed our britches. There was one thing in common every time. I will also get back to that in a second.

We were all completely convinced this Ouija board was the real deal. So my best friend asked me to bring it to his house to show his mom. I did. And it didn't work. We were both crushed! I remember wondering if the spirit only wanted to talk to us kids. That maybe it was because his mom was an adult that it wouldn't work. She looked at us like we were retarded while we sat there on the living room floor, across from each other, both of our fingertips sitting on top of that plastic planchette, begging the spirit to say something. Anything!

I gave up on the board after that. I think it might still be sitting in my parents' closet somewhere. Years later, I don't remember what brought it up, but my brother and I started talking about the Ouija board again.

And do you know what that fuck ass told me?

"Yeah, I was moving it the whole time."

I won't lie. Even as I type this, I'm still kind of mad at him for that. I mean…we had an agreement! Don't move it. Let's just see…*let's just fucking see*…if this is real. If there really is a way to talk to ghosts. And he betrayed me.

You see, that's why the spirit couldn't spell Limburger. And that's why my brother was the only one in the room who figured out what it was trying to spell. And that's why it didn't work at my friend's house in front of his mom…because my deceptive brother wasn't there! And that thing every session that worked had in common? Yep. My brother's fingers were on the indicator. I'm re-mad now. Where is that fucker?

Shit, I wanted that Ouija board to be real. I think maybe I'll hit up K-Mart after work today.

YOU DON'T NEED EYES TO SEE US

Zane and David jerked their hands away from the planchette at the same moment the board crumbled into pieces. What had been hard wood a moment ago broke apart like a wet cracker, the letters melting and sizzling as they dripped off the board's now-misshapen surface.

Shelly's fingertips remained on the now pulsating planchette, and she bared her teeth as she tried to pull her hands away, but couldn't seem to budge them. Her eyes shot up and landed on her two younger brothers, and she had a look on her face like she was ready to ask for help, but a scream erupted from her throat instead. Her hair blew upward as if a strong breeze was wafting from the floor and her eyes rolled back until only the white showed, rimmed with red veins that bulged until bleeding tears scuttled down her cheeks. Her lips were pulled back so tight that they were white with pink vertical lines running down them. Zane could see almost all of her gums.

"Shelly?" Zane said, wiping his hands off on his shirt. The planchette had moved just before they had all flinched their fingertips away from it, writhed like a slimy toad. Cold, hard oak had become warm flesh in an instant— it felt soft like belly fat, sweaty and moist. "Quit messing around…"

David was on his feet now, approaching their older sister. When the foam boiled out of her mouth and spilled down the sides of her face and neck, David yelped, ran to Zane and clung to him.

Shelly kept screaming, but it was muffled, sounded far away, under water. Her fingers still rested on the throbbing, fleshy planchette. It beat like a heart, thick veins now crisscrossed just under the surface. Then it moved, crawled onto the tops of Shelly's hands, inched its way up her arms and neck, then slid into her gaping mouth. Her arms shot out to her sides as the thing wiggled its way down her throat, making her neck bulge out and cutting off what remained of her screams.

Zane backed away from his sister, holding David close. He didn't know what to do, didn't know how to help her. Once her neck had deflated and the planchette had worked its way deeper inside her, she stood, arms still stretched out at her sides in a crucifixion pose. Her toes wiggled as if each one had a mind of its own, stretching and bending in different directions.

"Zane...help her. We have to h-help her," David said, but was now standing behind Zane, clutching the back of Zane's 49ers shirt.

"Shelly!" It was all Zane could think to do. He called her name again, louder this time, but still not daring to step anywhere near her.

That thing is inside of her... This can't be happening!

Shelly didn't respond to any of his cries, just stood in place, her muscles tight, limbs outstretched and stiff. Her jaw worked up and down like a nutcracker, and her head rolled in circles.

Everything had happened right after Zane had written down the last letter of the message that the planchette—or the spirit—was revealing to them on the Ouija board. The three of them stared at the indicator with wide eyes as it slid across the board in a figure eight pattern. They swapped accusatory looks with one another as if one of them was moving it, even though all three of them swore they weren't. Zane didn't move it, he knew that much. Barely had his fingers on the wooden tear drop at all, just lightly placed them on the hard surface.

And then the message began. Letter by letter, their arms bending and unbending as their hands were led across the board in a chaotic pattern.

"Write it down!" Shelly had said. "Hurry up, Zane, or we're gonna miss it."

They had been prepared for something like this, had a

pen and paper handy. And Zane had jotted down each letter as they were revealed.

Now, his eyes coasted to the paper beside the table, his messy handwriting scribbled across its wrinkled surface.

I'm free.

I see you.

The Ouija board, now broken like a sheet of glass, each piece soggy and glistening like melting globs of cream, lay just in front of Shelly's wiggling toes. As Zane watched, the pieces began to move, slowly slithering across the carpet toward Shelly's feet. When the globules made contact with her skin, started shimmying up her legs like fat caterpillars, a spray of foam shot from Shelly's mouth, misted into the air. Her head jerked forward, chin smacking against her chest with a thud. Her eyes, now a dark and irritated red, landed right on Zane, and in that moment, she found her voice again, screamed louder than ever.

Zane flinched, backed away from her, didn't stop taking blind steps until his feet touched the cold linoleum of the kitchen. He didn't want to feel the carpet anymore as he watched the Ouija board pieces continue to crawl across the maggot-like fibers and onto his sister's body.

Shelly's skin began to change color. She had always been a pale girl—her skin had always reminded Zane of marshmallows. But now, it started to turn a brownish-yellow, almost like polished wood. Black letters and numbers and symbols formed on her skin like tattoos.

The Ouija board, Zane thought. *Her skin is...*

Shelly's body quivered, the corners of her mouth pulled down tight to reveal her bottom teeth and gums, the cords in her neck bulging like fingers under her skin wrapped around her throat. The room smelled like struck matches and burnt hair.

It didn't look like Shelly could move her body as it continued to change, her face now covered with symbols—a moon on one cheek and a sun on the other. The only thing she still seemed to have control over was her eyes, and her pupils rolled until they landed on Zane, quivering and dilated.

"H-help me..." she mumbled, her voice hoarse and pained. "He's in-inside of m-me..." And then another throat-ripping shriek belted from her mouth and her pupils rolled to the back of her head again.

Zane and David jumped together, David now crying, hiding his face in Zane's side. He was saying something, blowing hot breath into Zane's T-shirt, but Zane couldn't understand him, could barely hear him over Shelly's cries.

Their grandparents' bedroom door flew open and Grandpa stormed down the hall and into the living room. He wore striped boxer shorts, his left black sock, and nothing else. The small amount of hair on his head stuck up in all directions, and as he stomped into the room, he looked about ready to kill someone, his bulbous belly inflating and deflating, covered in curly white hair. He looked right at Zane, pointed a thick-knuckled finger at him.

"What in...what in the hell did you do, goddammit?" he growled, his voice deep and thick with sleep. "You know what goddamn time it is? You-you kids have no goddamn business staying up this—" As he was saying the words, he turned his attention from Zane to Shelly, and his sentence cut off.

"Grandpa," Zane said through his own sobs. "Help her... something's wrong!"

Shelly fell backward onto the carpet, her body still stiff, looked like a statue toppling over. Her mouth got to foaming again, and as the bubbles sizzled out from between her lips, it sounded like she was trying to speak, trying to form words, but it all came out as gurgled nonsense.

"Shelly," Grandpa started, all signs of anger gone from his voice. He dropped down beside her, placed his hand on her forehead, then yanked it away quickly as if he had touched a hot iron. "Jesus Christ!" He turned his face toward Zane and David. "What happened? What's that all over her skin?"

Zane tried to answer, but couldn't find any words. All he could do was watch as his sister struggled against whatever had gotten inside of her.

The spirit. It's the spirit that's in her now. And it's killing her!

"The Ouija board," David said, then sniffled and wiped the wetness from his face.

Grandpa furrowed his brow. "What? Zane, what's your brother talking about?"

"Ouija," Zane was finally able to get out. "Shelly found it. She said it was-was under her pillow. She thought I put it there as a j-joke, but I didn't. I swear I didn't."

"We were talking to a ghost," David said. "We were asking it stuff…and it was answering. And then…then it…"

"It went inside of her," Zane said, and had to look at his feet when Grandpa's hard eyes landed on him. "The wood part you put your fingers on…it was moving, and it crawled into her mouth. And then the board…it got on her. It moved too and it got all over her. That's why her skin—"

Shelly sat up. Her eyes were closed but she had a smile on her face. The black symbols on her skin seemed to move slightly, writhe like leeches feeding on her, and she ripped her shirt off to reveal more letters and numbers, the words *Yes* and *No* where her nipples should be.

Grandpa moved toward her as if to cover her up, but when she spun her face toward him, her hair whipping him in the cheek, he flinched, stepped backward away from her.

"Shelly, baby, what's the matter? Talk to me, honey."

She pulled her hands up to her chest, placed one over the other, and then made an O shape with her fingers and thumbs. Her hands moved across her body and face in a figure-eight pattern, stopping over letters for a brief moment before continuing to slide across her skin. Zane watched through the O in her hands, put the letters together in his mind.

I see you.

"John?" The voice came from the bedroom, faint and weak.

Zane hadn't heard his grandmother's voice since they had arrived a few days ago.

"She doesn't have much time left," their mother had said.

"It'll be good for you kids to spend some time with her." She said this to Zane and Shelly, not David. As far as their little brother knew, they were just visiting their grandparents. He didn't need to know that Grandma was dying.

"But it's summer vacation," Zane had argued. "There's nothing to do there, Mom."

Shelly had just rolled her eyes and crossed her arms. She and mom hadn't been getting along so good, not since Shelly got caught with her boyfriend in her room. Zane and David had pressed their ears against their bedroom wall and listened to the argument when it happened. Zane had never heard his mom sound so angry before.

The truth was, Zane didn't really care about his summer vacation. All of his best friends had gone out of town, and he was stuck playing baby games with his little brother or doing chores around the house.

He didn't want to go to his grandparents' house because he was scared of his grandma. Ever since she had gotten sick, he couldn't look her in the face without getting the urge to run away. He knew it was stupid, knew that even though his chubby, huggable grandmother had shrunken down to a bony, curled-up corpse that was too weak to get out of bed, she was still the same sweet, loveable woman she had always been. Even if she couldn't remember who Zane was half of the time. Even if her bedroom was as hot as a sauna and smelled like old cheese and sweat.

Things had gotten worse over the past few weeks, Mom had said. Grandma wasn't even talking, wasn't eating. Grandpa didn't want them to go into the bedroom anymore, which was fine with Zane. The last time Zane had visited her in her room—and only because Mom made him do it— Grandma had soiled herself, looked Zane right in the eye and smiled while she did it too. That smile, that smell, haunted his dreams.

But even so, hearing her voice now, faint and barely audible, he couldn't help but picture her the way she used to be, and he wanted to hug her, wanted to crawl into bed with her like he used to when he was little. She would run her nails across his back and sing to him, tell him stories. And even though the urge to run to her, to crawl under the covers where it was safe, was strong, Zane didn't move, just stared at Shelly as she ran the O of her hands over her body, spelling out the same message again and again.

I see you.

"John...?" Grandma's voice seemed barely louder than a whisper, but was somehow loud enough that they could all hear it. "Who...who is this man...in my bed with m-me?"

Shelly's eyes burst open, as black as the letters decorating her mahogany skin. Her hand darted out, grabbed hold of Grandpa by the throat. She opened her mouth as if to scream again, but no sound came out. Her mouth stretched wide as far as it would go, her teeth as black as her eyes.

Grandpa grabbed her wrist with both hands, fought to free himself from Shelly's tightening grip. The tips of her fingers dug into the soft flesh of his neck. His hands clawed at her fingers quicker now as he struggled to breathe, his tongue sticking straight out.

Zane rushed forward, finally able to make his feet move. Grandpa locked eyes with him, but Shelly didn't acknowledge him as he beat on her wrist and arm, helped Grandpa try and pry her fingers loose. David bawled, both hands gripping fistfuls of his own hair as he watched.

Who is this man in my bed with me? thought Zane. *That's what Grandma said...* And even as he pulled and tugged on his sister's fingers, a shudder ran down his back as he glanced at the wall that separated the living room from the bedroom.

The bedroom door slammed shut then, shaking the walls. In that same moment, Shelly released Grandpa, rolled backward three times before rising to her feet again. Her mouth was still stretched wide in a muted scream, eyes once again squeezed shut. She kept moving backward, sliding her feet across the carpet until she wedged herself into the corner, knocking over framed pictures and porcelain crosses. Her hands were curled into claws, and she raked them across her belly again and again like a dog digging a hole in the dirt. As Zane watched her do this, something in his sister's stomach moved, bulged out.

That thing went down her throat, Zane thought. *And now it wants back out again.*

Grandpa coughed and kicked, gasping for breath and staring across the room at Shelly—a red handprint was wrapped around his throat. David cried and cried, kept calling for Zane to come back to him. Zane had his eyes on his sister as her stomach grew fatter, as her nails scraped black, leaking lines across her brown skin.

And then Grandma screamed. So hoarse and long that it sounded like a coyote howling. Something banged against the wall, denting it outward as if a wrecking ball had hit it from the other side.

Grandma shrieked again, sobbing and coughing. But there was another voice. Zane heard it under his grandmother's screams. Someone talking to her…singing. A man's voice, but high-pitched, the soothing tone usually saved for sick children.

"Zane," David said as he rushed forward and dug his fingertips into Zane's lower back. "Make it stop, make it stop…please. *Please make it stop!*"

"Ow." Zane pulled his brother's hands away, had to struggle with him to keep him from clinging to him again.

Grandpa sprinted down the short hallway toward the bedroom. He slammed his body against the door, tugged on the doorknob, but it wouldn't budge. His fists slammed against the wood as he grimaced and grunted.

"Patricia! Patricia, open the door!"

Grandma kept shouting, sounded like she was trying to say something, but her words were sloppy and interrupted with groans of pain. Something slammed up against the wall again and again, sending plaster dust sprinkling over the floor.

"Leave my sister alone!" Zane didn't know who or what he was talking to, but he had a sudden realization that if he didn't do something, didn't stop this thing, he would never see Shelly again. That still wasn't enough to make him approach her—he stayed in his spot with David at his side, both watching Shelly claw at her belly.

Shelly's hands stopped moving and her black eyes landed on her brothers. Her open mouth curved into a grin as a deep laughter echoed from her throat. It wasn't her voice, and her mouth didn't move as the laugh oozed out, but she still smiled, still glared at Zane and David.

"Zane!" Grandpa screamed, still fighting with the door. "911! Call 911, hurry!"

Grandma wasn't screaming anymore, but the banging never stopped. And the singing voice. Nobody else seemed to notice it, but Zane heard it clearly, recognized it as one of the songs Grandma used to sing to him when she was healthy.

"Zane, goddammit!"

"Did you see him?" David said, arm outstretched and finger pointing past Shelly and toward the sliding glass door that led to the backyard.

"What?" Zane said as he pulled the phone off the wall. He had to concentrate so that his fingers wouldn't shake. He dialed 911, bit his lip as it started ringing.

"The man," David said. "He's outside. He wants us to go with him."

It kept ringing and ringing, and Zane couldn't help but wonder if that was normal. He had never had to call 911 before, but he always figured it would be a fast process, more immediate. He paced back and forth, keeping his eyes on his sister and brother.

"He didn't have eyes," David said. "And I could see faces in his mouth."

"David, be quiet," Zane said and slapped the wall. "Come on, come on!"

Then the ringing stopped.

"Hello?"

No answer.

"He said that Dad's with him. Said that Dad wants to see us, Zane. Wants to show us something. He's outside...in the backyard." David started walking toward the glass door, Shelly's black eyes on him the whole time, still smiling, her belly now the size of a watermelon with the letters and numbers stretched out across the tight skin.

"David, what are you... Get away from there!" Zane wanted to drop the phone and grab his brother, but he didn't want to miss the operator once they answered. "Hello? Hello?"

Heavy breathing on the other line. Wheezing.

"H-hello? 911...police?"

"Zane," a voice said, whispery and strained.

Zane tried to drop the phone, tried to open his fingers and let it fall out of his grip, but his hand refused to move, and no matter how hard he tried, he couldn't let the phone go. It started to feel different, soft and wet like the planchette had just before it crawled down Shelly's throat.

"Zane," the voice said again, only now it wasn't alone. Other voices called his name, some sounding far away and others sounded like they were right there in the room with him. Though they all spoke his name, there was hurt in their voices, pain. As if they were being tortured, forced to speak the word again and again. Children's voices and adults' voices and the elderly's voices. All mixed together in a chorus of anguish.

With a hard tug, Zane managed to get the phone away from his ear, long strings of mucus stretching from the side of his face connected to the handset. The phone had transformed, an eye staring out at him from where his ear was just pressed. As yellow as cheddar and encrusted with a black substance like dried ink. It blinked rapidly as if irritated, stared into Zane's eyes.

As Zane stared back, the bottom section of the phone began to fold over on itself, a clear, viscous fluid dripping down and soaking into the carpet. Lips formed, chapped and dry, and the tiny mouth opened, releasing an odor like rotting fruit.

"Zane," it said. "I see you."

And then the lights went out.

It had happened so suddenly that Zane's reaction was to scream. The phone slipped from his fingers and he backed away from it, terrified that it was pursuing him in the dark, slithering across the carpet toward him.

Grandpa growled as he slammed his body against the door, yelling for Grandma to talk to him, tell him she was okay. There was a loud bang and hurried footsteps, and Zane knew Grandpa had finally gotten the door open, could hear his grandfather's voice from the other side of the wall, now in the room with Grandma.

Shelly didn't make a sound besides the constant scraping of her nails across her belly.

Then the sound of the sliding glass door opening.

"David?" Zane said, his hands out in front of him as he worked his way across the room toward the door. Even with the moon out, it was pitch black in the house, so dark that Zane couldn't see his hands in front of him, and he had to wonder if whatever they had let out of the Ouija board— *I'm free. I see you*—was responsible. Blocking out the light, drowning them all in darkness.

"David, where are you!" Zane just wanted to run away, bolt out the front door and run until he found someone who could help. But he couldn't leave his little brother behind, felt responsible for keeping him safe.

He took his steps slow, holding his breath, expecting something to grab him at any second. And then his hands touched something. Soft and wet and round.

Hands gripped his shoulders and a mouth pressed up against the side of his face. A soft giggle scuttled into his ear canal, and he knew he was touching his sister's belly, pulled his hands away from her. The grip on his shoulders loosened, then shoved him from behind.

Outside now. The air was warm, humid, made him sweat immediately. The moonlight lit the yard, and Zane spun to look back into the house but could only see blackness beyond the threshold.

"David!" he shouted as he turned back toward the yard.

His little brother sat cross-legged in the middle of the grass. Covering his eyes with both hands, weeping.

"What are you doing?" Zane said and hurried toward

him. "We have to go get some help for—"

Images flickered in and out of focus around David. Like lightning illuminating a dark room for a few flashes.

Children lay in pieces around the lawn, the limbs and torsos and heads flopping around like fish desperate for water. Blood splashed over the blades of grass, over David's face and shirt. And they cried. Each of the children's faces was twisted into an expression of agony as they bawled.

Another flash, and this time, Zane saw the man. Standing behind David, his long white fingers gripping the boy's shoulder and neck. He had no eyes, just smooth skin where his sockets should have been. He wore a black suit, the kind a preacher might wear on a Sunday morning. When he smiled at Zane, David pulled his hands away from his face.

"David!"

The boy's eyes had been scooped out, his sockets empty and gushing blood. David held his hands out to Zane, palms out, painted red. And then his body broke into pieces like a Lego sculpture being knocked over. The parts mixed in with the other children's, bounced and thrashed on the grass, and the next time the ghost light flashed, they were gone.

Zane sprinted toward the grass, slid on his knees, ran his fingers through the blades as if he would find his brother buried there. But there was nothing. No blood, not a single strip of flesh.

"Where is he?" Zane jumped to his feet, fists hard at his sides. *"Bring me my brother back! Bring him back!"*

No, no, no. This can't be happening.

The lights suddenly came back on in the house. A shadow moved over the window that led into his grandparents' bedroom.

The house, he thought. *Maybe he's in the house!*

Zane stormed back inside, holding back his tears. He had to be strong, had to save his brother, his sister, his grandmother.

That wasn't really David I saw, he told himself. *The spirit is messing with my head, that's all. David's fine, Shelly's fine...*

Zane didn't make it far into the house before a scream ripped from his throat and he collapsed to his knees on the living room carpet. All he could do was shake his head as he took in the scene in front of him, his hands quivering and covering his mouth.

Shelly lay on her back, legs spread, the black letters, numbers, and symbols on her skin pulsing. Her mouth was stretched wide again into a silent scream, the corners torn down to her neck. Though her eyes were still black, Zane could see the terror in them.

Grandma stood above her, holding Grandpa's severed head by the thin, wiry hair. She waved it over Shelly's body, letting the blood sprinkle over her. As the blood dripped onto her skin, the Ouija characters soaked it up, drank it in.

Grandma wore her nightgown, soaked with blood. The thin fabric clung to her bony frame, showing every sharp angle, every sunken cavern. Her hair was stuck to her scalp and forehead with sweat, and she slowly turned her face toward Zane as she waved Grandpa's head. She had no teeth, but her gums were as black as licorice, and she grinned at Zane and snickered.

Shelly shrieked, gripped her knees and sat up as far as she could. The bones in her hips popped as her legs were spread wider and wider, splintering and stabbing through her skin.

And something began to push its way out of her.

Grandma smiled her gums at Zane, crept across the carpet toward him, her back arched, the spinal cord pressed tight up against her skin.

Zane tried to run away from her, from the house. But some invisible force held him there, squeezed the air from his lungs.

Grandma ran an arid tongue across her lips, pressed her face against Zane's. "He's coming," she said. "He's coming and he's bringing hell with him."

And then she pressed her lips to one of Grandpa's eyes, slurped it right out of the socket. Her black gums squashed it down, popped it like a grape. The jelly squirted into Zane's face, but he was powerless to wipe it away.

The thing inside of Shelly pushed itself out. First an arm emerged, covered in a translucent film. The arm had a sleeve, black and soaked with Shelly's fluids. The hand gripped the carpet fibers, then pulled.

Another arm. The fingers were long, the knuckles thick and round.

The head came next, with hair matted down to the pale scalp, covered in scabs and open wounds. No eyes. Mouth stretched into a grin to reveal long, flat teeth like jaundiced piano keys.

Shelly stopped screaming.

Grandma slurped up Grandpa's other eye, rocking herself beside Zane as she chewed, singing the songs she used to sing, but with another voice, a deeper more sinister voice.

The man pulled himself free, smoothed his coat and pants. The room was filled with the scent and taste of rot and disease.

He pointed a long finger at Zane. "I see you," he said. "Now it's time for you to see me."

Grandma grabbed Zane by the back of the head, slammed her crusty, blood-coated lips to his eye. As she sucked it out, Zane saw the man. Saw who—or what—he really was.

And he saw the children. The infinite children. He saw David.

"You don't need eyes to see us," David said.

And he was right.

BECAUSE I WANTED TO

That's why I wrote this next story. Because I wanted to. It doesn't have any special meaning and it wasn't cathartic in any way. I just…wanted to.

This is the first of the new stories included in this collection. It's ridiculous and might not be funny to anyone else but me, but goddammit, I had to write this story for some reason. It's one of those times I had a title before anything else, and I just couldn't get it out of my head once it was in there. Something about it stuck with me.

So I asked myself. Do I want this to make any sense? Because for it to make any sense at all, I would have had to set it sometime around 1950. And for whatever reason, that just didn't seem fun to me. I didn't want it to be just a crazy guy selling skin masks and nipple belts. Not much of a story there. And having Ed Gein use the garage sale to lure victims seemed good at first, but the more I thought about that angle, the more bored I became with the idea.

So I decided to just go nuts with it. Do something completely ridiculous and over the top. And I had a blast writing it.

You know those old ghost stories where a guy, say, picks up a hitchhiker? She asks him to drive her to her house, and during the drive, he falls in love with her. He treats her nice, maybe gives her a kiss when they arrive to her house, and she thanks him, says she hasn't been treated with such kindness in years. He drives away, but can't stop thinking about her. So he goes back…and finds an empty field where the house used to be. He asks a neighbor, "Wasn't there a house here?" and the neighbor says something along the lines of, "There hasn't been a house there for fifty years. Not since that poor girl burned up in it."

That's more or less what I was going for here. Because it made me laugh when I thought about it. Before writing anything, I had my title, and I had my last line.

"Thank you, Ed Gein. Wherever you are."

I've always had a fascination with Ed Gein. Ever since I found out *Psycho*, Buffalo Bill from *Silence of the Lambs*, and my favorite movie of all time, *The Texas Chainsaw Massacre*, were all inspired by him, I read everything I could about the guy. One thing that jumped out at me were his issues with women. So, in order to make this story work, I had to use that angle. As harsh as some of the things said in the story may be, the overall tone is supposed to be silly.

So…let's see how this goes.

One day I imagined Ed Gein having a garage sale. And it was funny as hell to me.

So I wrote this story. Because I wanted to.

And if I ever get lucky enough to find Ed Gein and his garage sale, I'll probably stop and browse a little. I could use a new couch.

And who doesn't want a hand-sewn nipple belt?

ED GEIN'S GARAGE SALE

The family vacation was supposed to make things better. Not fix anything permanently, but at least relieve some pressure. Get his wife and kids smiling, getting along with one another.

He should have known it was a bad idea. Should have known it was going to be a fucking disaster. Just like everything else.

"You guys feel like eating something?" Willy said over his shoulder. He smiled at Daisy, but she didn't return it. He was pretty sure she had forgotten how to smile. Hadn't seen anything but a scowl on her face for the last fifteen years.

"We're almost home," Daisy said. "Just get us there. If I have to listen to any more of this—"

"Any more of what, Mom?" Ian said. "My problems boring you? Sorry my shitty life's bringing your mood down. Really I am."

"She's not the only one who's sick of hearing about it," Ramona said, and kicked the back of Willy's seat like a spoiled kid. Which of course was exactly what she was. "I mean, seriously, Ian. Isn't this what I said would happen? Isn't this what fucking *everyone* said would happen?"

"Guys, come on," Willy said, but was ignored. Which was what his life had become. "We can stop at a diner or something. Something local. Huh? Chicken fried steaks and milkshakes?"

"Not hungry," Ian said.

"I spent enough money on this stupid trip already that I don't have," Ramona said and clicked her tongue.

"It's on me," Willy said, then caught a look from his right like twin laser beams. "And your mother. Our last chance to have a nice time."

"Are you deaf? Nobody wants to eat shitty diner food

52

with you, all right? Jesus. Take a hint? This trip of yours was a bad idea. I knew it was bad when you brought it up the first time. What did you expect would come of this? We'd sleep in a roach motel on beds encrusted with dead skin and semen, take pictures of each other in front of the most tacky, touristy pieces of shit I've ever seen in my life, pretending we're having a good time, smiling for the camera so you can look back at them and imagine happy memories? It was a stupid fucking idea and I'm tired and I want out of this goddamn fucking car and I want you to take me home. Not that the shack you call a house counts much for a home. But it's what we've got, isn't it, Willy?"

That got everyone quiet.

The onslaught may have hurt Willy's feelings more if he wasn't so used to it. His wife could say those words and more with only a look, and he learned not to take them too personally. If she had it so bad, if she hated him and hated her life so much, she would have left a long time ago. She didn't stay because of love—that was painfully obvious.

She stayed because she had no place else to go. She stayed because, as unhappy as she was, starting over again was more trouble than sticking around and dying miserable. And her harsh words weren't her only form of revenge for a life full of disappointment and regret. When he met her, she was just shy of a year out of her first marriage. Ramona was already fourteen, and Daisy's figure was nice. Oh, she sagged in places, striped with a few stretch marks here and there, but Willy liked it. She was a woman, a real woman, who had lived a real life and showed it. She was sexy. Goddamn was she sexy. He asked her to marry him. She agreed, though Ramona made it clear from day one she hated the idea, hated Willy, and when Ian was born a year later, she hated him too. Daisy had gained some weight after the pregnancy. Willy figured it was normal. Figured the weight would sort of fall off naturally, the way he suspected it did after she had Ramona. But it only got worse. And year after year, when Willy failed to live up to the promises he made her, when he couldn't give her the life he wanted to give or that she thought she deserved, the weight just kept piling on. At that point, calling it baby fat was like calling a humpback whale a goldfish.

When he began struggling to find his wife attractive anymore, he didn't think it could get much worse. It did. Mounds of fat hung from every inch of her. Her face had swelled so that she hardly looked like herself, like the fat in her cheeks and chin were eating her old face, chewing on it, pushing her eyes back so that it looked like she was squinting all the time.

I still love her, he told himself. *No matter what, I still love her. Always will.*

Ramona snickered and shook her head. She made eye contact with Willy in the rearview, and gave him a look that told him how much of a loser she thought he was. Like she wished her mother had married any other man on the planet. Like if she had a better father figure, she might have made something of herself instead of being a thirty-six year old obese bitch who had never even tried moving out of their house, had never gone to college, and had never met anyone who could stand to spend more than a passing moment with her. All Willy's fault, of course. Never mind that her real daddy ran off and ended up in jail after getting caught trying to lure young girls into his station wagon outside of their middle school.

"I could eat," Ian said. "Haven't had a good chicken fried steak in a long time."

"That's it," Willy said. "You see? Be surprised what a little comfort food in our bellies will fix."

"I swear to God, Willy," Daisy said. "And Ian, you keep your mouth shut. I already gave my answer."

"Whatever." Ian pulled out his cell phone and started fiddling with it.

Willy tried to catch his son's attention in the mirror, let him know that he appreciated the support, but Ian kept his eyes on the tiny screen. His face pinched into a sneer and reflecting the blue glow from the phone's display.

He remembered how it used to be when he was a kid. He used to fantasize about what it would be like to be an adult.

His father was strong, handsome, and respected. His mother loved his father, always had a kiss and a meal ready for him when he walked in the door. Willy would rush home from school so he could do his homework before his father got home. Because he knew if he didn't, he'd be in a world of hurt. And it wasn't whoopings or spankings. Willy had been so terrified to disappoint his father that physical punishment wasn't necessary.

He wondered if things were just different back then. A simpler time.

He reached over and placed his hand on Daisy's thigh. After what she had said, and after a vacation full of rolling eyes and sighs and being ignored, he wasn't sure why he did it. Wasn't ready to give up on them, he supposed. Which was the entire reason for the trip in the first place.

It was obvious to Willy early on in their marriage that she wasn't as attracted to him as he was to her, but she always played along. Went through the motions. Tolerated his affection in hopes it would pay off somewhere down the line. Probably because she was getting older, had already failed at one marriage, and didn't think she had many chances left. And when they first met, like Daisy, Willy was slimmer, had more hair, still had ambition.

She looked at his hand first. Stared at it like it was a spider that had pounced on her. Her lip curled and her eyelids fluttered. Then she looked at him. The way a vegan looks at a plate of veal chops.

Using her thumb and forefinger like pincers, she grabbed his wrist and tossed his hand away like a used tissue.

"Vacation's over," she said, then looked out her window. Crossed her arms. Sighed.

Willy could see her reflection in the glass. Hatred and disgust as plain as a Halloween mask.

He was suddenly aware that his children were fighting again. They were already well into it, bickering about the same goddamn thing they had been bickering about since Ian moved back in after his own failed marriage. Nineteen years old, one semester deep in community college, and he had been convinced he was in love. Willy talked to him, tried to persuade him to finish school first, give it some time, but the boy wasn't having it. Marriage lasted a whole nine months.

"And that's my fault?" Ian said.

"Of course not. How could anything be your fault? Because you're so mature, right?" Ramona smirked again. When she got that look on her face, like she was better than everyone, Willy wished he would have spanked her more as a child. A lot more. Maybe once for every meal of the day.

"I loved her. But you wouldn't know anything about that, would you? Unless you count Twinkies."

"Oh fuck you. At least Twinkies don't go around fucking anything with a hard on. At least Twinkies don't get pregnant by some random wetback in an alley somewhere and then lie about it. When the baby came out brown, did you think it was tanning in there? I mean, its mother's pussy was wide enough to let some sunlight in, but—"

"Hey. Come on, guys. Enough of that."

"Look at you. A real hard ass. Hear that, kids? Your father says that's enough. Better stop before he says it again."

"At least I got married. At least I tried…something. What have you done?"

"Fuck you, Ian. You think you're special cuz you went and married the town slut? When you kissed her, could you taste all the ball sweat? Was it salty?"

The bickering in the back went on, and Willy did his best to ignore it, had become sort of a master at the art of conscious meditation. Being physically awake and alert, but sinking into his own mind and thoughts so that the goings on around him were muted and blurred. After all these years, it was the only way he had avoided going all Jack Torrance on his family.

Willy had been so lost in his own thoughts, a hurricane of insults and raised voices roaring behind him, the heat of his wife's displeasure pulling the sweat from his pores, that he didn't notice the traffic jam just ahead.

"Shit!" He slammed the brakes, held his right arm out protectively over Daisy.

The car skidded and the tires spat white smoke behind

them. Daisy rocked forward, her pillowy breasts pressing hard against his forearm as the car slid and finally jerked to a stop maybe an inch and half away from the semi-truck in front of them.

Daisy shoved his arm away from her, then covered herself like she just realized she was topless in church.

"Fucking idiot. Watch what you're doing! That why you forced this road trip on us? To kill us? If that's what you wanted you could have spared us the wasted time and burned the house down. Would have been less torture than this fucking vacation."

"Jesus, Willy." Ramona rubbed her shoulder and loosened her seatbelt. "Think something popped. That's great. You gonna pay for my doctor bill? Cuz you know I don't have insurance. Goddamn…"

"Oh, quit your fucking crying. Seriously." Ian nodded at Willy. "You all right, Dad?"

"Him?" Daisy said. She tried to turn and look at their son, but couldn't manage it. "He's just fine, Ian. Can't you tell? That's your father for you. Just fine. Always just fine. Never mind how the rest of us feel. Let's just forget about the rest of us."

"That's enough," Willy said. He twisted his fists over the steering wheel. More and more sweat spewed from his palms and made the wheel more slippery. His face burned as his pulse quickened, and he was suddenly washed over with the need to get out of the car. Not just out of the car, but away from his family. With every ticking second, it became more and more of an emergency.

"You've had enough? I warned you, kids. Your father has had enough again. We all better just—"

"Goddammit I said that's enough!"

Daisy flinched and stared at him like he'd just sprouted hair and howled at the moon. Ian and Ramona went silent, sat up straighter.

"Who the fuck do you think you *are* talking to me that way? You think because you raised your voice that I'm scared now? I've been married to you for almost twenty years, you worthless prick. Fear is the last thing you instill in me. I take that back. Second to last. Love is the very last thing."

"Jesus, Mom," Ian said.

"Still had enough? Or is there room for more?"

The traffic started to move, and just ahead was an exit. Without hesitating, Willy slammed his foot on the gas, swerving around the 18-wheeler and using the shoulder for the last few feet, then swung the car into the exit lane.

"What the fuck do you think you're doing?"

"Willy, don't be stupid. Just take us home already!"

"Dad? You…you okay?"

Willy's reflection in the rearview hardly looked like him anymore. Face as red as sirloin, teeth bared, sweat beads spread across his skin like transparent mosquito bites.

He had no idea where he was going. It didn't matter. The first excuse he found to park the car and get the hell out, he was taking it.

The complaining chirped on. The threats. The insults.

It all mixed into a cacophony of disrespect. And it fueled his rage. A rage he never knew he had inside of him. Like a hibernating bear that had slept through so many winters, when it finally woke from its coma, it was ravenous and out of its mind. Ready to maul anyone that was unlucky enough to cross its path.

Wherever they were, it looked to have been abandoned years ago. What structures were left sagged in on themselves, looked on the verge of crumbling completely. A few transients walked about, but even they were scarce in this wasteland Willy found himself rolling through.

And then he saw it. Rising from the horizon like a growing tree in a void desert.

The house was old, yet clean. Kept up. At least compared to the rest of the landscape surrounding it.

A picket sign was stabbed into the dry dirt just in front of it. *Garage Sale.*

It was as good an excuse as any. And Willy pulled the car up to the curb and killed the engine.

"If you get out of this car, I swear to God you'll be sorry."

Daisy tried to snatch the keys from his hand, but her bulbous arm didn't have the reach. The fat hung and wiggled like some kind of animal was stuck inside and trying to get out.

Willy smiled at her. Dangled the keys.

The blubber surrounding what was left of the pretty face he had married so long ago shook and darkened until it looked like a baked ham sitting between her shoulders.

"You made your point. Now get back in the car." Ramona shook his seat, but he was already out of it.

The fresh air filled him with relief instantly. Even with the hint of vomit and rot, it was better than the aridity inside the car.

Ian opened his door and got out. "Dad?"

"I need a minute. All right? Can you give me that?"

"Yeah. Sure. You all—"

"Ian, if you ask me if I'm all right again, I'm pretty sure my eyes will liquefy."

"Okay. Sorry."

"I need some fresh air. I need to stretch my legs."

"You need to get away from them."

"Yeah, that too. Let's look around. Browse a little. No harm in that, is there?"

"Browse? What are you—"

"One thing I know about your mother, no matter how mad she is, shopping is too enticing to pass up. Even at some shitty, dumpy garage sale."

"Oh, it might not be what you'd call glamorous, mister, but those're harsh words from a man who hadn't even seen what I got to offer. Wouldn't you say so?"

Willy wasn't sure how he'd missed him. Standing just beyond the rickety picket fence with his hands in his overalls' pockets. A scrawny guy in a red flannel shirt. Face weathered and sunken, studded with sharp, white whiskers. He looked at least fifty, maybe older, the cap on his head so low it covered his eyebrows.

"Didn't mean anything by that, mister…?"

"Ed," the man said, and extended his hand. "Ed Gein. You folks from around here?" He bent over to get a better look inside the car, then eyed the license plate. "Didn't think you were. But that don't matter. All're welcome. On vacation, are you?"

Ed had a firm grip on Willy's hand, shook it vigorously as he spoke. When the handshake was finally done, Willy couldn't help but smile. Something about the old guy that made it so it was damn near impossible not to smile.

"I'm Willy. And this is my boy Ian. And you can call it a vacation I guess. I tried anyway."

"Dad?" Ian stared at Willy, then let his eyes roam their surroundings.

"Women. Hard to please sometimes, aren't they? Yes. Yes they are. Found no matter how hard a man can try and please a woman, she'll find something he hasn't done to her liking sooner or later. Isn't that the truth, Willy? Ian?" He cackled and showed the spaces in his mouth where teeth used to be.

"Yeah. You're right about that, Ed. Me and Ian had our share of troubles. Thinking maybe we're better off staying away from women all together." Willy elbowed his son who looked even more uncomfortable and confused. Took a few backward steps away from the fence.

"Oh, I don't know. Better than going queer. Not that I got anything against 'em. Every person's got a right to be and do what they please, I suppose. Just can't imagine taking a look at a fella and wondering what his pecker looks like. You got me there, Willy? Ian?"

Willy exchanged a quick look with Ian, tried to share a smile and a laugh with him, but his son didn't look pleased. Had a look like he wanted to ask Willy if he was okay again. Like he wanted to be anywhere but standing there talking with Ed Gein.

"I'm gonna go wait in the car, Dad."

"You sure? We haven't even looked around yet."

"Looked around? Dad...forget it. Do what you need to do." And he walked off, hands shoved into his pockets. Glanced back at Willy once before getting in the car and slamming the door.

"Sorry about that," Willy said to Ed, who just shrugged and grinned. Willy pointed to the yard. "What you got there, Ed? Mind if we take a look?"

"Course not. Why I put it out, isn't it? Stuck a sign in the ground. Got lots of ladies things out here, too. Made 'em myself. Ever since Mama went and died on me, I sort of took a liking to ladies things. Got pretty decent at making 'em. Those girls of yours would love this stuff. Hand-sewn. Women...they like to buy things, don't they, Willy?"

"That they do."

Ed stood with his hands on his hips, just sort of staring at Willy. Studying him. Looking so deep into his eyes that it started to get uncomfortable. Then he put a strong hand on Willy's shoulder. "It's not right, you know. The way Daisy talks to you. And in front of your boy? A man should be respected by his women and his sons. Way the world was meant to be."

"Wait...how do you—"

"And that daughter of hers. Lord, she's a pain, isn't she, Willy? She is. Yes she is. I know it. And her being no blood relation to you, I'm sure you spent a thought or two on putting her down. Isn't that right, Willy? Course you have. Natural."

"Now hold on just a minute. I know you from somewhere?"

"See, it's no accident you showed up outside my house. No accident I decided to pull some things out of the house and sell them today, neither. Know why it happened?"

"Umm...God?"

"Hell no it's not God. God's nothing but a kid with an ant farm, shaking it up when he gets bored to see what happens inside. It's fate is what it is. Fate brought us together and I'll be damned if I'm gonna ignore a thing like that. You?"

"Listen, how is it you knew my wife's—"

"Hurry now. Don't have much time before that fat bitch stuffed inside your car starts throwing another fit and forces you out of here and back on the road."

"Watch it, Ed."

"Be honest, Willy. It really bother you I said it?"

61

He didn't answer.

"Come on in the yard. Let me show you a few things over here. Explain how a woman can crawl up inside a man, eat him up from inside there. You know, like one of those parasites. You heard of them? Heard of one that crawls in through your pecker slit. Rots you from the inside out, it does. Nasty business. Now tell me, Willy. How is Daisy any different than that parasite?"

The picket fence was short enough for Willy to step over, and he walked with Ed toward the long wooden tables lined up with items for sale. It all looked normal enough from a distance. Clothing, furniture, books, a few tools, and even jars of what looked like something preserved and pickled.

"Wasn't always this bad. We were happy in the beginning."

"Everyone's happy in the beginning. That's the easy part. I like you okay now, but in a few minutes, who knows. Might be I wanna slit you from chin to pubic hair and hang you upside down while I pull the insides out, you know?" Ed spat in the grass, hands stuffed back in his pockets. Then he smiled and shook his head.

"Only kidding with you. Like I said you and me, we were supposed to meet. And besides, I've never had any reason to kill a man. Men aren't the problem, like I was saying. It's the women. Can't trust 'em. Using their bodies to get inside a man's head. Like that parasite I was telling you about. Get all up inside you, then they get to work on you. Eat you up until there's barely a scrap of you left. Know what I mean?"

"Well…" Now standing just in front of the tables, Willy got an up-close look at the items for sale. Part of his brain told him to run. To get the hell out of there. Jump in his car and drive his family to safety, as far away from this psychopath as possible. But Ed was right. Fate was at work here. He knew it was true. And the longer he studied the items, the more interested he became about what Ed Gein had to say about women.

"Tell me, and be honest. You the same man now than you were when you met your wife?"

"No. No I'm not."

"And it's not your fault, neither. That asshole God, he gave men peckers. And he showed women how to use them against us. And they do. Every one of 'em. Just like that parasite I was telling you about."

Willy walked the length of the tables, Ed beside him. He stopped, picked up an especially interesting item. "What's this?"

"Nipple belt. Know how long it took to get enough nipples to fit all the way around my waist?" He cackled and slapped Willy's back. "Long goddamn time, I tell you that. But it's a beauty, isn't it?"

Willy checked the car. Ian, in the back seat, had his phone out again. Daisy and Ramona both glared at Willy through their windows. He waved and got twin, pudgy middle fingers in return.

"It is, Ed. I got to hand it to you."

Ed took the belt from Willy's hand, set it back on the table. "Don't think you're ready for that one yet, Willy. Not yet. But let me show you something else."

They passed furniture made from human bones, upholstered with human skin. A lamp, the shade a stretched-out, translucent face, a pair of dried-out lips hanging from the pull cord. Cranial bowls. Meat hooks and knives. Books on taxidermy, medical encyclopedias, Nazi picture books filled with photos of Jewish men and women being experimented on. Piles of women's panties that looked normal enough until Willy picked one up and found the dried out cunt sewn inside of it. Jars filled with human hearts and just about every organ he could think of.

"This is what I wanted to show you. Think you'll get a real kick out of it."

Five mannequins stood side by side, each posed similarly like a woman waving to someone in the distance. Each had a woman's face pulled taught over the heads. Mammary vests over their torsos. Human flesh leggings.

"Now see here. What do you think?"

Willy reached out just as the car's horn started honking.

63

First in small bursts, then one, long beep. He pictured Daisy having a heart attack and collapsing, her fat head resting against the steering wheel and causing that fucking horn to blast the way it was. The fantasy brought a smile to his face and pumped blood into his cock.

He reached out and ran his fingertips across the leathery skin. "Nice, Ed. Real nice."

"Nice? Hell, it's a lot more than that. What do you see when you look at that, Willy? And be honest with me now."

"Skin suits."

"Okay. And what is it you do with a suit?"

"Put it on. Wear it."

"When you take a woman's skin and slide into it, you're doing a hell of a lot more than wearing it. What did I say about women? About that parasite?"

"They get inside you."

"Bingo. They get inside you. You can kill a woman easy. God, the prick he is, made men stronger than women. It's no big task putting one down. But you do that, and all you did really is made her more powerful. Like Mama. Believe me, Willy, you don't want that. Not with Daisy or her offspring. Drive a man crazy. No. You gotta scoop 'em clean. Peel 'em. And once you do that, you climb inside the skin. Get inside 'em the way they were always inside you. Know what that does?"

Willy smiled. "Gives me power over them."

"If this was a gameshow, the dinger would be dinging right about now. You get the power. The way a man was always supposed to be. In charge. You're in control now. And once you tuck yourself into that skin, you'll be tickled at how things'll change. How your wife and step-daughter respect you. How much better you'll feel. You won't believe how much better you'll feel, Willy. And that, my friend. That's why fate brought us together."

Willy nodded. Nothing had ever made more sense. Deep down, though it was withering more and more by the second, he knew it sounded insane. He knew that the words coming out of Ed's mouth were awful, ghastly things. Yet it sounded right. It sounded like the obvious solution to his problems.

The kind of thing he should have thought of a long time ago. *This is why I took this vacation. To find Ed Gein. Like an angel in overalls.*

"You got what I need here?"

Ed grinned and slapped Willy on the back again. Walked up and down the tables until he had an armful of items, then shoved them into Willy's chest. The encyclopedia, the book on taxidermy, eight meat hooks, three differently-sized knives, and a couple pairs of the panties.

"What are the panties for?"

"Comfort."

"Get your fucking ass in this car, you son of a bitch! You've got thirty seconds before I call the goddamn cops and tell them you kidnapped us!" Daisy's hog head stuck out her window, sweat glistening like Vaseline.

"Like I told you at the start. We didn't have much time," Ed said.

"How much do I owe you?"

"Nothing but a promise. A promise that you'll go off and be happy. Live the life you wanna live. Like the queers we were talking about. People may not like their practices, but they're men just like me and you and they're living the lives they want to. Happy with a mouthful of pecker. I'm not telling you to go stuffing nobody's pecker past your lips or anything, but—"

"It's loud and clear, Ed." Willy extended his free hand, balancing the items in his other arm. Ed shook it. "I don't know what to say. Thank you just doesn't seem enough."

"It'll suffice. You have a good one, Willy. And if you need me. You know where to find me."

Willy smiled, hesitated for a moment, then strolled back to the car.

He hadn't felt so happy in twenty years.

***

Willy was a new man. Not the man he used to be, even before Daisy. He was better than that. Better than he'd ever been or imagined he could be.

And he owed it all to Ed Gein.

He drove back to the abandoned neighborhood where he first met the man. Remembered it perfectly. Knew exactly which exit to take, which turns to make.

Yet he pulled up to an empty lot. He turned around, checked his map, but there was no mistake. This was the spot. It had to be. And not only was Ed nowhere to be found, but there was no house, not even any kind of evidence that a house had ever existed there. Just empty, cracked blacktop with tufts of weeds sticking out here and there like Troll dolls' hair.

Willy stepped out of his car. He had to leave Ian at home. Locked in his room. He hated to do it, but his son still didn't seem to understand. Didn't see the big picture. Couldn't appreciate the power of what Ed had showed him.

One day he would. It was just going to take time.

He checked himself in the reflection of the car window. His eyes sparkling from behind Daisy's eyeholes. His grin was hidden behind her round, leathery face.

The mammary vest was the best part. His favorite. It was only after he had removed the skin that he saw the true beauty of all the weight she had gained. The way it poured off him in layers. The way the breasts spilled over the sides like droopy dog's ears. Stretch marks like red lightning climbing the folds of loose flesh. The stockings needed work. Inner thighs kept scraping together, eating holes in them. But when he was all put together, inside of his wife, he felt like there could be no wrong in the world. He felt like a man. A real man.

And all he had been able to think about since first climbing inside of his wife was showing Ed. Was even going to ask him to come over to the house and have a talk with Ian. Willy had saved Ramona for his son, and he figured if anyone could convince Ian that what they were doing was right, it was Ed Gein.

Or maybe I need to go and find his ex-wife. Might be more willing to participate if it's her hanging from the meat hooks.

He walked into the empty lot. Kicked weeds into the air and sighed.

He wondered if he had done something wrong. Offended the man somehow.

"If you was lookin' for somebody to warm you up, baby, you found him."

A homeless man staggering along the street had stopped and was facing Willy. A white man, though the grime coating his skin could have fooled you from a distance. He held a head of wilted, blackening lettuce in one hand, lifted it to his mouth and bit into it.

"How long ago did he move from here?" Willy asked, his hot breath filling Daisy's head.

"Holy fuck. You a man? What's that you got on? You fucked up on some shit? Got anymore?"

"Ed. Ed Gein. The old man who had a house here. Right here where I'm standing."

"Mister, I lived out here all my life. Ain't been nothin' there since I can remember. 'Cept that concrete your standin' on. Now you holdin' or what?"

"No. And I'm not on anything. This is my wife. Daisy. We've never been happier."

"Yeah I bet. Crazy motherfucker." And with that and another bite of spoiled lettuce, the man wandered off.

Willy sat down. Rested his elbows on his knees and his chin on his fists.

Something poked his rear. Scared he had just sat down on top of a used needle, he quickly jumped up. And smiled at what he found.

Sticking up out of a crack in the cement was a nipple. Sewn to another nipple.

Willy leaned over, pried at the cracked asphalt. Chunks ripped away easy, and he brushed the dirt away and yanked the nipple belt free. Blew it off, shook it.

He was ready for it now. And his eyes filled with tears as he wrapped it around his waist and fastened it.

He looked around, then up at the sky.

"Thank you, Ed Gein," he said. "Wherever you are."

DEAD
KITTENS

I get ideas from everywhere. No matter where I am or what I'm doing, my writing brain is on. I'm constantly trying to spin things into horror stories, and have found myself wanting to do things or go places that I might've hated before I became a writer. Like going to a baby shower. Or shopping for clothes with my wife. It doesn't matter. I get a kick out of watching people these days. Picking up little details that I can use in my fiction later.

I pay attention to everything. To the point that I even annoy myself. I can't just sit and enjoy a movie anymore, or even a song. I'll see or hear something, and I think, "Oohh! I can use that somehow!"

I was watching a show called *Hoarders* one day. My family (love you, guys!) may also have some issues with hoarding, so it was really uncomfortable for me to watch it, and I haven't watched it since. But the episode I did see was about a woman whose house was so jampacked full of shit, and overrun with so many cats, that she didn't know there were dead kittens scattered all over the fucking place like little hidden, festering treasures.

It got to the point that the people helping her clean the place out were almost bored with it. They'd move a big stack of boxes and find a dried out, flattened, furry carcass.

"Another dead kitten," they would say, and sort of kick it nonchalantly, toss it into their sack filled with baby pussycat corpses.

It was just difficult to imagine someone's house getting so bad that they couldn't even notice the smell of tiny pockets of rotting flesh tucked into every room. And it got me wondering what other crazy shit one might find within the house of a hoarder.

Now, this story goes way beyond dead kittens, but that's where the idea started.

I'm not saying there's anything wrong with dead kittens. They're fine if that's your thing.

I'm more of a dead puppy kind of guy.

HE'S JUST
A BABY

Styles straightened his tie, cleared his throat, and rapped his knuckles on the door. Not too hard, but just enough to alert the woman who resided there. He didn't want to scare her, didn't want to seem overzealous. All he needed her to do was answer the door, and after that, she would be his. Sing a few pretty words at her, whisper enticing promises, present her with some flashy paperwork, and she'd be melted butter through his fingers.

And he was goddamn good at it.

He'd been watching this particular house for a few days, taking note of the woman's comings and goings. She was perfect.

Styles faced the peephole and smiled wide, clipboard with the fake alarm company logo out in front so she could see it. Along the edge of the door was a mess of locks, and from what Styles could tell, half of them locked from the outside.

That's weird, he thought, but shook it off and re-stretched his smile. There was a flutter at the peephole, but the door didn't budge.

This he expected. A white woman sees a black man at her door, and no matter how well-dressed, no matter how friendly he looked, their trust was hard to come by.

"Hello. My name's Sebastian Howard, and I just wanted to offer you some security for your home." He flashed his pearly whites, hopped up and down on his toes. "May I please speak to the man or woman of the house? I promise I won't take much of your time, and your safety means everything to me."

Silence.

"I understand if you are apprehensive. I'll just leave a

pamphlet here for you." He placed the tri-fold paper on the doormat. "In these times, it really is vital that you secure your home and your loved ones. Never know who's out there."

He turned as if to leave.

"Don't need no security." The voice was harsh, a smoker's voice.

Styles spun back around and faced the door. "Yes, many people are under the illusion that their possessions are safe behind a locked door. But there are burglaries every single day, all day, not to mention home invasions. Would you be willing to risk everything you own, the very lives of your family? Is a simple lock really going to keep you all safe?"

A moment of silence. Styles flashed a countenance that said: "Shame on you for not heeding my warning."

Then the door creaked open, but just a sliver, just enough for the woman's eye to peer out and a stripe of her pale face. The pupil dilated when the sunlight hit it, and it rode the length of Style's body. He could only see the corner of her mouth, but it twitched as she spoke.

"You left your pamphlet, now get on and git."

"Yes, ma'am. But there are some things I'd like to discuss—"

"I done told you to git, now do it 'fore I call the police. You understand that?"

Styles put his hands out in surrender, never allowing his smile to retreat from his face. "No problem at all. I admire your cautiousness. My number's on the pamphlet, please consider giving me a call."

And he walked away. Okay, so this broad was a tough sell. It'd happened before, and he knew not to push too hard or it might ruin everything. So, nodding, smiling, and leaving was the best strategy.

The door creaked as it swung wider, and he turned just in time to get a glimpse of the interior of the home.

Just as he expected. A hoarder.

This could be good or bad news, but something worth checking out either way. Mountains of various junk and prized possessions loomed over the woman as she dashed out her door, swiped the pamphlet up. She locked eyes with Styles for a moment, squinted at him, scowled. Her flesh was the color of lemon yogurt, spotted here and there with open scab wounds. She wore a white robe, zebra-striped with brown filth. A slight gust hit just then, opened the robe just enough for Styles to get an unwelcomed glance at a pruned breast, the nipple like a smashed bug.

"And don't bring your monkey ass back here again," she said as she clamped her robe shut, then tore the pamphlet in two, and disappeared back into her home.

Styles chuckled.

Oh, I'll be back all right.

***

He sat in his Suburban just down the street, far enough away that the woman wouldn't notice him, but just close enough to see her driveway.

The clock said five o' clock. The bitch should be leaving soon, going to whatever errand demanded her presence at the same time every day. And right on schedule, she backed out of her front door, locked it, and scurried to her pewter-colored Taurus. As the car zoomed by, Styles ducked down, then watched it disappear around the next turn.

Hoarders. This wasn't the first time. He'd had a few let-downs, nothing but carnival-won plush animals, decorative plates, and plastic crap. Not to mention the heaping mounds of garbage.

And always the stink. Every one of them had a distinct smell all their own, but always with a hint of rot. He came prepared this time: a white surgical mask and latex gloves.

Though he had waded through the endless piles of shit, at times it proved worth it. Some hoarders were treasure hunters, filling their homes with precious antiques and timeless collectibles. He had his collectors waiting with open wallets for these items. Or, sometimes he would find enough electronics to sell to any mom and pop pawn shop, using his alias of course.

Styles eased the Suburban away from the curb and headed toward the home. His stomach tickled with anticipation and his palms grew sweaty within the latex gloves. The car squeaked as he brought it to a halt just in front of the home, then backed it into the driveway. He wasn't planning on being there long, had the ability to spot the valuables within a few minutes without wasting any time lollygagging.

The monkey's back, you stupid bitch.

He didn't even bother with the front door. After the mass of locks he'd seen, he knew that would be too tedious, and he needed to do this quick, in and out. He went straight for the side of the home to check the windows, checked over his shoulder periodically to make sure there weren't any peering eyes. The coast seemed clear, but when he looked up at the windows, he saw the black metal bars for the first time, then circled around to the other side only to find the same.

Shit.

The only thing left to do was hop the fence and try the back, and if that proved unfruitful, he would just have to call it a failure, move on to the next house. No problem, happened before, would happen again. The good thing about his profession: there was never a shortage of opportunities.

Experience taught him to poke his head over the fence and give a light whistle before just jumping over. His flesh had its share of teeth marks, and he wasn't too eager to add to the collection.

So, he lifted himself halfway over the fence, whistled.

The sound of hurried padding.

He expected to see the cliché pit bull or Rottweiler, which would spell failure with a capital fuck. But what came galloping around the back of the house induced a light chuckle, and he hopped over the fence and into the backyard.

A Pomeranian came storming across the grass, yapping and growling with dwarf-toned menace.

"Hey, little fucker," Styles said, and stomped his foot.

The dog barked again, then spun around and ran... through a doggy door. The clear plastic flap waved Styles over, promising him access.

He dashed toward it, sized it up with squinted eyes. The square looked just big enough, if he maneuvered right, to allow his skinny frame inside.

The dog poked its head out, saw him, yapped, and fled back into the safety of the home. Almost as if it was daring him to try, double-dog-daring him to invade its territory.

Shit, could snatch up the dog, sell his purebred ass to a loving family somewhere.

Too much time had passed already, and the clock was ticking. Only a matter of time before a suspicious neighbor called in the unknown vehicle parked in the driveway. The woman wouldn't be back for another hour, at least, as long as she stuck to her schedule.

Styles dropped to his knees, winced when he felt the soft mound mash under him, smear across his pants. The smell of fresh feces drifted into his nostrils.

"Goddammit…"

But there was no time to worry about that. He poked his head in first. The opening seemed big enough to fit his head, maybe an arm. Then he could just wiggle his way through, inch by inch. The dog sat on its haunches a few feet away, tongue lolling from its tiny mouth, an almost whimsical image.

Styles clenched his teeth and pushed with his legs, got his head, an arm, and about half his chest in. His other arm lay flush against his side, and something on the doggy door bit into his elbow, tore across his flesh as he squeezed in further. But he held back his cries of pain and pushed on, got his other arm free. After that, it was as simple as crawling the rest of the way in.

The dog yapped once and dashed away.

And there it was. The smell, waiting to greet him. But this was different, not like the spoiled, moldy smell most hoarders' homes provide. This was a smell he couldn't put his finger on. Though the odor of putrescence mingled with it, this stench seemed otherworldly, burrowing into his nasal cavity and filling his head with disease.

He pulled his mask out, slapped it to his face. But the stink was like a mist in the air, and it stung his eyes like chlorine, snuck behind the mask and made his mouth water.

The house was a wreck. At least there weren't cats in this place. He would never forget the cat house, countless felines mewing and hissing, covering every free space, their dead, festering offspring littering the floor, alive with the movement of flies and maggots.

And even then, with the smell of sewage and spoiled food and rotting kitten flesh, the stink in this house was worse.

What the fuck is that smell? Where is it coming from?

He figured he'd find out soon enough. His eyes darted around the living room, took in the mounds of trash all around him. And it was just that: trash. At first glance, he didn't like what he saw, didn't see a damn thing worth taking.

His heart nearly shattered his chest cavity when he heard the footsteps. He immediately searched the room for a weapon, anything heavy he could defend himself with when the woman's husband or roommate or whoever found him in the living room. But he didn't hear it again. He stood in his spot for a good minute, just waiting for it, but nothing came.

Must have been the fucking dog.

It sounded too heavy to be the dog, but he just dismissed it as nerves and moved on. Though the living room seemed hopeless, he still had the bedrooms to check. A lot of hoarders keep the good shit hidden: under beds, tucked in closets, maybe an attic.

He rounded the garbage heap, eyed the outdated magazines, the yellowed paperbacks, the various holiday decorations. Always the same kind of shit. What he suspected to be the master bedroom stood just to his left, and he sprinted toward it, checking his watch as he went. According to his calculations, he had about forty-five minutes before the flabby bitch got home.

Got to make it snappy. Just a quick look, no fucking around, then I'm outta here.

When he entered the room, the smell intensified. Pressed in on him like an avalanche of rot. He gagged, tasted a hint of vomit, swallowed it back down and took quick shallow breaths.

The bed was unmade, white sheets stained in much the same way as the woman's robe had been. An ashtray overflowing with butts sat on an end-table beside the bed. The ceiling fan blew the stench around, swirling it into his face. Every hot exhale was trapped in his mask, and he breathed it back in.

He stopped in his tracks when he saw what lay on the floor in front of him, made him wonder if maybe it was a better idea to just leave now, forget about this place and move somewhere else. A different neighborhood, shit, a different town. Get as far away from this fucking house as possible.

The carpet had been scraped away, leaving a concrete lesion in the center of the room. Something dark stained it, with chunks of what looked like dried meat scattered here and there. Flies scurried about, suckled and buzzed and sliced through the air. Black and red candles lined the circle on the floor, each one of them melted down to the base. Lying open and face-up between two of the candles was some kind of book. It looked ancient, something hand-bound from a time period he couldn't identify.

It looked valuable.

He grabbed it, but quickly let it fall from his hands. The binding was soft like baby flesh. *It must be my imagination*, he thought. It had to be. Because when he touched the book, he thought he felt it move, sort of pulse, responding to his touch. And in that instant, for just a second, images flashed through his mind, snippets of flesh being torn apart and wide screaming mouths and roaring beasts with teeth like scythe blades...and fire. Lots and lots of fire.

And words were branded to the inside of his skull, words that he knew had significance, but didn't know what they meant. Sacrifice. Resurrection. Guardian.

The second the book slipped from his grasp, the images sizzled out, but the words remained, nagged at him, floated in the vitreous humor of his eyes like bacteria.

The book lay pages-down, the peach-colored binding facing him now. Crude stitches ran across its surface, the flesh around the sewing red and irritated and fresh-looking.

76

"What the fuck…?" The words forced themselves out of his mouth, and he had to will his eyes to look away. The hellish slideshow lingered on the inside of his eyelids, and he ran the heels of his palms over them to smother the horrible images.

This bitch was into some freaky stuff, he knew that right away. Probably some kind of devil worshipper or fortune teller or some shit.

For reasons he didn't understand, he knew he needed to look under the bed. There was a certainty about it, that something he needed to see lay there waiting. So he got down on his hands and knees, and glared into the tight darkness.

A withered corpse lay there, its flesh as black as raisins, stared out at him with empty eye sockets. Though the face had no flesh to display its terror and anguish, it was apparent by the body's twisted position, curled in on itself like a burnt piece of paper. Even the flies refused to feed on it.

And the smell was as thick as chili, went through his mask with ease, filled his lungs with decay. Styles blew the air from his nose, coughed, rose to his feet and heaved.

Time to go.

He sprinted toward the bedroom door, would squeeze right back out of the doggie door so that the woman would have no proof he was ever there, no reason to seek him out. Whatever this woman was into, Styles wanted no part of it.

But he wasn't alone.

Standing between two mounds of garbage, sucking on its fore and middle fingers and staring at Styles with bashful, longing eyes, stood what appeared to be a baby. Except the thing was taller than him, at least six foot, with a misshapen and disproportionate body that was glazed with perspiration. Its protruding belly hung down almost to the knees of its bowed legs.

The thing yanked its fingers from its mouth, pulling a drooping string of drool that oozed to the floor. Its bottom lip looked swollen, bee-stung, and when it opened its mouth and gurgled indecipherable gibberish, its two bottom teeth shone with saliva, sharp like a staple remover. The gums were open-wound-red and resembled chewed-up raw steak.

It took a step toward Styles, giggled and blew spit bubbles.

Styles stepped backward. "Whoa, man. Stay…s-stay back, all right? I'm leaving."

The thing's brow crinkled, purplish and cone-shaped, and it took two more thundering steps. Its eyes sparkled as they studied Styles's face, one of them no bigger than a drill hole.

Fuck this.

Styles dashed for the doggie door, heard the giant baby's chasing footsteps. He dove, shoved his head through, squeezed an arm out, and pulled. The sun's heat soaked into his skin…he was almost free.

A tiny growl just in front of him. He looked up and into the face of the Pomeranian, its lips curled to bare the tiny canines.

"No…stay back…good pup—"

The dog leapt forward, nipped Styles's left cheek, broke skin and drew blood. It bit again, grabbed the mask and tore it free.

Then the hands wrapped around his ankles, squeezed, pulled.

He tried to grab something, but caught only air, and he was yanked back into the house.

***

After being dragged across the living room, Styles found himself in a bedroom. Flies cut through the air and made themselves at home here, attracted by the smell of the bodies on the floor in front of him.

Sitting in a circle, like some kind of graveyard Kindergarten class at story time, sat the skeletons of children. Strips of tendon and decayed meat clung to the bones, but there was hardly anything left of them. Filth-covered stuffed animals sat in the lap of each one, and mountains of more neon-colored plush characters towered over them from each corner of the room.

The mutant baby's grip nearly crushed Styles's ankle, and as he was being dragged along, he sat up, pried at the thing's hand with his fingers, but couldn't get a grip, couldn't loosen them at all.

Once inside of the room, the baby slammed the door, jumped up and down and giggled. Its body was webbed with dark veins, zigzagging along the bulbous fat mounds and inflamed boils. A crude diaper was wrapped around its groin and buttocks, and from the mass of flies swirling there and the gut-wrenching odor, he knew the baby needed a changing. A shriveled, blackened umbilical cord hung like a giant sun-dried earthworm from its belly button, curled like an upside-down question mark.

Styles lay on his back, the circle of dead children just behind him. The baby plopped down, squashing whatever mess lay in his diaper, and glared at Styles. The two fingers found its mouth again, and it sucked on them, scooting closer with small pelvic thrusts.

"I'm s-sorry...I'm sorry I broke into your house." He was sitting up now, hands extended with the palms facing the baby. "Just let me leave. Let me go."

But he got only a baritone chuckle for a reply. The fingers popped out of the mouth with a wet slurp, and a series of grunts and moans followed. It scooted closer, reached out for Styles's hand, but he pulled it away.

"Relax, now. Just...just calm down."

"Ungh...bababagh..." *Giggle giggle giggle.*

And the baby pounced, landed stomach to stomach on top of Styles, jammed its face into his and slathered mucus and slobber all over. The salty fluid crept into Styles's mouth and he gagged, tried to turn his head away.

The baby bounced, thrashed its limbs and guffawed. Styles couldn't breathe under the crushing weight, beat his fists against the spongy body, but the baby didn't let up, kept bouncing, kept giggling.

As Styles struggled for air, his vision going fuzzy, there was a sound at the front door. A series of clicks, a jangle of keys.

The baby gasped, releasing another waterfall of saliva that marinated Styles's face. It rocked its body, rolled off Styles, flung the bedroom door open, and raced toward the front door.

Styles writhed on his back, catching his breath—each inhale flooded his mouth with corpse-stink.

The baby whined and grunted, pounded on the walls with fists like boiled hams. When the woman stepped into the house, she was attacked by a rough embrace.

"All right, honey. All right," she said as she stroked the boil-covered fat rolls on the baby's back. "Mommy's home now. Calm down, sweetheart." She covered the baby with wet kisses, but it wasn't until she slammed the door behind her that Styles saw the child.

A small boy, maybe six or seven years old, had his hand clamped in hers, and he pulled, kicked at her, but she pretended he wasn't even there. Wet smears coated the boy's cheeks and he bared his teeth and whimpered as he yanked.

The baby stomped its feet, pointed toward its bedroom. Right at Styles. The woman locked eyes with him and a long smile cracked her face.

"Whatta we have here?" She strolled toward the bedroom, the crying boy in one hand, her deformed child in the other. "Take it that's yer car in my driveway, hm?"

"Look...I'm sorry. It was a mistake, okay? Just a stupid fucking mistake—"

"Watch yer dirty mouth 'round my baby." Her fingertips stroked the back of the baby's head, and she had to reach up to touch it.

"Lemme go...I want my mom...lemme go!" The boy looked exhausted, as if he'd been fighting this woman for hours.

"I just wanna leave now...I didn't take nothing, not a thing. Just let me go, and nobody has to know about any of this." Styles was on his feet, contemplating making a dash for it, but he didn't think he could get by the monster child.

The woman chuckled, her laugh thick with smoker's phlegm. Ignoring Styles's pleas, she turned to her baby.

"Honey, did you see what I brought ya?" She swung the boy in front of her, and the baby reached out and grasped the child by the arms, lifted him in the air, and bounced him like a puppet.

"Ow, ow! Stop...nghhhh..." The boy turned his head to avoid having to look at the baby's face, sobbed and kicked his legs.

The baby pulled the boy in, face to face, spat bubbles in his face and cooed a deep, wet growl.

"Go on and play, baby. Mama gotta talk to our new friend here." And from the inside of her coat, she pulled out a pistol, aimed it dead-center at Styles's chest.

Styles shot both hands in the air and tried to stop his bottom lip from quivering. "Come on, man. This ain't... It don't have to be this way."

"Why don't we spend some time alone, in my bedroom?" She coughed and a beige loogy catapulted from between her lips, landed somewhere on the carpet. "Sound good, my little monkey man?"

As Styles exited the macabre room, the bulbous baby ran back in, the boy bouncing by the arms and squealing. The door slammed and a shudder danced up Styles's spine, imagining the boy's meatless skeleton joining the congregation of dead children.

"What the fuck is going on...what is this?"

Sacrifice. Resurrection. Guardian.

The woman poked the mouth of the pistol into the side of Styles's head, motioned for him to walk.

"Who did you sacrifice?" he said as he shuffled into the landfill living room.

She stopped in her tracks, smiled and coughed. "You was in my bedroom, huh? You touched the book."

"Only for a second...I can't understand the shit floating around in my head."

A chuckle. "Oh, you'll understand soon enough, honey." She motioned with her gun again. "Now get the fuck inside that bedroom."

***

"Am...am I the sacrifice?" The more time Styles spent in the house, in the bedroom with this woman, the more he wished for a bullet. Just fucking end it now before any more horrors presented themselves.

"You? Baby, please," she said as she climbed onto the bed with him, gun still pointed. She had removed her pants and shirt, the flesh-toned bra and panties squeezing the loose flesh of her body that spilled over the edges like raw biscuit dough. The open sores oozed a clear fluid that she habitually wiped away. "The sacrifice was made months ago, almost a year now. The motherfucker lying right under ya, sweetie. I know you seen him."

The charred, twisted corpse spun back into his mind. His brow furrowed and he glanced up at the woman.

"The baby," he said. "The baby is the resurrection."

She nodded, wiped at a sore on her stomach. "And that good for nothing cocksucker under the bed was his daddy."

The sacrifice has already been made. The resurrection has already happened. She doesn't need me.

Styles had one attribute that he was confident about: smooth talking. He'd been a career criminal his whole adult life, learned what to say and how to say it to get what he wanted. And to get him out of a tight spot.

He took a long look at her repulsive body, figured the bitch just needed some dick, which is probably why she stripped down so fast.

He scooted closer to her, reached out and touched her hand. "So you been in here all alone with no man? For a year?"

She studied his face, coughed, then smiled. Her thick-knuckled hand reached across and plucked a pack of Camels from the end table. "What, you tryin' to sweet talk me now? That it?" she said with a cigarette bouncing in her mouth, pulling a yellow Bic from her bra.

Styles smiled. "Guess you can say that. I know a woman in need when I see one, and I see one right now. I think I just

82

might have the medicine for you."

The grin that spread across her face nearly made him gag. Just the thought of this woman on top of him, her spotted, wobbly flesh swaying as she rocked her pelvis was enough to make him grab hold of the gun and swallow a bullet.

But his survival instinct took over.

Get this bitch comfortable, do what you got to do, then ice her.

The scent in the air never let him forget about the dead man curled up beneath him, but he did his best to pretend it wasn't there.

Smoke billowed from the woman's mouth and she began to look shy, couldn't lock eyes with Styles without giggling. "Well, my baby sure could use a daddy. A good one, not like that fuck-ass under ya." She stubbed out the smoke. "And I'd be lyin' if I said I hadn't been lonely."

She reached back, broke the clasp of her bra and let it slump onto her stomach, revealing her withered breasts, the dark and hideous nipples like pieces of wilted lettuce stuck on the ends. Her tongue slithered from the depths of her mouth, glazed her lips with iridescent spit.

Oh Jesus Christ!

"Y-your son…what happened to him?"

She lowered her eyes, curled her lip. "Whatta ya mean?"

"Resurrection…what…what happened?"

Another cigarette found its way into her mouth. "Born dead. Just a tiny little thing he was. Spat right outta me while I was in the bath." Inhale, cough. "He was just floatin' there, all cute-like. I couldn't let him go."

"How did you bring him back?"

She laughed. "You don't wanna know the details, baby. Believe me. Somethin' passed down through my family for generations." Smoke stormed from her mouth, and she pointed at the mattress. "The fucker under ya, he gave his life so my baby could come back to me. Funny thing is…the little guy just won't stop growing. Could fit him in my hand one day, next thing I know, I'm ridin' on his back, ya know?" A hearty laugh rattled her chest, and she spat a fat ball of phlegm off to the side. "My boy…he's got him an appetite. First thing he did when his eyes opened up for the first time was eat the placenta. Just gobbled it on down."

The violent images of death and grotesque beasts that the book had induced inside of his head soaked back in for a moment. "Hell…it was hell, wasn't it? That brought back your boy?"

Stubbed the cigarette out. "I told ya, honey, ya don't wanna know." Panties slipped away.

Styles forced himself not to look.

Guardian.

"The guardian. Someone to protect your baby." He blinked rapidly. "Me? Is that me?"

"No more questions." And she dove on top of him, scrubbing him with her baggy flesh. The gun went to his mouth, slid past his lips, prodded the back of his throat. The woman eased him backward with the pistol until he lay spread eagle in the middle of the bed. With her free hand, she unbuckled his belt, yanked his pants and boxer shorts down to his knees. And with furious motion, she brought his cock to life. "There we go, honey, there we go."

As she mounted, Styles squeezed his eyes shut. From the other room, a scream coated in torment sliced through the air, along with loud banging sounds on the wall.

The woman rocked, her eyes fluttered, the gun pressed harder, almost down his throat. He gagged, coughed.

"Yeah, baby. Oh God, yes." Her free hand fondled a breast, reached down to his chest and raked five ashy lines down his skin.

Pull the trigger…just fucking do it!

A whimper escaped his lips as she rode harder, moaned and coughed and moaned and coughed. Something warm splattered on his chest and she rubbed it into his skin like cocoa butter.

Her head tilted back and she screamed, shuddered. The gun slipped from Styles's mouth as the woman bucked with orgasm, both arms in the air like a victorious Olympian. "Oh…oh, honey. Go—"

His fist struck the middle of her face, then again and again until he saw the gun tumble from her hand. Her sloppy pussy spat his cock out like hot food from a burnt mouth, and she fell backward spitting blood and teeth.

Styles dove for the gun, hopped to his feet, pointed it at the howling woman's head. "Hey," he said as he stepped closer. "At least you busted a nut first."

And he pulled the trigger three times, each one catching a piece of her face and head. Gore slapped the floor in piles and the woman slumped over, her mouth wide open, blood pouring down and drenching her chest and stomach.

Now get the motherfuck out of Dodge.

He fished through her pants pockets, found the keys, hauled ass into the hallway and toward the front door. Freedom was a few key-turns away, but as he twisted the first deadbolt, the child screamed again. The baby grunted and cooed, and the child muttered horrible cries of pain that made Styles wince and turn toward the baby's bedroom.

Resurrection.

This fucking thing is an abomination, he thought. *It's got to go.*

The Pomeranian yapped from across the room, its eyes demonic-looking with the light reflecting off of them. It spun in circles and barked repeatedly.

You're next, fucker.

Styles swung the door in, aimed the pistol. The stench of death came flooding out of the room, rushing over him. His gun hand shook and he bent over, splashed hot vomit over his shoes and the floor.

The child was no longer screaming, though his face was frozen and contorted with the final scream he ever had. From his chest and up, the boy still had flesh, looked almost normal besides the panicked terror on his face and the blood freckling his skin. But everything below that had been stripped and flayed down to bone.

The baby cradled the boy's body on the floor, sitting in a wide pool of blood and chunks of gore that soaked into its diaper. It looked up at Styles when the door crashed against the wall, its cheeks bulging with intestine as it chewed. It held the next mouthful of viscera in its hands, cupping it like a slice of watermelon.

"You…you motherfucker…" Styles raised the gun again, clenched his teeth and took one step toward the atrocity.

But the growl from behind stopped him cold. Small at first, squeaky, but it deepened, grew more menacing by the moment, along with a series of cracks and tearing sounds.

Styles spun in place, dropped the gun. "N-no. Please." His head shook and his shoulders bounced with sobs.

The little lap dog grew, its limbs snapping and elongating, its snout stretching, growing teeth the size of butcher knives that dripped foam and saliva. Its arms, legs, and chest thickened with muscle that twitched as they grew. Razor-edged claws retracted from its new fingertips. A deep rattling growl emanated from its chest as it stepped toward Styles and peered down at him with eyes the color of hot coals. Hot drool oozed over Styles's head and burned like boiling oil.

Guardian.

"I…I wasn't gonna kill him…I'm…I'm his new daddy. Me. I ain't gonna hurt him." Styles fell to his knees, winced when the baby wrapped its arms around him from behind, giggled and slobbered fresh blood over the side of his face. "S-see?" He reached up and stroked the baby's head, leaned over and kissed its cheek. "I'll feed him. I'll take care of him."

The demon bent backward, face to the ceiling, and roared. Hot spittle rained down and Styles whimpered, curled into a ball and hugged his knees to his chest.

It only took an instant for the creature to shrink back down. The Pomeranian padded toward him, licked his fingers.

The baby cradled him, cooed wet gurgles into his ear.

"I'll take care of you, baby. Y-your daddy's got you."

I'M A
TERRIBLE PERSON

Let me start by saying I don't do this anymore. But I admit I used to.

If it wasn't for my daughter, I might still be doing it.

Texting and driving.

There's no reason for it. First of all, if you want to talk to the person so bad, just call them. Now I know talking on the phone while driving isn't the safest thing in the world, but at least your eyes are on the road. But really, we could just put our phone away, couldn't we? Tuck it somewhere out of reach, then check it when we get to wherever it was we're going.

It's so bad now, that when the wife and I see a car swerving during the day, can't seem to stay in its lane, we look at each other and say, "Texting." And when we pass that car and look over at the driver, more often than not, that's exactly what they were doing.

Again, I did this myself. A lot. Once I had a child's car seat in the back, that stopped real quick.

I saw a commercial on TV one day while at the gym. I was just asked to write a new short story for someone, and I was lifting weights trying to think of something cool I could do. And in the mirror, I see this commercial.

I can't remember exactly how it went, but I remember there were three teenage girls in a car. The driver was texting, the other two laughing and dancing to some pop song blasting from the speakers. The driver doesn't see the traffic jam ahead, and as her car speeds toward it, her eyes on her lap, the entire scene pauses.

Everything is in slow motion, and the driver looks up at us and starts talking. Telling us how she'll never get to go to prom or graduate high school or go to college. Says the same about her two friends, who apparently, will also be dead soon. She talks about her family, how much grief she was about to put them through. All because she was texting when she should have been paying attention.

We get a quick glimpse of her phone and the conversation is about nothing at all.

Then everything speeds up. We hear screams and the sounds of crunching metal and hissing oil.

Pretty fucked up. And I knew right away I wanted to write a story about it.

What would you do if, after struggling for so long, things finally started to look up? After all your hard work, it was finally paying off. You take your eyes off the road for a second, just to playfully text with your loved one, teasing them about the good news you have.

And boom.

Nobody's around. Nobody saw it happen.

Would you do the right thing?

I'M ON MY—

Morris wanted to scream as he walked from the office building toward his Camry, but he breathed instead, held his composure. Ten years. Ten years he had been working for this company, and it was finally paying off.

I've been their best guy since day one. It's about time.

When they had brought him into the office, he was sure it was bad news. Not because he had done anything to warrant any kind of reprimand, but because he was pessimistic by nature. And he had never seen his bosses call anyone into their office for anything good.

"Morris," Mr. Whitehead had started. "You know I like you. You know I think you're a good worker, right?"

Morris had nearly passed out right then and there. He couldn't lose his job. Not now. Not with a baby in Melissa's belly. Not while they were waiting to hear back to see if their offer on the house was accepted.

"Y-yes, sir." He wanted to say more, but his words sizzled away on his tongue like water on a hot griddle.

"Stand up, son," Mr. Whitehead had said.

Morris did.

Then the scowl on his boss's face curled into a grin, his smoker's teeth like sallow toenails past his pasty lips. He reached out his hand. "Welcome to upper management, Morris. You earned it, you son of a bitch."

Morris had to clench his teeth to keep himself from squealing as he gripped Mr. Whitehead's hand which was as soft as a cinder block. His boss, who was usually devoid of all emotion, pulled him in and hugged him. He smelled like cheap cologne and stale cigarette smoke, and Morris held his breath as they took turns patting each other on the back.

There had been an awkward five minutes or so after the

strange embrace they had shared, then Mr. Whitehead told Morris to head home for the day, that he deserved a three day weekend. "Come Monday, get ready for some real work. Yeah?"

"Of couse, sir. I'm—"

"No more "sir" bullshit, all right? It's Abe from now on. You're the new sir around these parts." He cackled, coughed, spat something into a crumpled napkin that had been sitting on his desk beside a photo of him and his dog, then excused Morris.

Morris hopped into his car, slammed the door, stared at himself in the rearview. A pair of baby blue, miniature sneakers hung from the mirror, and he held them in the palm of his hand for a moment as his eyes welled up with tears.

No, getting a promotion didn't make them rich, but it sure helped. No more worrying about if they could afford their house payment—if their offer was accepted. No more worrying about the upcoming hospital bill. Melissa could stop freaking out about missing so much work while she recovered. He could feel the stress melting off him like candle wax.

One day, baby, he thought, *you won't have to work at all.*

He wiped his eyes with the heel of his palm, then pulled his iPhone from his pocket. Melissa's number was at the top of the list in his text messages—though it was labeled Babycakes—and he started typing, grinning as his thumbs tapped the screen. They hardly ever talked on the phone anymore—it was always text messages now, like little virtual love letters.

Huge news today! Got cut loose early. Get ready to celebrate!

It only took about a minute to get a reply.

Babycakes: Don't mess with me!!! What is it????

His reply was simply: *;)*

Babycakes: Evil bastard! Well hurry home!!!!!! I luv u.

Luv u 2.

They had been talking about the promotion for years, and Melissa had been the optimistic one. Always telling him

90

not to worry about it, to just keep working hard, that it would pay off eventually. Morris had been on the verge of quitting on more than one occasion, but she had talked him out of it, told him to hang in there, not to let his years of hard work be all for nothing.

And now, when it mattered most, it actually happened.

Holy shit!

As he pulled out of the parking lot, he threw in Melissa's Black Eyed Peas album, switched it over to "I Gotta Feeling." He always hated the group, especially hated that fucking song, but it was Melissa's favorite, and whenever she was in a particularly good mood, she blasted it, nodding her head and waving her arms, shoving Morris to get him to join in. Right at that moment, the song felt appropriate, and he smiled as he nodded to the beat and pulled out of the parking lot.

***

The deluxe sushi platter from *Uchiko*, a bottle of Crios Rosé, and a bunch of peach-colored roses sat in the passenger seat. Each one Melissa's favorite. Two of which pregnant women weren't supposed to touch, but even their doctor had smirked at this myth.

"If that were true, there'd be no French or Japanese people walking around, right?" she had said as she slathered Melissa's stomach in petroleum jelly.

Besides, he thought. *It's a special occasion. A few mouthfuls of alcohol and mercury never hurt nobody.*

Since leaving work, a couple hours had passed, and his phone had been blowing up with text messages since. He hadn't expected it to take so long, but *Uchiko* was packed and it took forty-five minutes just to get his to-go platter. *Central Foods* was swarming with customers, the lines filing back into the aisles. But none of that could spoil Morris's mood. He just smiled, waited patiently, sent generic replies to his wife as the texts rolled in.

Babycakes: OMG! Where are you already!?!?

91

Be home soon, babe.
Babycakes: Seriously, this is WRONG!!!!!
Luv u!
Babycakes: I want a divorce!!!!!!!!!!!
Kisses! Muah!

He knew she was probably pissed for real by now, but the second she saw what he had brought, the second he told her what it was they were celebrating, all anger would disintegrate. Morris had heard warnings from just about every person he knew, even some he didn't, about how Melissa's hormones would turn her into some kind of foul-mouthed monster, that he shouldn't take anything she said to heart because it wasn't really her speaking. None of that happened. She was a little more tired than usual, but that was all. Hell, her sex drive had even intensified since the pregnancy, and Morris wasn't the kind of guy who got weirded out by her bulging belly. They had some of the best sex of their entire relationship in the last nine months.

As he grew closer and closer to their apartment complex, his stomach started to churn, palms grew sweaty, mouth dried up. He couldn't wait to see the look on her face when he told her, couldn't wait to hear her make that *eeeeeee* noise she always did when she got excited.

His cell vibrated again, and he chuckled as he pulled the phone from the cup holder and glanced at the screen.

Babycakes: I'm pretty sure I hate you. WHERE THE HELL R U???!!!

I'm on my—

Something smacked the front bumper hard, throwing Morris's forehead into the steering wheel. His phone flew from his hand at the same time something collided with the windshield, bashing it inward and frosting the glass with cracks. As he slammed his foot against the brake pedal, there was a scraping and squealing sound coming from underneath the car as he dragged whatever it was the last twenty yards or so.

Morris threw the car into park, then cupped his face and moaned. The gash in his forehead cried streams of blood that ran down the sides of his nose, dripped into his eyes, sucked into his nostrils with every breath. Raw fish strips, broken glass, and rose pedals lay on the floor in a puddle of sizzling wine. The taste at the back of his throat made him gag, cough, and he threw his car door open and let himself fall out onto the concrete.

The car hissed and clicked. The scent and taste of burning oil stung his nose and throat.

A deer, he thought. *I hit a fucking deer.*

No. Not a deer. Not unless this was some kind of circus deer that had learned to ride a bicycle.

Morris forced himself to his feet, winced at the searing pain in his face and chest. A diagonal stripe of agony burned over his torso where the seatbelt had gone taught and restrained him from flying headfirst out the windshield.

But none of the pain mattered as he stared at the mangled bicycle sitting crooked and bent on the hood of his Camry. The seat had been planted into the windshield along with the handlebars. The back wheel, though slightly bent, spun in place, the metal spokes stained red with blood.

"Oh…oh Jesus…" Morris dropped to his hands and knees, praying he would see another pair of eyes staring back at him. Quivering with pain maybe, but open, with life behind them. "H-hello? Are you…?"

A hand lay just in front of him. Small, three of the fingers broken, the shredded skin revealing the meat and bone beneath. Instead of a pain-stricken face, he saw the back of a head, the hair matted with blood.

"No…nononono…"

Morris jumped back to his feet, launched himself into the car and searched for his phone. His hands shook so bad that when he finally grabbed it he accidentally tossed it to the back seat.

And then he stopped.

Took a deep breath. Glanced at his reflection in the rearview and then quickly looked away.

Check on the kid first. If he's alive, I'll call an ambulance, police. Anybody who can help him.

93

And if he's not?

Morris dropped to his stomach, grabbed the kid's wrist. He couldn't tell the kid's sex yet, and had expected some kind of reaction when he grabbed at the hand, but it remained limp, not a sound from the twisted child beneath his Camry.

He had heard somewhere that you're not supposed to move a person after an accident. That they're supposed to stay exactly how they were until medically-trained personal arrived on scene. But Morris pulled on the tiny arm anyway. He expected the body to be trapped, caught up on the undercarriage or something. It slid out easily, making a harsh scraping sound as it was dragged across the rough concrete, smearing blood across the blacktop.

A boy. Maybe seven years old.

One look at his face and Morris dropped the boy's arm, turned his head, and splashed hot vomit over the street. He looked around and didn't see anyone, no sign of the boy's parents.

What the fuck were you doing out here in the dark, goddammit!

The boy's eyes were closed. His forehead had been ripped from his skull and hung to the side like a flap of bloody leather. His shirt was so soaked with blood, Morris was too scared to look under the cloth to see the damage.

This kid was dead. He was alive five minutes ago, probably walking his bike home since he ended up under the car—flat tire maybe, or a busted chain—probably in a rush because it was already dark and he knew he was going to be in trouble for being late.

And now he was dead. He was dead because of Morris.

And there's not a fucking thing anyone can do about that now.

Morris checked over his shoulder, rose to his feet and spun, making sure nobody was around, that nobody saw what happened.

As quickly as he could, he popped the trunk, gently placed the boy inside. He would have to clean up the blood later, he knew, but right now, he had to act fast. Get the hell out of there before someone drove by or the boy's parents came calling for him.

It took a few minutes to yank the bicycle free, but he got it, forced it into his back seat. He didn't hit the gas too hard, didn't want to peel out and alert anyone, but he left the scene as quickly and quietly as possible.

He's already dead. I didn't mean to kill him. He shouldn't have been messing around out here at night like that! No reason to throw my life away. Not now. Not when everything is finally going my way. Melissa and the baby...they need me.

And I'd do anything for them.

***

"You okay, sir?"

"I'm fine. Just had a...a little accident. No big deal." Morris had forgotten about his own injuries, and he forced a smile as the teenage girl glared at him from behind the checkout counter. He reached up, slid his palm over his forehead, chuckled and wiped the blood on his pant leg.

"That'll be $11.39, sir." She took the money, then frowned again. "You sure you're okay? That looks pretty deep."

"It's nothing. Really."

Morris took the shovel from the counter and tried not to look too suspicious as he walked out of the store.

***

Babycakes: Okay...I've gone from pissed off to scared. Are you okay? Tell me what's going on, please! If you don't, I'm calling the police. I'm not kidding, Morris.

I'm fine, baby. Don't worry. I didn't mean to worry you, just wanted to surprise you. I'll be home soon. I love you, Melissa. I love you so much. I don't know what I'd do without you.

Morris turned off the phone and shoved it into his pocket. Before that message, there had been ten others, unanswered.

He knew Melissa was probably losing her damn mind by now, and he'd have to think up one hell of a story to get out of this mess.

The hole took much longer to dig than he had anticipated. It was a dry summer, and they were in the middle of a record-breaking drought. The dirt was as hard as concrete, and by the time he had the hole as deep and wide as he wanted, his arms and shoulders felt like they had been ripped free from his torso.

He tossed the shovel away, wiped the sweat from his face with the back of his forearm. Each breath wheezed out of his barren throat, and he shuffled toward the car, dragging his feet, and popped the trunk.

Just a boy. Tears filled Morris's eyes, rained down on the body as he imagined this as his own son. What would he do if someone did this to his child? Killing them and then taking them away like this. The parents would never get closure. They would assume their boy was kidnapped. Would probably be on the news, begging whoever took their son to please bring him back, that they love him so much and would do anything to have him back in their loving arms.

"I'm so sorry. I'm s-so fucking sorry…"

He scooped up the crooked body into his arms, slowly made his way toward the hole. He had made sure to dig it large enough to fit both the boy and bicycle, but once the boy was inside of it, Morris collapsed to the dirt beside the hole, glaring down at the boy whose face was pointed toward the night sky.

"If you would have been alive, I would have gotten you help. I swear to God I would have. But you understand, don't you? I have a family to take care of. My own son coming into the world any day now. They need me." Morris wiped the tears away, then climbed down into the hole with the boy, gripped his small hand, ran his thumbs over the knuckles. "I wish I knew your name. If I knew your name, I'd give it to my son. I would. To honor you. I—"

The boy coughed once. It was weak and barely noticeable, but it was a cough. His eyes fluttered open, and within the next few seconds, his bloody face twisted into a grimace and he began to cry. Asking for his mother. The cries became screams as his squinted eyes locked onto Morris.

Morris pulled himself out of the hole, kicked his feet and scooted away from it. His head shook from side to side as chaotic thoughts screamed through his mind.

Alive...he's alive...oh Jesus Christ he's alive!

Morris covered his ears and bared his teeth as the boy continued to bawl, begging for help, going on and on about how much it hurt.

I'm going to help him now, just like I said I was. He's alive, he can live through this. He needs an ambulance.

But instead of reaching into his pocket for his phone, Morris walked the few feet toward the shovel, picked it up, twisted his hands over the wooden handle, ignoring the splinters stabbing deep into his palms.

He hopped back into the hole, raised the shovel over his head.

Even as the boy screamed and pleaded, it was Melissa's laugh Morris heard in his mind. Her moans of pleasure when they made love. The way she said *eeeeeee* when she was excited.

It was the cry of his newborn baby boy.

"I'm sorry," Morris said, then swung the shovel down. Then again. And again and again and again. "My family needs me."

And I'd do anything for them.

ADDICTED
TO ADDICTION

Another common theme in my writing is addiction. Whether it be food, sex, murder, or just straight up drugs, addiction just really hits home for me.

Now, I've done my share of experimentation with drugs. I liked some more than others, and there were times I was doing more than I probably should have been doing, but I don't think it ever really got out of hand. I was never truly addicted to any drug. If I'm being honest, part of that was because I couldn't afford them.

But there were times when I scared myself. Because I liked it too much and wanted more before I was even done with what I had. I would justify calling the dealer in the middle of the night, asking if I could come back by for another baggie.

I know that sounds bad. It only happened a few times. And once the shit wore off, I was back to normal. Didn't need to do it anymore. But once I got that first taste, for the rest of that night, I was someone else. Not myself.

As I mentioned above, food has been a big issue with me and my family. Addicted to grease and carbs. Even though it made me feel like shit after eating it, the next day, I would go right back through the drive thru and order more.

I've had many moments where I stop and realize how disgusting I am as I stuff my face, grease dripping from my chin and glistening from my fingertips.

So, I wanted to write something about addiction that was a bit different.

Like what if there was a guy who was addicted to car accidents? What about the accidents did it for him? Why did he need it?

I chose car accidents because they have always scared

the shit out of me.

When I was about seven years old, my family and I were driving through Fresno. My parents were in the front, my brother and I were in the two bucket seats in the middle, and my older sister and cousin were in the back.

I had fallen asleep. And I woke up upside down. Hanging by the waist from my seatbelt.

After unbuckling myself and falling to the ceiling of the van, I heard my brother crying. Found him outside of the van, the back doors open, crying for our mom. Not knowing what to do or what was going on, I crawled to him.

The next thing I saw was our mom running toward us. I remember how bloody her hands were. The tops of her hands. Just dripping. My cousin was unconscious in the street.

My dad, and a large amount of people who had stopped to help, were trying to rock the van over because my sister was pinned underneath it.

All we could do was stand there and watch. They got my sister out. I remember she was able to walk. And she was completely covered in blood.

It was, by far, the scariest moment in my life.

Now, I work for the police department. My job is taking 911 calls. And every day, all day long, there are car accidents. Most are minor collisions, but multiple times a week, every week, we get very serious, terrible accidents. And they always bring me back to that day in Reno.

Another thing I remember about that day. We all went to the hospital. My sister and cousin were in critical condition. My dad destroyed his back moving that van.

I was with my mom and brother. My mom now with bandages over her hands.

I remember wondering why I didn't get hurt the way everyone else did. I remember actually feeling guilty about it. Wishing I was bleeding too.

So, with all those images and feelings in my mind, I wrote this story about a man who craves what I fear most.

RED
ASPHALT

It wasn't just the thrill of feeling his face smash into the steering wheel or the beads of safety glass raining down on him that made John do it over and over again. It was the moment of confusion and panic directly afterward that he savored. It was figuring out how many injuries he had sustained. It was how badly the other driver was hurt.

The need was bad tonight.

His hands shook as he gripped the steering wheel and sped down the interstate. It had been a while since he had done one on the highway. With that concrete barrier separating the northbound and southbound traffic, a head-on was out of the question.

Head-ons were his favorite flavor.

His deepest fantasy was hopping that barrier, rolling his car in the air until landing on the other side of the freeway and slamming into an 18-wheeler. He imagined crashing through the windshield and smashing his face against the semi's grille. He could hear the hiss of fluids sizzling on hot engines, the ongoing blaring of the horns, the screeching of tires as other vehicles tried to avoid it. The smell of oil and concrete and blood.

But it was just a fantasy.

He wiped sweat from his brow, licked his lips as he thought about it, going seventy down the freeway looking for that perfect exit. It would have to be a street he had never crashed on before. That was a given. Though he had some fond memories on certain roads around town, he needed something new each time. Some fresh pavement to rain twisted metal, shattered glass, and blood onto.

He checked himself in the rearview mirror. Scabs, along with patches of neon pink skin where a scab used to be, decorated his face from the last collision. He picked at the one on his forehead, peeled it off like a Band-Aid, and wiped the bead of blood that formed in the center of the new crater. His knuckles were maroon with scrapes.

The Plymouth was his fourth car that year. It was a good car, survived his last two crashes, but he was ready for a new set of wheels. Just like the varying location, changing the surrounding metal and glass box every so often was equally as important. And that, along with medical bills and insurance payments, was what made it more difficult each year to feed his need.

But he always found a way.

There.

His left middle finger extended, hit the turn signal. He took the exit for Oltorf St., checked his blind spot before scooting all the way to the right lane. Didn't want to get into a minor collision on his way to his destination. They did nothing for him.

Oltorf was a street he had been meaning to add to his list for some time. Narrow lanes, lots of pedestrians walking around. Not that he wanted to veer off the road and hit any of them, but witnesses were part of the thrill…they added to the panic.

"Oh my God, are you okay?"

"Don't move…are you injured?"

"I'll call an ambulance!"

Then there were the ones that thought they were certified paramedics from watching *ER* or any of the other bullshit television shows. Those were John's favorite. They would wrap their arms around his torso, pull him out of the smoldering wreckage, usually worsening his injuries. God bless 'em.

Another good thing about Oltorf was the speed limit. A solid fifty miles-per-hour. Not so fast that a head-on would kill someone with certainty, but there was endless potential for some serious injury.

When he first started, when the need first crept into his brain, he played around in residential areas—a nice, safe thirty MPH. But that proved to be boring, small potatoes. After that, he figured the highway was the ticket. But he found out that, though traveling at high speeds, rear-ending or sideswiping could only go so far. Of course, there were the occasional rollovers, but they were difficult to pull off with all the cars going one direction.

It was later he discovered the forty to fifty mile an hour streets with nothing but a double yellow line separating the traffic traveling the opposite direction of one another.

Those streets proved to be the most fruitful.

The Plymouth rolled down the road and John peered out his window at all the people walking along the sidewalk, sitting at bus stops, running across the street. He slammed his brakes as a male in his twenties, pants hanging half off his ass, walked at a slow pace across traffic. The car beside John screeched to a halt too, and they both got a long stare from the man as he continued his leisure stroll to the other side of the street.

It was times like this John thought about just barreling through a pedestrian. It wouldn't do much for his need, but the crunch of their bodies under his tires may prove satisfying. He looked over at the driver next to him and they shared a moment of camaraderie.

But John wasn't interested in the cars traveling westbound along with his Plymouth. It was the eastbounders he studied as he pushed his car that extra five miles an hour over the limit. He figured every mile an hour had to count for something.

Then he saw it: a bright yellow Hummer with a chrome grille that reflected the sunlight into John's eyes.

Now that *could probably total my Plymouth.*

As they converged, John squeezed the steering wheel with slippery palms, perspiration beading his face.

It was the reflected light that caused it. Hit me right in the retina and I veered over, didn't even realize I'd done it until it was too late.

Upon impact, there was a moment that seemed to stand still, suspending John in a gelatin of frozen time. He looked into the face of the other driver: a woman with a cell phone to her ear and a child's car seat just behind her. Her mouth twisted into a knot and her eyes looked ready to tear at the corners.

The next thing John knew his chest and stomach were wrapped around the steering wheel and the top of his head smashed the windshield. He wore no seatbelt—he never did—so his ribs took the full impact. There was no airbag to soften the blow—he'd made sure of that.

Blood filled his mouth and every gasping breath sent lightning bolts of pain through his chest, stomach, and back. His head rested against the shattered driver's door window, and when he leaned away from it he saw the red circle where his head had been. Long drips ran down the broken glass. Euphoria fluttered over his body as blood drops pitter pattered onto the seat and floorboard from his head and face.

And he smiled. He breathed in the smell, as best he could. Smoke spiraled from the metal accordion that was the vehicles' front ends, mashed together like kissing lovers.

John shuddered as the high swept over him like a warm bath. This was what he wanted, what he needed. What he deserved.

The woman in the Hummer screamed. People on the street spoke in rapid, quick-fire rhythm. Car doors slammed, shoes slapped across pavement, glass tinkled to the ground. A group surrounded his car, yanked on the car door, rocking the vehicle.

John was in heaven.

***

"What the hell is wrong with you, John?"

John sat in the passenger seat of Mark's minivan as they drove away from the hospital. He fumbled with the air conditioning vent until it blew against his wounded face. He sighed, leaned back against the headrest. "Nothing's wrong. It was an accident."

Mark snorted. "An accident? You really expect me to

103

believe that? You could have killed that kid."

"You can believe whatever you want," John said. He closed his eyes and enjoyed the warm throbbing in his chest. Though the crash was a few weeks back, he still had trouble breathing.

"That's bullshit, and you know it. You're…you're addicted. You need help."

John let his eyes roll open. "Addicted? That's stupid."

Stopping at a red light, "Look…it's not your fault what happened to Mom. You've got to let it go."

Just hearing the word 'Mom' nearly made John dig the tips of his fingers into Mark's throat. Nobody knew how he felt. Nobody else was there. He took a deep breath. "Just take me home, okay?"

Mark shook his head. They drove on in silence, and although John saw his brother glance at him from time to time in his peripheral, he never returned the look. He just stared right through the windshield. It felt like they were sitting still and the street passed under them like a concrete treadmill belt.

But as he inspected the inside of the minivan, he couldn't help but wonder what beautiful crashes it could create. With all the room in there and John in the passenger seat, he could imagine his body bouncing around the interior like a rubber ball. He looked at the steering wheel, thought about how easy it would be to jerk the wheel.

It had been so long since he was in a wreck from the passenger seat. Not since…

Mark veered onto the highway.

"Where are we going?"

"I've got something I want to give you." Mark side-eyed John, licked his lips. "Just a quick stop at my place, all right?"

John's knuckles slammed against the dash. "Just take me the fuck home!" His hand throbbed, a sharp pain penetrated his chest. Eyelids fluttering, he leaned back again.

"Just relax, man. It'll only take a second." Mark shifted in his seat, changed lanes on the highway.

John just shook his head, watched the surrounding cars dance with one another.

Metal with a flesh center, zooming this way and that, weaving from lane to lane. Such potential for carnage.

They approached a construction zone decorated with orange and reflective signs. A backhoe buried its massive claw into the highway's epidermal asphalt. In place of the usual concrete barricade were orange barrels and reflective posts. Workers scurried about like ants with hardhats.

They took the exit toward Mark's house, a good thirty minutes out of the way. John chewed his tongue, doing his best not to yell anymore. "What do you need to give me? And why right now?"

"It's something important. Just trust me, all right?"

"Why should I?" John jerked his head and winced. "Unless you have money for a new car, I don't need shit from you."

John saw Mark squint as they turned on another street, saw his jaw muscles twitch. They rode in silence until finally pulling into the driveway.

"You might as well come inside, say hi to Gloria and your nephew. They miss you, John. We all do."

John smacked his lips. "This is such bullshit. Is that why you brought me here? To make me feel guilty?"

"Just come—"

"That kid's not my responsibility! I have no obligations to your fucking family."

Mark's fist struck like a rattlesnake, bit John in the temple. John's head rocked to the right and his neck shrieked with pain. Then Mark's fingers were wrapped around John's throat. "Get the fuck out of this car and get inside that house. You think all your bullshit hasn't affected the rest of us? Huh?"

John tried to talk, but his voice was trapped under Mark's grip. His lips uncurled past his teeth.

"You think you're the only one that misses Mom? Every fucking time you do this, it brings us all back to that day. And how do you think Dad feels?"

When Mark released him, John could only gasp. Every breath was razor blades over the muscles in his torso. John opened the car door and stepped out, leaving his brother panting in the minivan.

John watched Mark take a deep breath, check himself in the rearview mirror, then exit the van. He cleared his throat, opened the front door to the house, motioned with his head for John to enter.

Not wanting to push this any further, John obeyed. His gaze remained on the ground as he trudged past Mark, but when he glanced up into the living room, he clenched his teeth, spun on his heels, but Mark slammed the door and crossed his arms.

"Fuck you, man. Fuck you!"

"It's for your own good. We just want to help, John," Mark said, reaching out to place a gentle hand on John's shoulder.

His family sat in the living room, all facing him, with furrowed brows and papers clutched in their hands.

A woman John didn't recognize rose to meet him. "Hello, John. My name is Gwyneth," she said. She motioned toward an empty seat beside his father and uncle like a gameshow host. "Your family is here because they love you and they're worried about you."

John's mouth went dry and his shaking knees nearly gave out. He wanted to scream, to pummel this bitch into the ground, but the sight of his family sitting there, worry etched on each face, softened him—especially his father who already had tears on his weathered cheeks.

He had only ever seen that man cry once before.

"They just have some things they want to say to you," Gwyneth said. "Will you hear them out?"

John nodded, hung his head as he shuffled to the empty chair. Mark followed behind and took his seat between Gloria and Charlie. The boy had gotten so big, and it was only then, as John looked at him, that he realized how long it had been since he had seen him. Or any of his family.

As the seat cushion deflated under him, his father reached

out, put a thin-skinned hand on his knee and squeezed. The old man's body rocked with sobs as he wiped his face with a flannel sleeve.

John's eyes burned and he couldn't make himself look anybody in the eye. He stared down at his hands, scraped and scabrous, and fought back the tears that threatened to emerge. His hands swam in his vision. A rough grip took his shoulder, patted his back.

"John, it's been a number of years since we spoke last," his uncle started. "I know you're probably wondering why I'm here since I ain't seen you since you was a kid, but I got some things to say to you that I hope can help." He cleared his throat and John heard a paper crumple. "John, I'm here because I love you. I miss my sister every day. She was my best friend, always was. And she loved you more than you could ever know."

The weight filling his gut began transforming into something else, something ugly. He tried chewing it down, but as his uncle continued talking about John's mother, it became unbearable. He watched his limp hands harden into fists.

"Look...I know you was in the car with her. I know you seen it happen. But—"

"You don't know shit!" John leapt to his feet, lifting his chair over his head. His entire body exploded with pain from the exertion, but his rage overpowered it. The man calling himself an uncle flinched, protecting his face with his arms.

Before John could smash open the man's head, someone yanked the chair from his grasp.

"What the fuck is all this? I don't want to be here!"

John turned to find Mark tossing the chair aside and stepping forward. John threw a closed fist into Mark's face, felt his brother's nose crack under his knuckles.

Mark stumbled back, his nose bleeding onto the carpet.

"Jesus Christ," Gloria said as she ran to her husband's side. "What the hell is your problem, John?"

Charlie's face pinched and he started crying.

"What do you people want from me, huh?" John turned

to Gwyneth and pointed a finger like a gun barrel. "And who the hell are you? Why are you here?"

She stayed seated, smiled. "I'm here to help. To offer you a second chance."

"A second chance at what?"

"At life, John."

As John gasped for breath, it felt like something in his chest had torn. A twisting blinding pain that John was wasting in his brother's house. He wanted to be home where he could enjoy it alone, where he could ride the high.

"John, sit down." The voice was thunder, absolute.

The barbed anger that pulsated in his stomach, like he had swallowed a fistful of nails, shied away at the sound of that voice.

Mark sniffled and wiped at his face as Gloria whispered into his ear and kissed him. Charlie's cries had turned to soft whimpers. Uncle Paul muttered cuss words under his breath.

"You need to listen and listen good, boy."

John didn't bother looking for another chair and just let his body unfold itself onto the floor. He looked up at his father and melted under his gaze.

"This has to stop. Your mother would be so ashamed of you, do you know that? I'm sorry you had to see what you saw, I would have changed places with you in a minute," he said. He leaned over, rested his elbows on his knobby knees. "I love you, boy. Your mother loved you. You had nothing to do with what happened, you understand? It was an accident. Now forgive yourself before you end up in the ground alongside…"

The old man's lip trembled. He took a deep breath, sat up taller.

"This woman, Gwyneth, is going to offer you something, and you damn well better take it. For all our sakes."

John turned his head, ignored the searing pain in his neck, and stared at the woman through blurred vision.

"John, there's a facility we want you to spend some time in, talk to some people that can really help you. Your family has set everything up for you, and all you have to do is agree to go."

John looked around at the faces surrounding him. He buried his face in his palms and allowed the tears to flow.

He nodded, wiped his face with the collar of his shirt. A collective sigh of relief blew around him like gale winds.

"I...I just need some air."

"Go ahead, John. Take a minute to take this in. We'll all be here waiting for you."

His father helped him up with a strong callused hand, pulled him into a tight embrace. They held each other for what felt like an eternity, though once the old man released him, it didn't feel long enough.

Mark smiled through his bloody face, patted John on the shoulder as he walked by. Uncle Paul extended a hand and John shook it, got a nod of approval.

But John had to get outside. Had to get away from them all.

The day's crisp air, with a hint of freshly-mown grass, filled his lungs as he eased the front door shut behind him. He looked at the keys that he had swiped from the end table by the door before exiting the house.

The need was too strong to deny.

***

He had to take the U-turn on the service road of the freeway so he could loop around. The minivan sideswiped a green sedan, but John barely felt it as he continued his journey. He clenched his teeth so hard he felt a couple of them crack. Blood basted his tongue.

The minivan bounced off a guardrail on his left, then into a motorcycle that had just changed lanes on his right. He saw the leather-clad man bouncing on the pavement like a rag doll through his side mirror, but John kept going.

"I'm sorry, Mom," he said. He slammed his palms against the steering wheel as tears blurred his vision. *"I'm sorry!"*

He took the entrance onto the northbound highway, the same one Mark had taken just an hour or so before.

But it wasn't the highway he saw zooming past the windows…he was nine years old again. Sitting beside his mother.

He couldn't even remember what he was upset about anymore. Some redundant game or toy maybe that was being denied him. Or maybe they were on their way to the dentist. He didn't know.

He only remembered reaching over, wrapping his pudgy fingers around the steering wheel, and jerking it to the right. The car skidded and nearly spun out, flew into a side street. His mother screamed, clawed at the wheel and slammed on the brakes.

John saw the truck coming and squeezed his eyes shut.

She wasn't wearing a seatbelt, always said they were too uncomfortable, though she made John wear his, and the car was an older model Toyota with no airbags.

The impact was like a bomb going off, but John's seatbelt held him in place. His breath was knocked out of him and his chest and stomach ached a bit, but other than that he was fine, he was okay.

He couldn't remember if he said anything. But he remembered staring into his mother's eyes. Wide open, coated with the blood dripping into them from the opening on her forehead.

Her torso was twisted toward the driver's door, but her face rested on the steering wheel, facing John. Glass twinkled from her curly hair.

"I'm sorry. Oh-oh God…."

John couldn't tell his family what he had done. The truck came out of nowhere, he had told them. Mom didn't see it.

He pressed the gas pedal down to the floor, pushed with all his weight until his knee hurt. The minivan shoved a station wagon aside as he swung into the left lane.

The construction zone came into view, materialized over the concrete horizon. The first orange barrel bounced off the front bumper, smashed into the windshield and rolled away. Then he hit the next and the next.

There were no workers there, but the backhoe sat like

a yellow metal beast, and as the minivan's tires rolled onto the clawed bucket, the van ramped off, launched into the air sideways.

John's forehead cracked against the steering wheel and his body slammed against the driver's door.

The minivan landed on the passenger side, skidded and spun toward the southbound traffic. Glass shards and hot sparks peppered his face. Through the blinding pain consuming him, John could see the oncoming semi-truck. Blood covered his eyes and the world became red as the truck's horn blew.

Then there was the satisfying crunch of metal and glass, and a glorious pain erupted, held him in a strong and tight embrace.

And he knew he deserved it.

He was in heaven.

PEANUT BUTTER PIZZA

What happens when you combine two things that you love? Well…I guess it depends on what they are. As much as I love pizza, and I straight up lust over peanut butter, I'm not so sure it would be a good idea to put the two together. Not that I'm not open to giving it a try.

I once ate a hot fudge sundae hamburger. It was on the menu as a joke, so naturally, I ordered it. Because I was being a smart ass. And they made it and brought it out to me, almost as if daring me to actually eat it. So I did. Every bite. And you know what? It was kind of awesome.

So, the moral of the ramblings above, if you combine two things that you love, it might come out pretty awesome even if it doesn't seem like they should work together. Then again, it might be a disaster.

So that's what I did with this next story.

I love slashers. Something about big, dominant serial killers in masks has always filled me with excitement. Probably because I grew up watching *Friday the 13th* and *Nightmare on Elm St.* and *Halloween* and all the others. I liked monsters. But masked killers were always my favorite. Which is why I wrote *Muerte Con Carne*. Because I *needed* to create my own.

Another thing I love…is fishing. I've been fishing with my dad and grandpa since my first memory. I could spend all day long sitting on a pier with my line in the water, sipping beer and just relaxing. Even if nothing's biting, I'm at peace and happy.

So I thought, "Hey! I love slashers and I love fishing. I'm gonna combine them and see what happens!"

And this ain't no fishing themed serial killer wearing a catfish mask and impaling his victims through the lips and

cheeks with giant hooks. Though that's not a terrible idea...
I wasn't sure if it would work. But I had a ton of fun
writing it anyway.

I can only hope it's as good as that hot fudge sundae
burger.

THAT'S A KEEPER

Ezra watched the old car creep across the dark, deserted road from the top of the small hill a good quarter mile away.

The night vision binoculars turned everything green. Made him feel like Dorothy in the Emerald City. He lay under the sign for Robertson's World Famous Fried Pies. A good spot. *His* spot. The way the sign sat, it blocked most of the moonlight, sort of laid a blanket of shadow right over him.

And he'd had plenty of luck in that spot. Caught some serious keepers.

He stayed still. Perfectly still. Hadn't showered in a week. He heard the scent of soap and other perfumed cleaning products could drive them away. Like they could detect it, though he wasn't all that sure he believed it. But just in case it was true, he practiced it.

This year was important. This was *his* year. He could feel it deep down in his gut.

The woman behind the wheel was a knockout. Maybe in her mid-twenties. College girl. Hardly any makeup on her face. Just a little black liner to make the eyes pop. A soft pink over her lips. But that was all. Girl next door. Natural beauty.

The car was old. Paint flaking off like dead skin. Puking a steady stream of white smoke out its tailpipe as it puttered on down the road. Nothing around it but hills and night. It was a full moon, but even the moonlight was having trouble cutting through the darkness. Like the black was thicker than usual.

Light and dark battled all around them and it looked like dark was winning.

The car coughed and choked and finally died. Rolled to a halt in the middle of the road, right next to the sign that said she only had a few miles to go before she reached the next town. Civilization.

The sign said that if the car would have only held on for a little while longer, she wouldn't be alone. In the dark. Things might have been different.

But there was no fun in that.

Ezra adjusted his binoculars, zoomed in on the woman behind the wheel. Even with that angry expression on her face, she was gorgeous.

This one was perfect. After so many others. So many disappointments. This one was different. He knew it. He knew it the same way he knew this was his year. Because he goddamned deserved it, that's why.

He sighed softly. Telling himself to be patient. Wait for it. It would happen. He just knew it would.

***

Bart watched the couple from the trees.

He didn't like to use any kind of equipment for watching. Didn't trust anything but his own eyes.

He'd come out to the spot a few nights back. Dug a good sized hole so he could fit all two hundred pounds of himself in there comfortably. Laid a tarp camouflaged to look just like the forest floor over the top of him. The color of soil with dead leaves and twigs glued to it. He even had a hat that looked just like a rock. Could walk right up on it, stare at it, could even pop a squat on it and you wouldn't know it was anything but a rock. That way he could stick his head up out of that hole and use his eyes to watch.

The couple was only about fifty yards ahead of him. Their tent fully built. Not one of the big fancy ones either. Just a simple, old-fashioned one. But they weren't inside the tent.

The couple lay on a sleeping bag close to the fire. It wasn't a cold night by any means, but just something about those thrashing flames that was relaxing. And camping wasn't camping without a fire.

Orange, flickering light twitched over the woman's naked back and buttocks as she rocked on top of the man. They both moaned. Took turns so it was a deep moan, then a high-pitched one, back and forth like it was some kind of language only the two of them could understand.

They were perfect. Others had been good in the past, but nothing like these ones here. They were the ticket.

This was his year.

He thought last year was it, had been sure of it, but it was a fluke. He'd been cheated. Not this time. No fucking way. This was his year and with this couple fucking by the campfire, he knew he had it in the bag.

The man and woman had been at it for a good while now.

Watching them, sunk into the ground all alone, he couldn't help but think about how long it had been since he had a fine piece of pussy on top of him like that. He missed it, sure. But there were more important things to spend his time worrying about. Preparing for.

When it was all said and done, maybe he'd reward himself.

He deserved it.

But for now, he stayed hunkered down in his spot. A good spot. Always his favorite.

And he waited.

***

Ezra didn't see him at first. The bright green of the night vision was giving him a headache, so he had set the binoculars down and squinted toward the distance.

It was too dark and too far to make out any details. But he could see the car. Could see the shape of the woman behind the wheel. Could see the street sign mocking her just in front of the sedan, its green surface sparkling in the moonlight like one of those vending machine stickers he used to buy for a quarter.

So from where he was, without the night vision binoculars to cut through the distance and darkness for him, he almost missed him.

It was like the night spat him out. One second there was nothing but nothing, and then there he was. Standing at the foot of a hill just on the other side of the sign.

"Shit." Ezra lifted the binoculars, pressed them to his sockets, then pulled the strap over the back of his head.

He could hardly breathe. Couldn't believe what he was looking at. After all these years. Finally. It was finally his time.

This one was nice. No, more than nice. It was goddamn spectacular. A keeper. Biggest and baddest he'd ever seen.

I got it in the bag for sure this time. No goddamn question about it.

But still, he waited. Watched. If he got too anxious, if he let his excitement and the adrenaline now pumping through his veins make him impatient, he might lose him. It had happened before and he would be damned if it was happening again. And none of the others that had gotten away from him before were anywhere near as beautiful as this one.

No. He was bagging that son of a bitch. No other way about it.

A hitchhiker. And a nice one. A lot of folks gave up on hitchhikers. Said they weren't what they used to be. Going extinct. Not worth the time or trouble waiting for one.

Ezra knew they were full of shit. Problem was, none of them were willing to put in the work. All looking for the easy way out. Out there in the woods or breaking into old houses looking for slashers. He liked a good slasher himself every now and then, but he wanted something special this year. And he knew if he got the right bait and stayed patient, it would all pay off.

This one was massive. Never saw a hitchhiker as big as this one.

But he knew the big ones got big for a reason. They were smart. He would have to time this just right.

The hitchhiker wasn't only big, but damn impressive looking. Wore a white mask like a bleached skull, featureless besides the eyes. Deep, black pits. Even darker than the

117

surrounding night. The neck was red like blood pouring from the bottom of the head, disappearing into the black trench coat beneath it. His hands were stuffed into the pockets, and for a long while it just stood there, watching the woman, not moving.

Ezra started to get nervous. He feared he'd been made, that the hitchhiker had sensed him hiding up there by the sign for fried pies.

But then the hitchhiker moved. Pulled his hands from his pockets, as red as his neck. Some kind of gloves pulled over them, long needle-like talons on the ends of the sleek, crimson fingers.

Wait for it. Wait for it.

***

The bastard walked up behind him. When Bart heard the crunching footsteps, he gasped, then lowered his head down into his trench with the rest of him, slapped his hand over his mouth. Waited for sharp metal to be driven into his back.

But the footsteps walked right on by him, then stopped. Replaced by heavy, rattling breaths.

Bart chanced a peak. Lifted his head just enough to let one eye get a sliver of vision to the outside.

A massive, mud-caked boot sat right beside him. The beginnings of a girthy, muscular calf rose from the ankle and out of sight. The shoe looked big enough to pack a family into and take a drive.

They stayed that way for a while. Bart holding his breath and getting an eyeful of giant boot, and the owner of the boot staying perfectly still. Breathing deep and steady.

The couple fucked and fucked. Never slowing.

Then he moved. The biggest goddamn slasher Bart had ever seen. Bigger than his last winning catch by a mile. Like a Kodiak bear wearing a man suit. Shoulders as wide as a semi's bumper. Arms like battering rams hung at his sides, fists the size of truck tires curled at the ends. A long-handled axe extended from one hand, the blade wide and rusted with old blood.

Bart only saw him from behind, but he could see the bush of scraggly beard hair puffing out on both sides of his head. The red and black flannel shirt heaved as he breathed. Slowly creeping toward the copulating campers.

That's it, Bart thought. *Take 'em. Go on and take 'em.*

The slasher's slow trudge burst into a running leap, and he buried the axe into the top of the woman's head. Split it down the middle, all the way to her neck.

And still she fucked. Hips thrusting.

The slasher ripped his axe free, revealing the sparking wires within her head, then grabbed her by the neck and yanked her off. Threw her aside like an inflatable sex toy. Her body slammed into a tree and broke apart. Splashed oil over the bark and dirt floor. The hips still thrust back and forth in the soil, making a whirring sound.

The man still moaned. The slasher stared down at him, head tilted. He raised his axe.

The net exploded from between the man's legs, wrapped around the slasher like a sticky ghost and tossed him onto his back. Kicking and punching and grunting.

Bart set the remote down and popped up out of the hole. "Yeah! Got you, you big, scary fucker!"

***

The hitchhiker scraped its talons along the car's side, peering in at the woman who still looked angry, slapping the steering wheel.

Hold it, Ezra. Hold.

The shiny, red hand raised, tapped the driver's window.

Ezra hit the scream trigger. The woman's head spun toward the hitchhiker and she shrieked. Ezra rolled the volume control up some, got her really wailing.

The sound seemed to awaken something in the hitchhiker. He reared his head back and howled. Tore his black trench coat from his body and let it fall backward, revealing the blood red flesh of its torso like exposed, skinless plates of

119

muscle. It thrust one hand through the window, shattering it, then reached toward the woman's face.

Her mouth spread wider, the scream so loud the hitchhiker actually flinched.

Now!

The dart spat from the woman's mouth and stuck the hitchhiker in the neck. He hardly reacted, seemed more confused than injured. So Ezra hit it again. And again. It took five darts to finally put the son of a bitch down, and the hitchhiker dropped to his back and twitched before finally going still.

"Got you. I got you! You're goddamn right, you ol' son of a bitch, I got you!"

Ezra grabbed his equipment and tossed it into the passenger side of his tow truck that was parked on the far side of the Robertson's World Famous Fried Pies sign, then drove it down the hill and toward his bait and his catch.

After hooking up the car to his truck, he grabbed the woman out of the front seat, who was only a torso, arms, and a head, and set her in the front passenger seat of the wrecker. Best lure he ever bought. Better than anything that ignoramus Bart would have. Stubborn old bastard.

But Bart had tasted victory before. Had the trophy sitting on top of his fireplace at home. Loved to take it down and show it off. Ezra wouldn't be surprised if that old fool slept with the thing.

Not this year. No, sir. This is Ezra's year. That trophy's mine.

He circled the hitchhiker, studying him. A fine catch. Breathtaking.

"Look at you. Just look at you. What a beauty."

He knelt down and ran his hands over the red flesh. He thought it was some kind of costume, but it was a growth. Prickly and moist. Felt like scabs, but the color was too bright. He suddenly wondered if it was a good idea to be touching it, whatever it was, and pulled his hand away, wiped it on the seat of his jeans.

"Well. Let's get you hooked up."

The hitchhiker's eyes watered as they stared up at Ezra. The poison wouldn't kill him. With five darts, the paralysis should have lasted an entire day, but seeing as how the son of a bitch was as big as he was and how long it took to drop his ass, Ezra wasn't taking any chances.

I'll put him down after the judges get a look at him. Damn shame, really.

He tried to roll him over with his boot, but it was like kicking a fallen tree. Had to get down on his knees and push the bastard over. Then he hogtied him, opened the rear door of the bait car, and hauled his catch into the back seat. Barely managed it. Had to take a minute to catch his breath, rub the spot on his lower back that felt tweaked.

The CB in the truck crackled and Ezra shook his head and grinned. Strolled toward the driver's door, still minding his back.

"That you, Bart?"

Laughter. "Who the hell else could it be, you old geezer? Goin' senile on me already?"

"Better laugh now while you can, old boy. Cuz what I got tied up right now's gonna make you wish your daddy never taught you to hunt."

***

"Shit, Ez. You see the son of a bitch I just bagged, and you'll be shittin' your Depends."

"Let me guess. Got you a slasher, didn't you?" Ezra laughed, his voice tinny and muffled, oozing from the radio's speaker.

"It ain't the species, it's the size. You go hitchhikin' again?"

"It ain't just the size of it. You get you something rare. Something special, size won't mean shit. But just in case it does, my hitchhiker is the biggest I've seen. This one's so damn pretty it's almost a shame to kill it."

"Bullshit."

"Would I lie to you, Bart?"

121

"You'd lie to your dead mama if it meant a chance at that trophy."

"Think what you want. The judges will see soon enough. See you out there, old boy. Not that it'll matter, but bring that slasher you got with you. Might as well."

Bart frowned and let the CB drop from his hand. His buddy and nemesis had to be lying. Silly bastard had been chasing hitchhikers for years with nothing to show for it. Wasting money on the tournament and never once showed up with a catch.

He's full of shit. There aren't any hitchhikers left worth a shit. He's got him a slasher and don't know it, and there ain't no way in hell it's as big as mine.

There was only one way to find out. So he put his truck in gear, all his equipment already packed up, and drove on toward the tournament's base camp. When those judges, and all the other hunters, saw what he was hauling in, they'd shut the damn thing down.

***

"Don't take it too hard, old boy," Ezra said and admired the trophy in his hands. His grinning face was reflected against the golden surface. "I tried to tell you. Caught me a special one today."

"Ah, hell, Ez." Bart patted his old friend on the back, pulled two cold beers from his truck, handed one over. "I don't mind losin' to a beauty like that. I mean goddamn, son. That's a keeper if I ever saw one. Nobody's gonna forget that catch for a long time."

"I tried to tell you," Ezra said and cracked his beer open, drained half of it. "Just a little patience. And the right lure."

"Mine did the trick, but that mean bastard busted the woman all to shit. Gonna cost a fortune to fix her up."

"Not a scratch on mine. And believe me, she'll be gettin' put to good use. More than welcome to join me if you wanna lesson."

"Lesson. Here's your lesson, you cocky prick." He smiled

and chugged from his beer can. "But yeah, I'll take you up on that. Now I won't be satisfied till I get me a hitchhiker for myself."

As the other hunters strolled by, looking defeated, some seething with jealousy, they either acknowledged Ezra with a pat on the back and a nod, or they scowled and growled as they passed.

The catches all hung from their ankles, lined up side by side from a thick block of wood above the stage. The judges were still up there, admiring the year's haul. Pretty nice, even besides Ezra's winner. Some real big ones. All slashers. If Ezra wouldn't have bagged the hitchhiker, he was sure his buddy Bart would have taken home his second trophy. The slasher was so big it could have eaten the others and still have room for Jell-O.

"Next weekend, then?"

"Sounds good to me."

The judges turned, found Ezra, and waved him up. All smiling, shaking their heads in admiration. Nobody had expected a catch like that.

"Go on. Now's the fun part. Where everyone starts kissin' your ass and givin' you the celebrity treatment. Hope that ugly mug of yours don't break their cameras."

"Yeah, yeah."

"Go. Enjoy it. You deserve this one."

The two old friends shook hands, then hugged, patting each other on the back. They clinked their cans together and both drained the rest of the beer.

Screams. Wood snapping.

"What in the hell?" Bart grabbed Ezra by the shirt, pointed across the way toward the stage. "Tell me you put a bullet in that thing's head, Ez."

Ezra's grin melted off his face. He shook his head and slowly turned to face the sounds.

"You stupid son of a bitch…"

"I…I put five darts in him. Five! Should've put him down till morning…at least!"

"Till morning? You're supposed to kill the fucker!"

"Well I forgot! Too excited about—"

The hitchhiker wiggled from his ankles raking at the neighboring slashers hanging on either side of him. Ripping big chunks of flesh from their carcasses. The wood made another loud cracking sound, then shattered.

The catches all slammed to the stage, their massive bodies crushing the judges.

And then the hitchhiker was on his feet. Tilted its head back and howled. One judge still whimpered from below the pile of bodies, shoving against them to free himself.

The hitchhiker's claws drove through the man's head just under his nose, silencing him. Then he flicked his talons as he tore them free, flinging a mound of bloody brain peppered with skull fragments at Ezra.

Ezra ducked and heard the splat behind him.

"Ah shit! What in the goddamn..." Bart wiped the muck from his face, spat and cursed.

As the hitchhiker leapt from the stage and started tearing hunters to shreds and painting the ground with their blood, Ezra couldn't help but admire it.

It was a beauty.

AIN'T WHAT IT USED TO BE

Remember when Halloween was…I don't know. Better? As an adult, I get to make Halloween whatever I want it to be. Before my daughter was born, it pretty much consisted of inviting over a bunch of friends and watching horror movies all night long, smoking and drinking ourselves braindead. Or, we found a costume party to attend, with the end result being about the same.

Those were good times. I still look for any excuse to have a bunch of buddies over for some horror movie watching, popcorn munching, beer guzzling pandemonium.

But when I think of Halloween, I think of trick or treating. And it wasn't just collecting pillowcases full of candy that I look back on so fondly. It's being creative. Coming up with that perfect costume. See, I was a shy kid. I'm still shy, though I've learned how to fake confidence in social situations. So putting on a mask and running around with a group of my best friends with no adults around was my idea of the perfect night.

We weren't bad kids. I smashed a pumpkin once, and felt terrible about it for a week. The next day, there was a sign in the yard, the parents saying they hoped whoever smashed their pumpkin had as much fun destroying it as their child had picking it out. Yeah. I'm a fucking evil son of a bitch.

We would just roam the neighborhood. I would talk to girls as we passed them by because I was protected from embarrassment by whatever mask I decided on that year. And yeah, pillowcases full of candy were pretty bad ass too. Especially the Reese's peanut butter cups. If I could find a way to liquefy them and inject them straight into my veins so that I just walked around all day tasting them, I would do that. Hey Science, get on that, will ya?

Even more fun than all that? Scaring people.

The best Halloween I ever had was when I decided to skip trick or treating for the first time ever. Convinced my buddies to do the same. I had the whole thing set up perfectly.

It was nothing complicated. But fuck was it affective.

The way my parents' house is set up, there's a small walkway that leads from the driveway to the front door. The side of the garage on one side of the walkway, and big bushes on the other. One friend, the owner of Sinister Grin Press, was hiding in those bushes, wearing a simple clown mask.

I had my setup in front of the garage. I also wore a clown mask. And a huge jacket and huge pants that I stuffed with newspaper. Plus an old, rusty axe. I sat in a lawn chair and pretended to be fake. Gave my head a tilt. Stayed as still as possible, which is really hard when people are staring at me, face to face, inches away. Prodding at my chest and arms.

I fooled every one of them. They would decide I was just a fake decoration, then move on down to the walkway. Now, once they move to the walkway, they can't see me anymore.

I would hear a knock at the door. The door would open. "Trick or treat!"

And then the clown in the bushes would stick his face through the leaves, roar, and push the limbs forward so the bushes almost seemed to be reaching out for the trick-or-treaters.

There was a scream. And they would come running.

As soon as they were in eyesight, I would jump up off my chair, raise the axe over my head, and do the infamous slasher walk as they ran away shrieking.

Oh my God, it was fun.

The best scare by far happened when I was taking a break. It had nothing to do with me, but goddamn it was satisfying. I'm not sure if these kids heard from someone else in the neighborhood about our setup, but when they walked up, I was sitting with my elbows on my knees, chewing a mouthful of peanut butter cup.

These guys, a little too old to be trick or treating really, were dressed like cholos. One walked up to me, gave me the tough guy face, and said, "Why joo movin', clown?"

I just shrugged and continued enjoying my candy.

They moved on to the walkway, chuckling to one another. Knock. Trick or treat! Clown face. Roar.

Nobody screamed louder or ran away faster than those guys. What I remember the most about that moment was the little girl behind them. Dressed like a princess. They trampled her as they scrambled to get away, didn't even pause to see if she was okay or to apologize, just booked it down the street.

She was a little badass, though. Just got up, brushed the dirt from the front of her pink dress, and went and claimed her candy. Because candy is far too important to waste time crying about getting trampled by coulrophobic cholos.

It was a great night. We scared a ton of people, laughed our asses off, then finished the night with candy and horror movies. Already planning next year's house of horrors.

And nobody showed up. There were a few, but only a fraction of the amount from the year before.

I started noticing that it didn't seem like anyone was trick or treating anymore. For me, it happened in one year. We had the greatest Halloween ever, followed by the most disappointing. I don't know if it's because parents were getting too protective or if we just didn't have many kids in our neighborhood at that time, but it was a real bummer.

Now, with my daughter, we go all out on Halloween. She loves it. She's three years old, so I still have to tag along. She still thinks I'm the coolest person in the world, so she doesn't mind. We ended up with a pretty good neighborhood for trick or treating. Lots of festive people, lots of kids. It's great. But it's still not what it used to be. I just see a bunch of over protective parents, following along, putting a limit on how much fun their kids can have on the day they're supposed to be able to run free, dressed as monsters, collecting candy from strangers.

Halloween is for the kids, damnit! No adults allowed!

That's where I got the idea for this next story.

It's time for kids to stand up and take back their holiday.

GIVE ME SOMETHING GOOD TO EAT

Dan tightened the ropes around his son's wrists, then walked around the chair to face him.

"Are they tight enough?" Esmeralda said.

"They should hold."

Esmerelda bit her lip and turned her gaze away from Corey.

Dan wrapped his arms around his wife. "I pray to God they hold."

Their son's face dripped sweat as his eyes bounced from parent to parent. "Please. You don't have to do this…"

Esmeralda buried her face into Dan's shoulder. He reached up and squeezed the back of her neck, his eyes on Corey's feet, unable to look him in the face.

"I'm sorry, Corey. We have no choice."

Dan led his wife up the stairs and out of the cellar, leaving the light on for Corey and ignoring his pleading. It never got easier, year after year, keeping their only child locked away like that. But it was something that needed to be done. Their lives depended on it. Everyone's did.

Dan locked the cellar door, took deep breaths to collect himself before turning to face his wife. He had to stay strong in front of Esmeralda. The woman seemed especially on edge lately, and he worried her composure would shatter if he let her see how stressed he truly was.

"The pumpkin?" he said.

"On…on the counter…"

The kitchen smelled of cinnamon and charred pumpkin. The jack-o-lantern sat atop the counter, just as she said, the candle already burning within, casting dancing shadow demons on the walls. The face was simple: triangularly cut eyes and nose, a smile with four square teeth.

He scooped up the pumpkin and walked with his wife toward the front door.

The other parents would be waiting outside.

They walked to the curb and placed their pumpkin there, signaling to the others that Corey was secure. Other jack-o-lanterns lined the sidewalk in front of each home—one for every child. The street was alive with orange, writhing light.

Their neighbors, Preston and Walter, walked out just a few seconds after Dan and Esmerelda and set their pumpkin in its place. Their adopted daughter, Sonia, had only been with them for a year, and it was their first Halloween as a family. The balding men embraced each other and wept as they stared at their jack-o-lantern, taking turns lifting their eyeglasses to wipe the tears beneath.

"You guys stay strong," Dan said. "The night will be over before you know it, and we can all get back to our normal lives."

The men said nothing, didn't turn to acknowledge Dan. They just stared at their pumpkin, sniffled and whimpered.

Dan eyed the street, counting the jack-o-lanterns. Couples stood at the end of their driveways, nodding to one another as they made eye contact. Everyone knew what had to be done. Dan pursed his lips and gave each one of them a nod. Esmerelda wrapped her arms around him and squeezed and he squeezed back, rested his chin on the top of her head.

The sound of shuffling footsteps grew louder as they approached from his left.

Simon trudged toward them, the moonlight behind him deepening the shadows on his heavily-lined face. His back was hunched and a shaky hand repeatedly rubbed at the back of his head, which hung limp from his neck. When he reached Dan and Esmerelda, he finally let his eyes roll up from the cement.

"I need to talk to you, Dan. It's the McKrackens." When he said the name, he jerked his head to the rear.

Dan peered over Simon's shoulder toward the McKrackens' one-story brick home. The curb was empty and dark, no pumpkin in sight.

Not again, Dan thought.

"You talk to them yet?"

"I was hoping to have you along 'fore I tried it. Never know, know what I mean?"

Dan nodded and gave Esmeralda a tight squeeze. She kept her arms locked around him, looked up into his face. "Dan?"

"It's fine," he said, doing his best to hide the panic threatening to cave in his chest. "I'll go talk to them. I'm sure they're just behind, lost track of time. No big deal."

Esmerelda nodded but kept her face pinched as she unwrapped her arms from his torso. Dan kissed her three times before walking down the street with Simon. He had to force himself not to look back at her again.

The two walked in silence until they reached the empty curb in front of the McKrackens' home.

Simon cleared his throat. "They got twins, don't they?"

"They sure do. Good boys…nice boys."

"Not tonight they're not." Simon ran his hand over his face as he glared at the home's dark front patio. "What in the hell are we gonna do if—"

"Let's just hope it's a misunderstanding, that they just—"

"A misunderstanding? The sun's almost down, there's no fucking time for a misunderstanding." Simon whisper-yelled the last sentence.

Dan held up his hands and nodded. He sucked in a stomachful of cool oxygen and marched toward the front door. The air smelled of grass and burning pumpkin. Dan couldn't help but remember the McKracken boys mowing his lawn—front and back for five bucks each—every other week. Good boys. Nice boys.

Simon followed closely behind cursing under his breath. He had been there the last time a parent buckled under the pressure. He knew what this meant.

Dan rapped his knuckles against the red, wooden door, checked his watch, then turned to look at the sky. The sun just peeked over the horizon. They had to do this quick if they weren't already too late.

"Hello? Anybody home?"

"No time for this shit!" Simon pounded his fist against the door, then jumped back when it creaked open.

They locked eyes for a brief moment before entering the home.

Dan felt the energy in the air change. The sun had sunk. The night had risen. Halloween had begun. The air was as thick as caramel, and as they stepped into the home and down the front hall, he could smell it. The meaty scent of fresh blood.

Oh Jesus...

"Something's wrong," Simon said.

"I know."

They crept past the living room and into the kitchen, then stopped cold. Simon gasped, slammed his knuckles against the countertop.

"Fuck! This is so... *fuck!*"

The McKrackens lay face-down on the tile in a pool of their own blood that continued to widen as Dan and Simon stared. The blood ran along the grout lines in red zigzag patterns.

"Stupid fucking bastards," Simon said as he paced the living room. "One day a year. *One day a fucking year!* Now look at 'em."

"Simon—"

"No. No, these fucking assholes are putting us all in danger. Goddammit! How stupid can you be, huh? How fucking stupid!"

"Simon, they're already—"

"You remember what happened the last time, Dan. You remember. Ah shit, Dan, I don't know if I can handle another night like... *Stupid fucking bastards!*"

"Simon! They're dead. Cussing them out won't change shit, okay? We need to warn the others."

Dan *did* remember the last time it had happened. Would never forget it. He'd seen more than six of his friends and neighbors die that night. They'd found Bill and Donna— Dan and Esmerelda's best friends at the time—sprawled out in their lawn. Bill's throat had been scooped out so that his spinal cord shone in the moonlight. Donna lay on her back, her arms tense, fingers digging into the grass. Her eyes bulged, mouth wide open as hoarse whimpers oozed out.

Their daughter Eliza—just barely two—was between her mother's legs. Her tiny toes dug into the lawn as she pushed herself forward, crawling back into her mother's womb, already waist-deep when Dan had seen her.

Dan shook his head and pulled his mind out of the past. There was no time.

"Oh shit, Dan. Their...they—"

Dan crouched down beside Simon who had Felicia McKracken's body turned over. Dan knew it was Felicia's body because of the flowery dress she wore, now drenched in dark red. But he was looking into the face of Oscar McKracken, her husband. A butcher knife had been shoved into Felicia's neck stump, hilt first, but buried deep enough to hold. Oscar's severed head was pressed down onto the blade, a gap just wide enough between where his head ended and her neck began to see the gleaming metal of the knife. Dan looked at Oscar's body and saw the long blond hair flowing from the head. He didn't need to see the face.

"We have to—" Dan jumped to his feet when the screaming started from outside, and he sprinted toward the door without waiting for Simon.

He stumbled across the threshold, nearly losing his footing. The night poured over their street and he could feel the evil crackling in the air, could sense that Halloween was in full swing. And the children would have their night.

All it took was one. He'd seen it before. One child would free another, and then they would free two more, and so on and so on. Dan's nightmares were still filled with what he did the last time to get through Halloween night. But he wouldn't put his family at risk. Not this time.

I have to get to my family.

As soon as he reached the sidewalk, he stopped short when he heard the giggling. It came from his left, high-pitched and whispery. Dan's muscles tightened and he clenched his teeth as he turned to face it.

Sonia skipped toward him down the middle of the street, her eyes shining a hellfire orange. Her jump rope made a wet sound when it skipped off the pavement, and she hummed between giggles as she approached.

Dan was frozen in place as the little blond girl hopped closer and closer. Staring at her for too long made the backs of his eyes burn and pulse. And as she grew nearer, he saw that her jump rope was a fresh, slimy rope of intestine, splashing blood over the street as she swung it over her head and skipped along.

"Stay back, you little bitch!" Simon rushed across the McKrackens' lawn toward Sonia, fist raised above his head, but didn't make it too far before his body was thrown backward following the loud blast.

Dan flinched at the sudden sound of the gunshot. He ducked and covered his head with his arms.

Simon's body slammed against the concrete as blood rushed out of the hole in his belly. His legs writhed and he gurgled and groaned.

"You w-won't touch my daughter!" Walter limped forward with his shotgun held at stomach-level. Smoke spiraled from the tip of the barrel.

Sonia dropped her slimy rope and dove onto Simon's quivering body, tearing away his shirt like it was a food wrapper. She dug her fingertips into his wound, pulling it open, and plunged her face into the red and yellow fat just below his skin. She slurped it up like buttered grits.

"Dan! D-Dan…get her off…" Simon's words grew fainter until his mouth fell open and his eyes stared sightlessly at the pavement. Sonia moaned and chortled as she gorged.

"You stay away from my Sonia. Don't you touch her," Walter said through his high-pitched sobs. "My beautiful little Sonia…"

"Where's Preston, Walter? What did she do?"

Walter collapsed to his knees in the middle of the street and bawled. He rocked back and forth, the barrel of the shotgun scraping against the asphalt. Sonia's eyes lit the night around them. Dan sidestepped away from the wet sounds of Sonia's feasting, kept his eyes glued to Walter.

"I need to get to my wife, Walter. I need to make sure she's safe."

"Preston...he..."

Sonia screeched and turned to face Walter, fresh gore dripping from her face in globs. She did a handstand as she tittered, shining her hell light over her foster father's face and washing it in orange. She walked on her hands toward him, slowly, singing as she went.

"Trick or treat..." Another few steps with her hands, her hair hanging over her blood-stained face. "...smell my feet..." Her voice went deeper, but held the childlike shrillness simultaneously.

Walter covered his face and wept.

"Give me something good to eat!"

She cartwheeled back to her feet as her demonic voice exploded from her tiny throat, startling Dan and nearly making him fall backward. She dove for Walter, but he had his shotgun at the ready, and pulled the trigger just in time. Sonia's body flew backward, her chest blown wide open. As her body flopped around, the orange light dissipated until fading out completely. The smell of burnt gun powder mixed with the pungency of blood and cooking pumpkin flesh.

"No! *Noooo!*" Walter pounded his knuckles into the street, cracking the skin and flinging blood as he pummeled the black concrete. *"Sonia!"*

Dan felt a deep sadness for the man, but he had no time. Esmeralda could already be in trouble. Corey could have been released, maybe by one of the twins, maybe by Sonia. For all he knew, every damn kid on the block could be free, raising hell and feasting on the flesh of adults.

Esmeralda could already be dead.

Walter cracked the gun open, dug into his pockets, shoved a shell in and snapped it shut. As Dan ran by him, Walter already had the barrel in his mouth.

I'm sorry, Walter.

When the blast rang out, echoed off the houses and

parked cars, Dan flinched but didn't look back, didn't slow his pace. No time.

Screams exploded into the sky from every direction, and Dan whimpered as he pumped his legs faster, passing the orange grinning faces of the jack-o-lanterns lining the street on both sides.

Please be okay...please be okay.

He passed Simon's house, winced when a woman shrieked from inside. His house was only a few strides away. He could already see the Corolla's rear bumper in his driveway.

The boys stepped into the street from opposite sides, merging together in the middle. The McKracken twins, covered in blood, locked arms and faced Dan. Their eyes illuminated the lawns and houses around them.

They juggled something, flinging glistening objects over their heads. One boy tossed them into the air, the other caught them and handed them over, again and again and again.

Dan squinted against the orange of their eyes, tried to find a way around them, but found himself rooted to his spot. They closed the gap between them and him, and the blue moonlight revealed what they were juggling.

Pieces. Some unrecognizable. There was a hand, crudely severed at the wrist, jagged flesh and skin flapping as it flew through the air. A small breast, already turning blue, followed the hand.

The nipple is pink, not brown like Esmeralda's, Dan thought. But it did little to calm his panic.

After the breast came a foot, then a wad of red and yellow flesh that could have been a chunk of belly. The boys snickered as they marched forward. Their eyes bathed the juggled meat the color of candy corn.

"Trick or treat," they said in unison.

Shit!

Dan thought about trying to plow through them and make it to his house, but he didn't know what tricks they held up their sleeves. The children were crafty little devils. He about-faced and ran back to Walter. The man had blown a hole in the middle of his face, from the chin through the top of his balding cranium. Dan tried not to look as he scooped up the shotgun. He cracked it open to find it empty, then dug his hand into Walter's pocket, grimacing as he felt the man's motionless, warm thigh through the fabric.

Just as his fingers wrapped around a fistful of shells, something collided with the side of his head. It hit with a splat, spraying blood and fluid into his face and mouth. He spat and wiped his face with his shirt sleeve as he pulled his hand from Walter's pocket. The severed breast jiggled to a stop at his feet, the pink nipple staring up at him like an albino's eye.

The twins leap-frogged each other, getting closer to Dan with every hop. Their voices gained bass as their childish giggles bloomed into maniacal cackling.

Dan fumbled with the gun as he loaded it with shells, nearly dropping it a few times as his shaking hands grew greasier with sweat by the second. He snapped the shotgun shut and took aim. He only hesitated for half a second, looking across the barrel at the twins, remembering how Esmerelda would make fresh lemonade for the boys to drink while they worked in the yard.

Good boys. Nice boys.

The shot tore through the first boy's head, splattering the other with his brother's brains. His scrawny body fell over and his eyes faded out. The other boy came at him on all fours, galloping like a rabid dog, but he was blown backward and splashed over the street. He gurgled blood, bubbling and oozing from the corners of his mouth. The orange light flickered. The boy smiled up at Dan as he passed.

"There's nowhere to run, Dan." The voice had lost all traces of child now. A deep, gruff chuckle rattled from the throat. "We'll use your children to eat you alive. We'll use them to eat you and fuck Esmerelda."

Dan lifted his boot and stomped down on the face. The boy cackled as blood sprayed from his nose and mouth, and Dan's boot continued to slam head to concrete. Dan didn't stop until the orange in the boy's eyes faded to black.

A scream. *Esmeralda!*

As he ran, he reloaded the gun and prayed to God that his next shots wouldn't be at his own son. Prayed that Corey was still tied up in the cellar, that none of the other children got to him yet. Prayed that his wife was alive and well, barricaded inside of their home, waiting for him to return.

Orange light lit the neighborhood. The air swam with the laughter of children and the screams of parents. It came from all directions now, but Dan kept his focus on getting to his home, to his family.

He ran past the Corolla and stopped at his front door. It stood open, swipes of blood dribbling down the wood and pooling on the patio below.

He rushed into the house and slammed the door, securing the deadbolt and chain.

"Esmeralda!"

No answer. Dan ran to the cellar door. His heart plummeted to his groin when he saw it standing open.

Oh God no.

"Esmeralda! Where are you!"

"I'm…h-here…"

The shaky, faint voice of his wife came from the cellar. She was down there. She was alive. Dan stepped over the threshold, slammed the door shut and locked it, then took the steps three and four at a time, nearly tumbling down. The cellar was engulfed in orange light.

Corey sat in his chair, the ropes still secure. As Dan approached, Corey's head spun and his eyes shone, making Dan squint and grimace. But the boy was tied up. *Everything will be okay*, Dan thought. *I made it in time.*

"Dan? I-I'm s-so sorry…" Esmerelda sat in the corner, her face beaded with sweat, hair pasted to her forehead.

"It's okay, baby. We made it. Our family is safe. The others, the neighbors, they—"

"No. Stop t-talking and listen. I…I…"

Dan took slow and careful steps around Corey and approached his wife on egg shells. She flinched at every one of his steps, whimpered and shook her head. Her legs were spread into a wide V…and an orange light glowed from beneath her dress.

"I will eat your fucking heart and rape your soul!" Corey roared with a voice that wasn't his.

"Esmeralda? What—"

"I'm so sorry, Dan." She raised her head, her eyes bright red and swimming in tears. "I'm pregnant."

The rubbery body burst free, sliding across the stone floor. The thing was tiny, no more than five months developed. The eyes shone just as bright as the other children, and a tiny smile spread across the glistening face. Esmeralda moaned and kicked her feet, scraped her nails across her belly and thighs. The baby crawled toward Dan, but was stopped by the umbilical cord still attached to its mother. It crawled in place, stretching out the cord, reached out with tiny hands as it giggled.

"Trick or treat, smell my feet…" Corey sang, his prepubescent voice squeaking through the demonic growl.

Dan took blind steps backward, shook his head, covered his ears to block out Esmerelda's screams and the baby's tittering. The back of his knees hit something and he lost his balance. And landed in Corey's lap.

The boy's eyes burned out Dan's vision, engulfed his brain with intense heat. All he could see was orange. All he could smell or taste was pumpkin.

"Give me something good to eat."

The teeth tore into his neck. His mouth filled with blood as he choked and gurgled and tried to shriek. Something wet hit his leg, clawed at his pants as it climbed.

Esmerelda screamed in rhythmic bursts.

The teeth bit into his throat, pulled, ripped. Another mouth, toothless and wet, lapped up the blood.

It was Halloween.

And the children would have their night.

BABY
HITLER

I don't remember which class I was in when I heard this, or even which grade it was. Maybe the philosophy class I took at community college? That sounds right.

Anyway, the question was, "Would someone be justified in killing a baby if they knew that baby was going to grow up and be the next Hitler?"

Most people, I think, would say no. A baby is a baby and we can't justify hurting a baby no matter what.

Wait till the fucker grows hair on his nuts, then we'll curb stomp him!

I don't really have an answer. There are valid arguments for both sides. And I'm not nearly smart enough to plead a case that matters.

But what I can do is write a story about it!

What if the above question was asked to the child's parents? And what if the father was already noticing strange things about his daughter?

His instinct tells him to protect his child. No matter what. And I get that.

I'm sorry, you guys. If a time machine landed in my fucking backyard and some time traveling barbarian popped out of it and told me that in the year 2050, my daughter was the cause for the apocalypse, that she was single-handedly responsible for the extinction of the human race, and that he was sent to the past to take her out and save mankind!

Yeah, he'd be buried in the yard by nightfall. Sorry people of the future!

SO MUCH PAIN, SO MUCH DEATH

"What the fuck do you want me to do? What else *can* we do?"

Erin glared at him from the kitchen table, her eyes rimmed red and sunken. She pointed at him with a shaking finger, the nails chewed down to slivers. "You're glad this happened. Aren't you?"

Shawn had been pacing, but at the sound of his wife's words, he stopped. His eyes burned from lack of sleep. "What did you say?"

She jumped to her feet, throwing her coffee cup to the floor and shattering it. The coffee had grown cold, and it crawled across the linoleum until it touched the tips of Shawn's toes.

"I said you're glad. *She's our baby! Where...where is my baby?*" The last sentence belted from her throat at a high pitch, and afterward, she crumbled to her knees and wept, the black cold coffee soaking into her pajama pants. "Oh... oh my God, Shawn. I can't live like this. Without her. I'd rather be dead."

Shawn let himself fall beside her, and he pulled her in and held her, let her sob into his shoulder. He wanted to cry too, but he had cried so much over the past two months, only anger was left. His wife's words still rang in his skull, and part of him wondered if she was right.

No, no. I miss my daughter. No matter how...difficult she was. No matter how frustrated I got. She's my goddamn daughter!

Shawn wasn't sure how long they stayed that way on the floor, Erin clinging to him as if they were on the edge of a cliff with strong winds slamming against them. At some point during her cry, she had fallen asleep, and Shawn didn't have the heart to wake her. Sleep didn't come easily those days.

The phone rang.

Every time that fucking thing rang, Shawn's chest tightened, his stomach dropped. So far, every time it rang there was no good news on the other end. Just useless information. Detective Hudson ensuring them that everything that could be done was being done. If it wasn't that, it was reporters, even a few prank callers.

Erin jerked awake, slapped him hard on the chest again and again. "Answer it. Hurry up, Shawn, and answer the goddamn—"

"I'm going." He raced toward the cordless, unable to keep his hopes from rising. A deep breath, then he answered. "Yes?"

Detective Hudson's voice swam into his ear. But the words he was saying couldn't possibly be true. After all this time…

The man kept talking, but Shawn didn't hear another word of it. His mind just kept repeating those first three words that were spoken.

We found her.

***

Oklahoma. They had found her in Oklahoma. A seven hour drive from Austin.

It took Shawn five to get there, and though Erin was always the kind to tell him to slow down, be careful, you're going to kill us, she didn't say a word as he weaved his way through traffic to get to their little girl.

Alive. She was alive. That's what the detective had said.

"A man was walking his dog, heard the screaming. Thirteen of them. We found thirteen children, but only nine alive."

And Lily was one of the living. Shawn knew it wasn't right to be glad that the other kids were dead and not his daughter, but he was happy about it nonetheless. He couldn't imagine what the other parents must be going through, but he forced himself not to think about it.

My baby girl is alive. She's alive and that's all that matters.

"Turn left here," Erin had said. She hadn't stopped shaking the entire trip, didn't say a word that wasn't directions she was getting off her cell phone.

Shawn didn't blame her. Until they actually saw Lily, it still didn't seem real. Felt like some kind of cruel trick.

Detective Hudson stood by his car. He had driven from Texas as well, a day before calling Shawn and Erin. "Wanted to make sure it was the real deal," he had said. "Wanted to see her for myself first." The man had been good to them, had actually given a shit. Shawn got the feeling Detective Hudson wanted to find their daughter as much as they did.

Shawn hadn't killed the engine before Erin was opening her door and racing toward the detective. She screamed and bawled as she went, and just watching her, Shawn couldn't stop the tears from flowing. But after all the time he spent crying, these tears were different. These were tears of relief, a relief so heavy and strong it nearly crushed his ribcage. He stayed in the car, found it hard to open his door as he watched the detective take Erin into his arms, whisper something to her, and then guide her to the back seat of his Lincoln.

The door was thrown open. Erin dropped to her knees and wailed, then threw her arms into the car.

Shawn saw the tiny hands—covered in a layer of black filth—grip the back of Erin's head as the two of them hugged, Erin's body shaking as she clutched their daughter in her arms and bawled harder than ever.

The scene swam in Shawn's tears, and all he could do was rest his forehead against the steering wheel, cry, and thank God.

***

"I want to see it."

Detective Hudson pursed his lips, placed his hand on Shawn's shoulder. He shot a look toward the house where forensics was going in and out, taking pictures, bagging up evidence. "Can't do it, Shawn. Even if this was my jurisdiction, it'd be damn near impossible. Probably not much to see by now anyway."

Shawn shrugged the hand away, stared past the detective toward the house. The house where his daughter was held captive for over two months. Where twelve other children were held for God knows how long, four of them now cold and rotting.

"I want to see where that sick fucking bastard was holding my baby. Show me."

Erin held Lily in her arms and whispered into her ear. Lily looked as happy as ever, her smiles and giggles coming as easily as they always had. Besides the layer of grime on her skin and her slightly thinner frame, she looked okay.

It was Shawn's turn to grab the detective's shoulder once it dawned on him. "Did he…with my daughter… Did he…?"

"No. We had her checked out before you guys got here. The other kids too. No sign of sexual abuse of any kind."

Shawn kept his hand on the detective and squeezed, lowered his head. "Thank God for that."

"The man posed as a crossing guard. From what we can tell, he traveled from town to town, volunteered at the schools. Most of the kids all came from Texas, two from Oklahoma. Not a single one from the same town. Who knows how long he's been at it though."

"A crossing guard. Son of a bitch."

"Shawn," Detective Hudson started as he ran his hand over his graying hair. "It's not pretty in there. The smell… I don't see any reason why you should see it. You've got your daughter. You've got Lily, unharmed and—"

"Unharmed? My daughter might be…special. But she isn't stupid, Hudson. Unharmed? She'll be fucked up the rest of her life over this shit!" Shawn winced at the volume of his words, shot a nervous glance at Erin and Lily. Erin ran her fingers through Lily's hair, glaring at Shawn through slits, but Lily just smiled, played with Erin's cell phone.

"What I was going to say is, I've got video. Shot it on my

phone, so it's not the best quality, but you can see the inside of the house, can even see the bastard as they were pulling his ass out of there. Was screaming some shit about finishing his work, how much pain and death there would be if—"

"Show me. I... I just need to see it. For my own sake. Please."

The detective smiled at Erin over Shawn's shoulders, gave her a slight nod as if they had some secret between them, then led Shawn to his car.

***

The video started outside of the house. An officer approached Hudson, told him he couldn't be there, and even after Hudson flashed his badge, the officer didn't look happy about it. But then they dragged the man out of the front door of the house, and his screaming got the officer's attention. Hudson moved closer, the video shaky as he trotted.

The man looked to be in his late fifties, early sixties. The white whiskers covering his face looked sharp, coarse. His eyes were wild, as red as painted toenails. The cords in his neck bulged and stretched as he tried to fight himself free from the officers on either side of him. A thin man. The kind of man who could only victimize children because he couldn't overpower anyone else.

"No!" he screamed as he kicked and bucked. "You have to let me finish...*you have to! So many will die if you don't let me finish my work!*"

"Jesus," Shawn said, balancing the phone in his palm.

As the man grew closer to Hudson and his camera phone, his gaze oozed over and stared, seemed to be glaring right at Shawn.

"Monsters," he growled. "Monsters, all of them. You don't understand what you're doing! If I don't kill them...if I don't kill them, thousands will die! *Thousands!*"

As the officers pushed him forward, he continued to scream. Reporters were there, trying to get statements, but were being ignored. When the man was shoved into the back of the police car, he smashed his face against the glass, smearing it with tears and saliva as he kept shouting and begging. The look in his eyes made Shawn's stomach twist with dread.

He thinks Lily is going to hurt people...kill people?

Shawn thought about the way his daughter made him feel when he was around her. Yes, he loved her, of course he loved her, but there was always something...there. In the pit of his gut. Something he didn't even think she was aware of. Something Shawn didn't know how to explain even to himself, but it was something that always bothered him.

You're glad this happened. Aren't you?

The footage showed the officers get in, wave off the reporters some more, and then drive away. Then it cut to the house just as Hudson had been entering.

"They tried to give me shit about going inside too, but I can be a persuasive son of a bitch," Hudson said, then pointed at the small screen. "Brace yourself, Shawn, okay? This shit is...well, it's fucked up is what it is."

Shawn didn't respond, but tightened his grip on the phone, tried to swallow some spit to moisten his throat, but couldn't get any down.

The house was a story and a half, the upstairs area a small loft. It was here that the children were kept, cages lining the back wall like some kind of animal shelter. Dog bowls sat in the corners, some still containing whatever slop he had been feeding them. Looked like oatmeal with raisins, but then the raisins started moving and Shawn realized they were flies. Clear water bottles hung from the cage, the same kind used for pet hamsters or mice. More flies cut through the air, crawled along the walls and ceiling, dove in and out of the dog bowls and scuttled across the floor.

"Fucking son of a bitch..."

Detective Hudson didn't say anything, just sighed and shoved his hands into his pockets.

The floor was padded with cardboard, the middle section stained a dark brown. The flies were there too, sucking up what they could. A few maggots scooted over the stain. A hospital gurney sat in the center of the room, thick leather straps hanging off the sides. The gurney's metal frame was spotted with dried blood. A tray sat on top, an array of surgical tools lined up neatly on its surface. Each one painted with blood, old and new.

"He had been working on a young boy when they caught him. They didn't make it in time to save the kid," Hudson said.

On the other side of the room, across from the cages, were sheets of college ruled notebook paper stapled to the wall. Each page had names written on them with a neat hand. The video showed some of the names, lingered there long enough for Shawn to read them, but they meant nothing to him.

The papers were arranged in columns, some shorter than others. The page at the top of the column had a name written in larger, bolder font, underlined.

"Those are the children's names at the top there," Detective Hudson said. "But so far nobody knows what any of the other names mean."

The video showed all of the names as it scanned the wall from left to right until finally coming to rest on the paper with Lily's name written at the top.

"Other kids maybe? That he was planning on kidnapping?" Shawn said.

"That's possible. If that's the case, thank God we found the motherfucker. Excuse my language."

Thank God indeed. There had to be thousands of names written on these pages. And as far as the length of the columns, Lily's was the longest by far, stretching down to the floor and then back up again. The names were tiny, hardly legible, while the other pages were easier read.

If I don't kill them...if I don't kill them, thousands will die! Thousands!

Shawn didn't know what it meant, but he had had enough. He handed the phone back to Hudson, stared blankly out the windshield.

"Listen. You've got a lot on your mind, all of you do. Why don't you let me put you guys up in a hotel, get you some dinner, hmm?"

"You don't have to do—"

Hudson held a hand up. "Don't say another word about it. Now come on. The three of you need to be together, and I don't want you trying to drive home tonight."

After a few more seconds, Shawn nodded, smiled. He rushed toward his family and hugged them, picked up his daughter and peppered her face with kisses.

***

Back home, things had gone back to normal. The experience seemed to have brought the family closer together, and Shawn and Erin's relationship hadn't been so good since they were newlyweds.

They watched Lily closely, wondering when the PTS would start, or when she would lash out at them. But that never happened. She seemed completely fine, and for some reason, that worried Shawn even more.

"You should have seen it," Shawn said to Erin in bed one night. "Dog cages. He must have killed those other kids in front of the live ones too. There was this gurney...and the tools... Oh Jesus, Erin."

Erin lowered his head to rest on her breasts, ran her fingers over the back of his head. "She's home now. Don't think about it. It's going to drive you crazy."

Don't think about it?

"The man. The things he was saying when they were dragging him out of that house. I just keep hearing it again and again in my head and...I don't know. How is it I'm in worse shape than our daughter is?"

"A father is supposed to feel pain when his child does. It just means you're a good dad, that's all. Now enough of all this for tonight. It's time for you to be a good *husband* now."

She kissed him, slipped her arms out of her nightie. Though Shawn let himself melt into her flesh, and though it felt damn good, his mind was elsewhere.

And it wouldn't stop racing until he had some answers.

***

"You sure about this?" Detective Hudson said as they pulled up to the prison. The man had offered to drive Shawn out there, and Shawn had agreed. He had hoped they could bounce some theories off each other on the drive over, but the two of them remained quiet for the most part.

"It's driving me crazy. What he said about the children. How thousands would die. I can't get his voice out of my head."

"He's just a crazy asshole, lost in his own fantasy. Don't subject yourself to this, Shawn. There's nothing this man will tell you that will help, I promise you that."

"And Lily. I thought she'd be...I don't know. Messed up after everything, you know? But she's not. She's completely fine, as happy as could be. I asked her about it, and she remembers everything, even told me how the man would hurt the other kids. I didn't tell Erin that part. When she said it...she was smiling. Like she was remembering a trip to Disney World or some shit."

"Okay, so what are you saying? That your daughter... enjoyed it? Because if that's what you mean, if you're buying into this shit that asshole was saying—"

"I don't know what the fuck I'm saying, okay? I'm confused and pissed off and scared. I don't know what else to do. I figure if I can talk to the guy, maybe it could help. Maybe he'll say something to help me understand."

After a few moments, Hudson just nodded. "You want me to go with you?"

"I think I better do this alone. Erin doesn't even know I'm doing this. Told her you had some more questions for me, that I'd be at the station all day. I'd appreciate if you kept this between us, Detective."

He nodded. "I won't sit here and tell you I know what you're going through. Because I don't. Never had any kids myself. If you need this, I believe you. Just be careful, all right?"

"I will. And thank you."

After going through all the procedures—filling out paperwork, handing over everything in his pockets, walking through the metal detector, getting patted down—he was led into a room with gray walls. There was a thick glass partition separating Shawn's side with the other, and a phone on both sides. Shawn took a seat on the orange plastic chair, wiped the sweat from his palms onto his jeans. His heart thundered in his chest, and he started to wonder if this really was a bad idea.

Maybe I should just walk out right now. Go home to my family.

A door opened up on the other side of the glass, and a guard walked in backward…followed by the crossing guard. The man's whiskers had grown to give him a full white beard, his pink bottom lip in the center of it. He wore an orange jumpsuit, the handcuffs biting into the flesh of his wrinkled, spotted wrists and hands. Another guard followed, and they set the man in his seat across from Shawn, said something to him before stepping back, but still only a few strides away.

Shawn and the crossing guard stared at each other for a full minute. Shawn knew this man's name was given to him at some point, but he couldn't remember it. Just *Crossing Guard* stuck with him.

The crossing guard picked up his phone first, his hands quivering, lip moving from side to side like he was tasting something.

Shawn hesitated for a moment, then grabbed the phone and pressed it to his ear.

"I know who you are," the crossing guard said. "You don't see it. You don't know what she'll do."

Shawn almost dropped the phone. The man had whispered the words as if telling a secret. He breathed heavy, stared at Shawn with panic in his eyes.

"Why do you say that?" Shawn said. "What makes you think my daughter, or any of those kids, would ever hurt anyone? You're the monster here, you fucking bastard. You hear me? Not my little girl!"

149

The guards behind the man started forward, but Shawn took a deep breath, apologized to them with his eyes, held up his hand to let them know everything was fine. They held back, but looked ready to pounce on the inmate.

The crossing guard licked his lips, his eyes never leaving Shawn's for a second. "You're trying to convince yourself, not me. Because you know. Deep down, you know I'm right." He leaned forward. "Don't you see? By killing them, I would have saved so many lives. Thousands of lives. You think that made it any easier for me? I'm no monster...but I'm cursed with the sight. I can see what they'll do, those kids. But that didn't make killing them any easier."

The tears started pouring, and the sight of them made Shawn want to break through that glass and strangle the asshole.

The crossing guard cleared his throat. "But I did it because it had to be done. To save countless other lives. With those kids still out there...there's going to be so much pain. So much death. Oh God, help us all."

"My daughter...she's only seven years old. How could she possibly—"

"Not yet. I don't know when it'll happen. I just know that death surrounds Lily. More than any other child. She...she scared me," the crossing guard said. "Watched me. Always watching and smiling."

"Keep my daughter's name out of your mouth. You fucking piece of shit."

The man stood up, pressed his forehead against the glass. He dropped the phone, but Shawn could still hear his voice. In his head, piercing like needles in his brain.

"You have to stop her. You have to see. Finish it, Shawn. Finish what I started. With Lily and the others. And there's more out there. So many more. There will always be more."

The guards were trying to wrestle the inmate away from the glass partition now, but couldn't budge him as he glared at Shawn.

And then the heat was there. Like his head was in a microwave.

Shawn backed away from the glass, grabbed his head with both hands and screamed. The heat was so intense he expected flames to shoot from his mouth.

The partition shattered, raining thick pieces of jagged glass all over the floor. In that same exact moment, the fire went out in his head, and Shawn dropped to his backside, grimacing, moaning and massaging his temples. Blood poured from his nose, trickled from his ears.

The crossing guard leaned forward, ignoring the guards as if they were nothing but a couple of annoying flies.

"Now you see. Finish it."

The man picked up a piece of glass and pressed it to his throat, sawed back and forth until he worked his way from one ear to the other. Blood poured out in sheets, and the guards were finally able to move him, were calling for help and scrambling to stop the bleeding.

Shawn just sat there, trembling, clenching his teeth as his head throbbed and pulsated.

Part of him wanted to rush home, be with his family, hold his girls in his arms and never let them go again. The other part of him was terrified to see them.

***

"You gonna be all right, Shawn?" Hudson said as they pulled into the driveway of Shawn's home. "You sure you don't want me to come inside, talk with Erin about what happened? Shit, man...don't you think she should know?"

The sun had gone down a couple of hours ago. He knew Erin would have questions.

Shawn opened the passenger door. "I'll tell her. But not right now, okay? I just...I just need some time. My fucking head is killing me, my thoughts are all over the place. Give me a day. I'll tell her tomorrow."

Hudson twisted his fists over the steering wheel. "Goddammit, Shawn. I told you it wasn't a good idea. Shit..."

"Just... Tomorrow, okay? Thanks for the ride." Shawn

shut the door, patted the hood. He heard the car reversing and driving away as he strolled toward the house.

Now you see. Finish it.

He wrapped his fist around the knob, smelled the savory scent of dinner cooking, and in that moment, he knew everything would be okay. The crossing guard was just some crazy asshole. And now he's dead. *Good riddance.*

He walked in, went into the kitchen for a glass of water. Erin stood at the stove, mixing a big pot of spaghetti sauce with a wooden spoon. She smiled wide, wiped her hands on her rear as she rushed toward him, wrapped her arms around him, and planted a wet kiss on his lips.

"How'd it go? What did the detective want?"

"Just more paperwork. Nothing much. Boring really." He smiled, kissed her again. "It's good to be home. Where's Lily?"

"In her room. She kept trying to get a taste of the sauce, and I kept slapping her hand away. She's been asking for my spaghetti for days."

"It smells amazing. Let me go say hi to her, then I'll help out."

She rose to her tiptoes and kissed him on the forehead. "No need. I got this. Go play with your daughter. She was asking for you today. Seemed upset about something."

"Really?"

Shawn decided to skip the water. As he walked down the hall toward Lily's bedroom, he realized his headache was gone. The violent throbbing had ceased completely.

Lily giggled from the other side of the door. Shawn smiled, sighed.

When he opened the door, he immediately shrieked, tripped backward and slammed the back of his head against the wall. He sat there, staring into the room, at his daughter sitting Indian-style in the center, bouncing her Cabbage Patch doll up and down, up and down, smiling so wide, giggling.

The smell was the worst part. Like spoiled, burnt pork and hair. Thick and greasy and making the back of Shawn's throat sting with acid.

"Hi, Daddy," she said. "Did you see the bad man? The crossing guard?" She smiled again, wider than before.

Festering corpses surrounded her. Piled one on top of the other. Their flesh was charred, cracked to show the dark red beneath. Hairless. They were piled from the floor to the ceiling, so packed into the room that Lily hardly had any room to play.

Men and women of all ages. And children. Children younger than her, their faces twisted and frozen in anguish, their eyes liquefied and running down their blackened cheeks, sizzling and smoking as the jelly flowed.

The babies looked like roasted whole chickens, thrown in sloppy piles all around her. Smoke filled the room as it swirled off the broiled flesh.

And Lily just bounced her doll and laughed. As happy as ever.

"What's the matter!" Erin said as she ran down the hall. She took one look at Shawn's face and her run became a sprint. She jumped over Shawn's legs and into the room.

Shawn tried to stop her, to warn her, but he couldn't do anything but stare at the genocide stuffed within his little girl's bedroom.

Erin didn't acknowledge the bodies. It looked like she was about to collide with the wall of cooked flesh, but instead, she walked through it as if it were nothing but a projected image. She knelt beside Lily, hugged her, rocked her as she stared at Shawn.

"What the hell is your problem?"

So much pain. So much death.

Now you see. Finish it.

I will, Shawn thought. *I have to.*

A KID
FOR LIFE

Look, we all gotta grow up. I know that. Nothing we can do to keep ourselves from aging. As an adult, we are expected to make our own way and take care of our responsibilities.

I accept that. I have a family to take care of and a mortgage and car payments and all the other bills everyone else has. In order to handle all of that, I have a day job that I'm not crazy about, but I go and I'm a good employee because I know my family is depending on me to keep things above water. I'm not complaining either. I do it because I want to, not just because I have to.

I love teaching my daughter new things and watching her grow and experience the world around her. It's a lot of pressure, as a parent. Constantly asking myself if I'm doing enough or if I'm doing it right or if I'm a terrible father. The same thing can be said about marriage, I guess. I got lucky and married my best friend, so things are pretty flawless there. But I still do those little extra things to let her know she is not being taken for granted.

Anyway, my point is, I'm living the life of a responsible adult. I pay my bills on time. I put in the time with my wife and daughter. I go to work. I mow the lawn (another strange expectation as an adult homeowner…they suddenly expect you to give a fuck about grass). So I guess I'm an adult now.

But that's just a word. The above may be the definition of that word, and I may be living that definition, but I'm no fucking adult.

At my core, I'm a kid. I'll always be a kid. The shy kid who loves horror movies and monsters and superheroes and rap music and Reese's motherfucking peanut butter cups.

I'll never grow up! Not really. I won't let my responsibilities or my day job or my bills change that.

Being an adult sucks. Too many reasons to be unhappy as an adult.

I like being happy. I like having fun. I like being a goofball at home and making my wife and daughter laugh. I like horror movies and monsters and superheroes and rap music and Reese's peanut butter cups. I always will. And my age and society can't stop me.

That's what this next story is about. Kids fighting against adulthood.

Because no matter how bad your problems are or how much of a failure you've convinced yourself you've become…it's nothing a nice bowl of ice cream won't fix.

DON'T YOU WANT TO PLAY WITH US?

"Game!" Flip rubbed his palms together to stop the shaking, then picked up his beer and drained it, slammed the empty glass on the bar. He stared at his darts, none of the three a bull's eye, but still just enough points to win the game.

Jerry stared at the dart board for another minute before cussing under his breath and pulling out his wallet. His buddies elbowed each other and snickered. The woman he'd come in with chewed on her bottom lip as she studied him. She looked ready to run away, as if Jerry would explode at any moment.

Jerry slapped two twenties into Flip's hand, then wiped his own hand on his pant leg. "Fuckin' street trash," he said, then checked his palm as if Flip had smeared shit on it. "Come in here and try to hustle me? Cal, why you let this stinky motherfucker in here anyway?"

Flip knew the guy was intentionally trying to hurt his feelings or piss him off, but he wouldn't accomplish either one. Flip's skin had grown as thick as rhinoceros hide. He slapped one of the twenties onto the bar and smiled.

Cal moved his toothpick from the left corner of his mouth to the right and snorted. He knocked his knuckles against the bar on top of the bill. "Next one's on me, Flip." Cal filled another glass full of Blue Moon, slid it to Flip who grabbed it and drained half of it down right away.

The woman ran both hands through her hair, sighed, then joined the other two men who continued to snicker. She widened her eyes at them and they both shrugged and continued to laugh. Jerry shot a quick glance at his group, then let his fiery stare land back on Flip.

"It was your stink, asshole. It was throwing my game off. You learn to throw darts by flinging shit against the dumpster walls?"

Cal pulled his toothpick from his mouth and flicked it at Jerry, crossed his arms and rippled his forearm muscles. "You best watch your words, Jerry. 'Fore they get you in trouble."

Jerry's face burned red and his friends finally stopped chortling.

Flip only smiled and sipped his beer, reached out and tapped his finger on the crumpled bill on the bar. "Why don't you pour us a couple of whiskey shots, Cal. See if we can't extinguish the fire a little bit, hmm?"

Jerry's jaw muscles fluttered and his eyes rolled from Cal to Flip, then roamed back toward his friends. The woman turned her gaze, wouldn't look Jerry in the eye.

Cal filled three shot glasses with Jack, slammed two on the bar, and swallowed the liquor from the third. He hissed, wiped his lips with the back of his hand. "You lost fair and square. You give Flip here anymore shit about it, and we'll be using your ass for a dartboard next, yeah?"

Jerry reached over, plucked the shot, swallowed it. Flip did the same, then sat back on his stool and grinned.

Jerry ran his tongue across the front of his teeth, then spun and joined his friends. He grabbed the woman rough by the wrist and yanked her toward the table in the back. The other two men followed, exchanging glances and shaking their heads.

"Thanks, Cal," Flip said.

"You're gettin' sloppy, you know that?" Cal ran a damp towel over the bar, pulled another bacon-flavored toothpick from his shirt pocket and jammed it into his mouth. "You used to hit the bull's eye with every dart, you know it? Used to remind me of that Robin Hood movie. With ol' what's his name…"

The glass shook in Flip's hand, and he downed the rest of the beer, set it down, then massaged the meat between his thumb and forefinger. That always seemed to help once the shakes got too bad. "Still good enough to kick the snot outta any of your customers, ain't I?"

The creases on Cal's forehead deepened. "Ah, shit. You

know…that fella that was dancin' with Indians. Shit…"

Flip chuckled, flexed his fingers. The shaking let up some, but it was still there. It was always there at least a little these days. Seemed they started the same day Flip walked in on Constance with her lips wrapped around a mouthful of hard cock. The fucking pool boy. Even through his rage, Flip couldn't help but acknowledge how cliché the whole situation was. But God how it hurt. Crushed him. Constance wasn't only his wife, but his best friend. His only friend. That was also the last day Flip ever had a real roof over his head.

"Kevin Bacon? No…no that can't be right. Shit, what was his name?"

"Fill 'er up, would you, Cal?"

Cal mumbled to himself as he fetched a new glass and pulled the Blue Moon tap. He stared at the ceiling and chewed on his lip as he continued to search his memory.

Cal was a good man. Always treated Flip with respect. They had known each other since high school, though Flip was two years older and too damn cool back then to hang out with lil Stinky Calvin. But these days Cal wasn't so little, and Flip was for damn sure not cool. Cal had recognized Flip the first time he stepped into the Thirsty Dog, told him he could come by any time. Flip could tell the guy just felt sorry for him, but he didn't mind. The Thirsty Dog was a great place to waste time, and these days, that's all Flip had was time. He always tried to wash up beforehand so as not to chase away Cal's customers with his sharp aroma, but finding a place to scrub his ass wasn't always easy.

Cal set the fresh glass down, shook his head. "The hell with it. Shitty movie anyway. The point is you could split darts back in the day."

Flip grabbed the glass, but his shaking hand made a good portion of it spill onto the bar. He set it back down, put his hands in his lap where he got to massaging again. A forced smile sliced across his face. "Look, you're gonna hurt my feelings here. Didn't I just pay for this beer with my winnings?"

"Nope, it was on the house, remember?" Cal arched his mouth and gave a light chuckle. "You doin' okay, Flip?"

Flip shrugged. "Living the good life, brother. Can't you tell?"

They both laughed, but were cut short when something crashed from across the bar. The woman was on her feet, the neck of a beer bottle in her fist, the other end jagged and broken. Jerry clutched at his forehead as he stood, his teeth bared and clenched. A dribble of blood rode the creases of his nose, and he wiped it away and snarled.

"I told you not to fuckin' touch me!" The woman waved the broken bottle out in front of her.

"Oh, you're gonna get it, bitch. You're gonna get it so bad." Jerry stomped his foot at her, and when she flinched and yelped, he chuckled.

"Goddammit," Cal said, then reached under the bar and pulled out a big, chrome pistol. "Not in the mood for this shit."

Flip spun in his stool so he could watch, drained his beer in three big gulps. Never a dull night at the Thirsty Dog.

"You fuckers take that shit outside, you hear me?" He took turns pointing the pistol at each of them. "Go on and get!"

Jerry's friends tried to coax him into leaving, but he shoved them off, ignored Cal and his pistol, and faced the woman again. "Yeah, that's a good idea. Just wait 'til I get your ass home." He wiped another palmful of blood from his forehead.

"The lady will stay here with us," Flip said. "Ain't that right, Cal?" Flip wasn't sure why he butted in like that. He'd seen dozens of bar brawls at the Thirsty Dog in the last few years and never spoke up before. But he couldn't feel good about letting this lady go home with Jerry. Regardless of the sour feelings he had toward women these days.

Jerry's eyes, burning as red as heated metal, landed on Flip, and he curled his lip until it nearly touched the bottom of his nose. "I suggest you shut your fuckin' mouth, asshole. Before I shove my arm down your throat and toss you back in the garbage where you came from."

"Come on, Jerry, let's just get the hell outta here," one of the men said, both forearms covered in tattoos. He eyed Cal's pistol which was still swinging from face to face.

Jerry shoved the man in the center of the chest and sent him crashing into the pool table. "Mind your fuckin' business, Barney. I mean it."

Barney held his hands up, head shaking, lips mashed together. The other man, a red-headed scrawny guy at least six foot six, caught Jerry's blood-thirsty stare next, and didn't say a word.

Cal shot Flip a quick look, wrinkled his brow for a moment, then nodded and blinked rapidly. He turned back toward Jerry, jabbed the gun in his direction. "You heard him, dickhead. She stays. Now get the fuck outta my bar before it gets real messy."

Barney and the tall guy started inching toward the door, but Jerry held his ground. He ripped his shirt off, tossed it into the woman's face, then faced Cal. Took three long, heavy steps toward him and pressed his forehead against the gun's barrel.

"You better be ready to pull that trigger, motherfucker. You hear me?"

Cal smiled, cocked back the hammer. "Oh it would be my pleasure."

Flip hopped off his stool. "Come on now, fellas. No need for this shit. Jerry, you just had a bit too much to drink, that's all. Go home, clear your head. Don't do some shit that you'll regret later, okay?"

Jerry flared his nostrils and glared into Cal's eyes, showing no signs that he had even heard Flip.

The woman still held the bottle out in front of her, tears streaming down her face. Her hand shook and her lip trembled as she watched the standoff between Cal and her man.

"We're just gonna make sure she's safe, that's all. I'll even give her my winnings so she can get a hotel." Flip grabbed the twenty back off the bar and pulled the other out of his pocket, waved them in the air. "Everything will be—"

The bar door flew open, thumped against the wall. Cal's framed picture of Clint Eastwood fell and cracked, and a man stepped on it, splintering and crunching glass as he made his way into the bar. The guy was pale, the color of whipped cream. His red hair was disheveled, sticking out in all directions and thick with some kind of glue-like substance. A red balloon floated above his head, the string tied to his wrist. But the string looked weird, thick...slimy. He turned, closed the door, ran his hand along its frame.

What in the hell? Flip thought.

The guy wore a smile like the Mad Hatter as he slid his feet along the floor and took a seat on a stool across the bar from Flip. He ignored the commotion around him, tented his fingers on the bar, and kicked his feet. Flip couldn't help but think the guy's movement reminded him of an impatient child. The guy's smile never even twitched, eyes never blinked.

Flip rubbed the back of his head, shot a glance at Cal who was staring at the guy too. Even Jerry and the others now had their attention on the balloon-toting stranger.

"Ice cream," the man said. "A bowl of ice cream please." His voice was high-pitched, sounded like he was on the verge of laughing as he spoke. A glistening tongue slid out from between his teeth and soaked his lips.

It was like the energy in the room was shifted. Flip felt it the second that guy spoke, as if the very words he muttered transformed the atmosphere. A smell like baking cookies began to swirl through the air, and Flip's stomach got to churning in response. He had a slight urge to laugh, but he couldn't explain why.

Cal removed the gun's barrel from Jerry's forehead, gave the man a long, hard look. "Now get the fuck outta here, Jerry. I've got a business to run here, goddammit."

Jerry scowled and squeezed his fists until the veins on his forearms bulged, but didn't say another word. He wiped his nose with his palm, spat on the floor, then made his way toward the door.

The woman wept, set the bottle on a table, and crossed her arms.

"Ice cream...hot fudge...*ice cream!*"

Jerry and his buddies were at the door, and Jerry tugged on it, kicked it. "Well if you want me to leave so fuckin' bad, unlock the door!"

"Nobody's leaving." The man spun in his stool, kicking his feet and going around and around, a soft giggle clicking from his stretched-out smile. "You're not ready yet."

Flip squinted at the balloon wobbling in the air above the stranger. He even rubbed his sleeve over his eyes to make sure he was seeing this clearly. Intestine. That's what it looked like. A rope of intestine was tied to the balloon and the man's wrist. Translucent slime dripped from it and pitter-pattered over the bar.

"Hey, Cal," Flip said. When Cal looked in his direction, Flip widened his eyes, nodded toward the man.

"Cal, let us the fuck outta here!" Jerry slammed his fists against the door now, threw his shoulder into it hard enough to hurt himself, but it still didn't budge.

"The children are outside," the man said. "When you're all ready, they'll be waiting for you."

"Look, motherfucker," Jerry said as he stomped toward the stranger. "I don't know who the fuck you are or what your problem is, but—"

"Hold it now," Cal said and used his tree trunk arm to hold Jerry back. "Let me see what the problem is here." He pulled a fistful of keys from his jeans pocket, tried the door first, and when it didn't open, slid the key in. "What in the hell?"

"A big bowl of ice cream please," the man said. He turned and sat straight, facing the bar, hands folded in front of him. "With hot fudge."

Cal ran his hand along the frame, and when he pulled it away, strings of what looked like syrup stretched from his fingertips. He smelled it, wrinkled his nose, and turned toward the man with a hard scowl. He made his way behind the bar, leaned forward so he could look the man eye to eye.

"Who in the hell are you? And what did you do the—" Cal's brow furrowed when he noticed the slime droppings on the bar, then looked up at the balloon, at the intestine it was tied to. "What the fuck is this?"

Jerry slammed his fist into the wall, then paraded toward the stranger, fist raised. "Open. The motherfuckin'. D—"

The stranger moved so quickly, Flip wasn't sure what he had actually seen. The man's smile seemed to widen even further, even as Jerry's blood sprayed him in the face.

Jerry's scowl melted and a deep grunt seeped from between his bloody lips. He grabbed the stranger's shoulder, coughed, then fell on his side. He twitched as he pressed both hands to the wound under his chin as the blood steadily pumped out, made a whistling sound with his throat, then was still, eyes wide.

Flip saw the knife now. No, not a knife…a peppermint stick? The candy was sharpened like a shiv, and Jerry's blood flowed over the red and white swirled stripes. The balloon danced as the air conditioner blew against it.

"A bowl of ice cream please."

Cal bared his teeth and jammed his gun into the stranger's face, placed the barrel against his left nostril. "Get up. Now."

The man chortled, lifted the hand holding the peppermint stick over his head in a stabbing motion.

The gun went off, and Flip jumped, screamed when he ran into something behind him. It was the woman, and as soon as Flip was close enough, she clutched him, pressed her body against his.

Flip's ears rang, and he had his eyes squeezed shut, scared to open them and face the gory scene in front of him. Then Cal screamed, and Flip's eyes burst open.

"Jesus!" Cal looked to be on his knees, only his face visible over the bar from where Flip stood. Cal's hand was pinned to the bar by the sharpened candy, his fingers rigid and spread wide as the blood puddled around it.

"A bowl of ice cream please. With hot fudge. Lots and lots of hot fudge." The back of the stranger's head was blown open, a pink goopy substance oozing out. But he sat as happy as ever, still kicked his legs. Still smiled. He ran a finger over his face where the bullet had entered. Fingered the hole, then popped the tip into his mouth.

The woman whimpered, shook so hard she was beginning to give Flip motion sickness. She kept saying Jerry's name, shaking her head, crying. He peeled her hands off of him, and took tentative steps toward the stranger. Jerry's two buddies were still huddled at the door, staring down at their dead friend. Neither one of them making a sound.

"Fucking hell, get it out! Please pull it out!" Cal had his free hand wrapped around the candy, tugging on it, but it wouldn't budge. His face sparkled with sweat and glowed a deep maroon. Blood pumped from the wound, but as Flip watched it, the color began to change. The dark red started to lighten, turned a pink color like liquefied bubble gum.

Flip rushed forward, hesitated when the man turned his ghastly grin toward him, then reached out with both hands and gripped the peppermint stick. He leaned back, pulled with everything he had, but it wouldn't move.

The pink stuff dribbled down the man's face, and he leaned forward so he was almost touching noses with Flip. "A bowl—"

"Ice cream. I got it. Let him go," Flip said and nodded toward Cal, "and we'll get you some. Ain't that right, Cal?" The urge to laugh started to rumble in Flip's belly again, but he chewed it up and swallowed it back down.

"Yeah…yeah just pull it out…*please!"* Even as Cal screamed the last word, a slight smile pulled at the corners of his mouth. But only for a second before the grimace returned.

Flip realized that he was standing in the puddle of blood seeping from Jerry's throat wound. When he moved his feet, they felt stuck to the floor, tore free with a ripping sound. The pink blood stuck to the bottom of his boot, stretched out when he pulled his foot away.

The man wrapped his fingers around the peppermint stick, yanked it out with ease. He sucked the red and pink blood off of it, leaving it glistening with saliva, then went to stick it back into his pocket. But it wasn't his pocket…

he lifted his shirt and plunged the candy directly into his torso, his skin looking as soft as marshmallow. The candy disappeared into his pale, pillowy flesh, and he pounded both fists on the bar. *"Ice cream!"*

A scream ripped free from Flip's throat as he backed into something, and once again it was the woman. She waved her hands like she was swatting at bees, grabbed Flip's arm, and squeezed. Her eyes, surrounded by mascara-stained and swollen flesh, bounced from Jerry's body to the stranger over and over again, and she still kept muttering Jerry's name. The other two men had turned and began tugging on the door, grunting and cussing under their breath.

Flip didn't think Cal would have any ice cream in the bar, but the man ducked down, opened a black miniature refrigerator, and pulled out a pint of Haagen-Dazs rocky road. He peeled the top off, and Flip could see it had already been half eaten.

"Here's your fuckin' ice cream, you son of a bitch." Cal slid it across the bar.

The man's eyes lit up and he grabbed the pint in his fist, squeezed it until the brown ice cream squashed out, then slammed his face into it. He moaned as his head rolled, looking like a man giving intense cunnilingus, both of his hands gripping the lip of the bar counter.

Then Jerry's body began to flop.

Flip and the woman screamed at the same time, and when the two men at the door spun in reaction, they joined in.

Jerry's body thrashed, hopped from stomach to back, arms flailing loose. As he bucked, his eyes popped open and the corners of his mouth crept upward.

"What the fuck is going on?" the woman said, grabbing fistfuls of Flip's shirt and shaking it. *"What is this shit!"*

Flip once again pried himself away from her, sprinted across the bar, and grabbed a pool cue. He broke it in half on his knee and wielded the sharp, jagged sticks as he slowly marched back toward the commotion.

"Cal?" Flip called, not seeing his friend. "Cal, get your ass out here. Where the hell—"

Cal's laughter exploded from behind the bar. A loud cackle with no pauses for taking a breath. His hand appeared, covered in thick pink goop, and it gripped the edge of the bar as Cal hauled himself to his feet. His eyes were pinched shut from the massive rictus pulling his face apart.

The man had finished the ice cream and was now licking the bar clean of the melted chocolate puddles. His tongue ran across the counter lovingly, swirling in circles as that deep moan oozed from his mouth.

Jerry's body made one final leap, landed hard on its back. His head suddenly tilted so that his chin was pointed to the ceiling, his back arching to the point of his spine snapping. And then something started to grow from his mouth.

"Oh Jesus Christ…" Flip thought it was an internal organ working its way up Jerry's throat and out past his teeth, but something wasn't right. It wasn't until the thing grew more and more, continued to inflate out from between Jerry's lips that Flip realized it was a balloon. A purple color.

Cal climbed up onto the bar, got on his hands and knees, and opened his mouth as wide as it could go. His balloon was green, and it curled his lips back as it swelled from his throat.

"Cal!" Flip turned his pool stick halves so the broken ends were facing down, and he charged toward the man with both weapons held high. He had watched a gunshot blow straight through this guy's head with no effect, but he didn't know what else to do. The sticks stabbed into the man's back with ease, just slid through with no resistance. The pink sludge squirted from the wounds and slapped Flip in the face, some spraying into his mouth. Tasted just like bubble gum.

Flip tried to yank his sticks back out so he could stab again, but they wouldn't pull free. The man spun in the stool and grabbed Flip by the shoulders. His eyes widened, chocolate-stained smile stretched further across his cheeks. Pointed peppermint sticks slid out of his chest and stomach like porcupine quills, and he chuckled as he slowly pulled Flip toward them. The savory smell of baking cookies grew stronger as Flip was pulled closer.

"Fucking asshole!" The woman jabbed the broken glass bottle into the man's face, twisted it and shredded his nose and lips. Pink bubbled from beneath his puffy, white flesh.

But he still only giggled as the bottle peeled away meat from bone, the glass screeching when it hit his teeth. He tossed Flip away, flinging him across the room. Flip's body smashed into the wall and he landed on his side, rolled in place as he tried to catch his breath. His ears rang and his mouth tasted like blood and bubble gum.

A choking sound, coughing. Something splashing across the floor.

Flip rubbed his eyes to rid them of the blurriness, sat up and leaned against the wall. His hand landed on something sharp, and he flinched it away when it broke skin and drew blood. A dart. The dartboard lay on the floor beside him, along with a shattered beer logo neon sign and a few picture frames.

The woman hit the floor, legs kicking, both hands clutching her belly where a deep cavern had been carved into it. Her scream was gurgly and wet as the man dove on top of her and shoved his face into the opening on her stomach, ripping a chunk of meat away and chewing it happily.

No, Flip thought as the room came back into focus. *Not the man...that's Cal!*

Cal's green balloon floated above him, the gleaming intestine tied to it, the other end disappearing into his mouth. He lifted his face from the woman's bleeding flesh, gripped the slimy rope, and ground his teeth back and forth until the intestine was severed. The pink blood exploded out, drenched his face and stretched between his lips as the tube slid itself around his wrist like a constricting snake. Shredded red meat and yellow fat was spread across his face as he dove into the woman's belly for more, and it was only a matter of seconds before her head tilted back and a yellow bulge inflated from her mouth.

This isn't real. This is impossible...

Jerry stood by the door with his balloon already tied to his wrist, the tall red-headed man bleeding on the floor between Jerry's feet. Barney wrestled with Jerry for a moment, but was no match, and then Jerry ran something across Barney's throat. Looked like a giant lollipop. The candy was razor thin and opened up Barney's neck like his skin was made of frosting. Barney landed on his backside, kicked his feet as he struggled to breathe and clawed at the new red smile opening and closing across his throat. Jerry dove on top of the redhead, tore into his stomach, and chewed on the purple organs inside.

"The children want you."

Flip flinched, jumped to his feet. He held the dart in his shaking fist as the stranger approached.

"It's time to play. Don't you want to play with us?"

Flip was ready to curl into a ball and wait for his death. The sounds of sloppy eating filled the room. Whatever this guy was, it wasn't human. He couldn't be killed. Some kind of demon.

I'll stick this fucking dart in his eye anyway.

Flip clenched his teeth, pressed his back hard against the wall. His hand shook so bad, it looked like he was writing his name in the air with the dart. A sharp pain rode his palm up into his wrist, and a cramp seized his hand and squeezed like vice grips. He tried to throw the dart anyway, but he was way off target, and it sailed over the stranger's head…hit the balloon. The red balloon popped and a torrent of black liquid exploded out, more than could have possibly fit into it. The oily substance rained down over the stranger, soaked into his flesh and clothing.

"The ch-children…ice c-cream…play-play with u-us…"

The man slowly lowered to the ground as his body melted, his flesh sloughing off in sloppy chunks that hit the floor and sizzled, bubbled. He reached a dripping hand toward Flip, then fell face down and continued to liquefy, what was once the scent of cookies now more resembling shit.

Flip squatted, collected the rest of the darts that lay scattered on the floor, then stood up and faced the others.

The red-headed tall man was on his knees, chewing on

the intestine snaking from his mouth, the other end tied to the blue balloon floating over him. Cal, the woman, and Jerry were all on the floor, chewing on Barney's body. The man's blood was already beginning to turn pink, and the three of them sucked it up as quickly as it oozed out of the wounds. It wasn't until the orange balloon started inflating from Barney's mouth that they left him alone and faced Flip. Each of their faces were pulled tight in wide grins, and they pulled candy from their bodies as they approached. Their cackles intensified as they grew nearer.

You could split darts back in the day.

Flip picked a dart and held it up by his cheek as he squinted and aimed. He wanted to take Cal out first. Couldn't take seeing his friend like this anymore.

"I'm sorry, Cal." His hand shook, but he took a deep breath, locked onto his target, and let the dart fly. It sailed across the bar, but he didn't throw it hard enough. It stuck into Cal's left eye, inducing a fresh round of roaring laughter. The bubble gum blood dripped down into his face, and the group, now including Barney, quickened their pace.

"Shitshitshit..." Flip ran to his right toward the pool table, hopped on top of it. He flexed his fingers, shook his hand, massaged it. "Please...oh God please."

Candy rained from the open stomachs of the woman and Jerry's friends like broken piñatas. Jerry plunged his fist into his belly, pulled out a lollipop by its stem. He guffawed as he flung it across the room toward Flip.

Flip ducked just before the candy collided with his face, and it lodged into the wall behind him, sheet rock dust raining down.

He stood back up, his hand as steady as it could be, and threw the next dart. It cut through the air and hit Jerry's purple balloon. The black liquid burst and poured over Jerry who hit the floor and moaned as his flesh bubbled and slid off of him.

Jesus...

Flip tossed another dart and another, hitting pink and blue. Balloons popped, flesh melted.

The woman shoved her entire forearm into the gaping wound on her stomach, pulled out a red, braided licorice rope aligned with long thorns. Cal was just behind her, the dart sinking deeper and deeper into his eye as his eyelids chewed on it like a toothless mouth, swallowing it down into his socket. His teeth were stained pink as he smiled.

Flip cocked his hand back to throw the next dart and take the woman out, but an intense cramp seized his hand, turned it into a gnarled claw. Flip grunted, dropped the dart, nearly dropped to his knees in pain.

"The children only want to play. Don't you want to play? You can eat all the sweets you want. Forever and ever and ever…"

"Fuck you!" Flip rose to his feet holding the dart like a knife. The woman was just in front of him now, and she swung her licorice thorn whip over her head, but before she could fling it toward him, Flip reached out, grabbed the intestine string, pulled the balloon close, and drove the dart into it.

The woman dropped to the floor and kicked her legs, turning herself in a full circle again and again as she dissolved into a pink and black puddle of flesh and candy.

"Don't fight it, Flip." Cal reached into his mouth, and when he pulled his hand out, he had a fistful of something brown, dripping. Rainbow sprinkles were mixed in with the brown goop, and when the droplets hit the ground, spirals of smoke drifted into the air and the floor sizzled. "The children only want to play. You'll be so happy…finally you'll be happy, don't you see?"

Cal tossed the acidic chocolate toward Flip, but Flip rolled off the pool table, landed hard on his back and grimaced. The chocolate ate through the felt and wood and dripped to the floor where it continued to sizzle and pop.

"Goddammit, Cal." Flip shrieked when more icy pain stabbed his hand like glass lightning bolts. But he had his eyes on the butt of the pistol sticking up from Cal's waistline. Every movement sent more agony into his hand, but he worked his way back to his feet, teeth clenched and spittle raining as he hissed.

"Constance is with us. I can feel her. She's as sweet as red velvet cake." Cal snickered as he pulled out another fistful of chocolate. The brown liquid oozed from his mouth and striped his chin as he spoke. "She misses you, Flip. You can be together again. The children want you to be."

Just hearing her name injected poison into Flip's bloodstream, and he roared as he charged forward. His shoulder collided with Cal's stomach and they both flew backward onto the floor. The chocolate flew from Cal's hand and splashed across the wall, eating a hole into it on contact.

Cal cackled as he opened his mouth and reached for Flip's neck, lips curled back over his teeth, tongue whipping.

Flip rolled off, ripped the pistol free from Cal's waist, aimed and fired.

The balloon erupted and the inky substance was like a waterfall rushing over Cal's spasming body. His limbs thrashed and his teeth clicked as he melted down, and Flip covered his ears to escape the horrid sizzling sound.

Tears streamed down his cheeks as he cradled his hand in his lap. The air was thick with the scent of shit, and Flip gagged and coughed as he forced himself to his feet and made his way toward the door. He spotted a loose peppermint stick, and he strode across the room to retrieve it before facing the door. He tucked the gun into his waistline before grabbing the handle and tugging on it. Still wouldn't open. The syrupy substance was thick along the frame, and Flip used the peppermint's sharp end and chiseled away at it. The stuff came off in chunks, and before long, he was able to swing the door open.

The cool night air felt like heaven against his sweaty, aching flesh. But the night was alive with ruckus. Screams and breaking glass and gun shots. But mostly laughter. So much laughter.

Countless people roamed from business to business. Balloons of all colors bobbed in the air above them. The bakery across the street was full of people feasting on cakes and pies and muffin tops. Others lay on the pavement, balloons swelling from their mouths.

"Oh my G—"

Then he saw them. The children. Holding hands and floating down the street, smiling at the chaos around them. With roller skates on their feet, they leisurely kicked as they rolled their way through town. Their mouths were as red as strawberries, eyes sparkling like sugar cubes, all the colors of the rainbow.

Flip pulled the gun out and stared at it as the moonlight danced off the chrome surface. He couldn't help but wonder if Constance really was a part of all this. If she was somewhere out in the street right now, maybe looking for him. Maybe she really did want to be with him again.

The gun's barrel found its way into his mouth.

It tasted like bubble gum.

MY FIRST CRUSH, JESSICA RABBIT

To be fair, it was either Jessica Rabbit or Paula Abdul. I can't remember which was first, but Jessica Rabbit is still the Jessica Rabbit I remember from when I was a kid, and I still want so badly to play patty cake with her. Paula Abdul has become a pill-munching goblin, so the image has been ruined forever.

So, let's focus on Jessica Rabbit. I know for damned sure I'm not the only one who had a crush on her, whether she was real or not.

I was furiously jealous of Roger Rabbit. How could that rabbit get a woman like that?

In my eyes, she was perfect. On more than one occasion, I would pause the movie during her performance and stare at her, with those vibrating tracking lines slicing through her torso since it was a copy of the movie I had recorded from HBO onto a VHS tape. I did that a lot. You could fit two movies, sometimes three, onto one tape. My collection was incredible. I probably own DVDs of every movie I ever recorded, but it's not the same. I put a lot of time and energy into those tapes. Finding the right ones to pair with each other. Timing it just right so the second movie started directly after the first, minus the HBO intro where the letters were in space and we sort of soared into them, and minus the part where it tells you why it's rated R. I even took time to make the labels on the front of the tapes look cool.

Damn, I want my tapes back!

Now. I'm not saying the following novella is my way of getting revenge on Roger Rabbit. It's not. At least I don't think it is. I did just get done telling you guys I'll be a kid forever, right? Maybe, deep down, this is me releasing all my jealous child rage.

The real reason I wrote this story is just because the idea of it really intrigued me. It was, again, one of those ideas that wouldn't get out of my head once it was in there.

It came to me while making a list of high concepts I could use to pitch book ideas. I was in the "blank meets blank" zone at the time, using well-known shows or films to get my idea across. Like *"Dora the Explorer* meets *Scarface."* Holy fuck I'm writing that next.

This one was *"Who Framed Roger Rabbit* meets *Hostel."* Something about a couple of kids tying up their favorite cartoon character and torturing him just really tickled me.

In the cartoon world, we all know cartoons don't die. You can drop them off a cliff or shoot them in the face. They always bounce back.

So I got to thinking…what if they've never felt pain before? How would they react if they were dragged into our world and injured? Not just feeling pain for the first time, but tied up and slowly tortured?

I may have had too much fun with this one. But having fun is fun.

So. Mrs. Rabbit. Wherever you are.

Just be glad I never got my little pudgy hands on one of these devices back in the day.

Cuz I might have a cartoon rabbit foot hanging from my keychain.

STAB
THE RABBIT

"Mom and Dad ain't gonna like it," I said, but Randall wasn't having none of it. He took that little device right into the living room and sat down with it in his lap.

"Close the door already," he said, his eyes on the screen. The color of it shined up in his face and was so bright it looked like fruit juice was splashed over him. "And you won't say shit to Mom and Dad. Cuz if you do, I'll kick your ass so hard you'll be shittin' out your nose."

I had only taken my eyes off the salesman for a second. A short man. Kid short. Midget height, since he was an adult. Red clothes. So red it hurt if you looked too hard. Red hat, too. One of them hats with the little propellers on top. And it spun. There wasn't any wind, but that thing spun the whole time he was giving his spiel. And after Randall took the little device from him, the salesman thanked him, then started to leave. Backing away from the door. Smiling real big. So big it was like the corners of his mouth unpeeled from his face. I blinked and he had his back to me. Walking away. Slow. Like he was on roller skates with slugs for wheels. When Randall said he was gonna kick my ass real hard, I turned away from the salesman to look at him, but only for a second. Real quick. When I turned back, the salesman was gone. Didn't seem possible for him to have disappeared so fast.

"Close the door, Boyd, ya retard."

I did. "What you take that thing for? What if Mom and Dad can't afford it?"

"You didn't hear the man? It's free. You were standin' right there with me when he said it."

"There ain't nothing free. Why would a man go door to door giving away free…what is that anyway?"

Randall hadn't taken his eyes off of it since he wrapped

175

his hands around it. He squinted, licked his lips. Swiped his fingers across the wide screen.

"One of them iPads. Or a knock off or somethin' like it."

"Okay then. You think that man's just gonna let you have it? For nothing?"

"Why not?"

"Cuz he's a salesman. They sell things. He ain't Santa Claus."

Randall finally took his eyes off the iPad knock off so he could make an ugly face at me. "Will you shut up and come over here already. This thing is pretty cool."

Something about the whole deal made me feel funny. Like when I gotta pee at night and its dark in the house and I gotta run by the guest room with the door that don't shut all the way. I can't see nothing in there and I know it's stupid to be scared of a dark and empty room, but that don't mean I don't run by it as fast as I can just to make sure. It was like that. Something about the device, and the salesman who gave it to us, made me wanna run real fast.

But I couldn't let my big brother know I was scared of some stupid computer or whatever it was. I didn't really know what it was. Was pouring myself a bowl of cereal when the man knocked at the door. By the time I had made it over there, he was already halfway through explaining it to Randall, and he didn't start it over on account of me. Probably because he could see on Randall's face that he already had a sale. Even though he gave it to him for free, there had to be a catch. I was just a kid, and I knew that. Nothing's free. Ain't no such a thing as free.

Mom and Dad had to go visit Aunt Priscilla over in Houston. Boyfriend went and beat her up and she didn't have nobody else to call about it. Since me and Randall were old enough to take care of ourselves, they let us stay home. Said they'd be back in the morning. It was a weeknight, but since it was summer vacation, we didn't have nothing to do. Left us twenty bucks for pizza, but me and Randall agreed to save it, use it to buy some comics or a new video game. The only problem was they gave the money to Randall and I had a feeling I wouldn't ever get to see it.

"You didn't give him that twenty, did you?" I asked, just to make sure.

"I told you, retard. It was free. Quit bein' a dumbass and check this out. It's got TV on it."

He held up the device so I could see it clear. And when I saw it, most of the weirdness I was feeling just sort of went away. Floated off me like a hat carried off by a strong wind.

Harry Hare. My favorite cartoon show since I could remember. Randall's too, even though he wouldn't admit it at the time. Was too old and cool for a cartoon like Harry Hare anymore. But still, when he held up that computer, he had a smile on his face the way he used to smile on Saturday mornings. Back when he was nicer to me. Back when it still felt like we were friends. We would always make sure we were up early enough to catch the show. Wouldn't miss Harry and all his crazy adventures for anything. The way he'd get the better of all the bad characters trying to get him and make rabbit stew out of him, bonking them on the head with his mallet and shoving carrots up their noses.

At one point in every episode, it always looked like the bad guy was gonna get him. But no matter what, Harry would get loose somehow. Harry Hare always came out on top.

I took a seat next to my brother. Tried to swipe the computer out of his hands, but he turned and threw an elbow in my ribs that knocked the air out for a second, but I didn't make a stink about it. I hissed and rubbed the sore spot, then scooted up close to him. He seemed like he was in one of his good moods that night. He was having less and less of those. Like the older he got, the madder he got. Stopped wanting to play with his dumb little brother because he said I was too much of a faggot baby. So I didn't want to start a fight. Especially not when there were cartoons to watch.

He started to tap the play button in the middle of the screen. Finger hovering over it, he smiled at me.

"You gonna tell Mom and Dad now?"

"No. I won't. I swear I won't. Just play it. Come on... push it. Randall!"

177

He laughed. "Okay, okay. Don't shit your diaper."

He lowered his finger. But something…strange happened. Instead of his finger tapping the touch screen where the play button was, it sort of sunk into it. Like the screen was made out of liquid. It only sunk down the length of his fingernail, then he pulled his hand away like he just touched a hot stove, looked at his finger like he never knew he had one until then.

"What…what was that?"

"Don't know," Randall said, then dipped his finger in one more time. This time deeper. Then his whole hand.

"Randall," I said, tugging on his shoulder. "Stop. Take your hand outta—"

When Randall screamed, I screamed too. Jumped away from him and covered my head with my arms. I don't know what I thought was gonna happen, but it sure wasn't like anything that actually did. Even as I was looking at the thing flopping around on the end of Randall's hand, I wasn't sure what it was. I mean, I knew what my eyes were telling me it was, but I didn't believe it. Not at first. Because a thing like that wasn't possible. At least that's what I thought at the time.

Randall swung his arm, ran around the room trying to get it off. Knocking over things. One of Mom's tables fell, the one with all her collectible Jesus figures, and each one of those glass Lords crashed and broke apart.

After about a minute of Randall panicking and yelling for me to help him, he finally calmed down. Smiled. Poked at the thing and laughed.

"It don't even hurt."

The thing was a fish. But not no regular fish. It was a cartoon. Straight out of Harry Hare. I've seen those same fish on the show a million times. After Harry finishes up with whatever adventure he has that week, he always drinks carrot juice from his flask and goes fishing at the pond by his rabbit hole. And when he catches a fish, it always looked just like the one dangling from Randall's finger. A blue one. But not the kind of blue you'd see on a normal fish. No shiny scales that turned blue when the light hit them just right.

This fish was blue. Pure blue. Like someone colored it in with a marker. It had a darker blue color where a shadow might fall, and a lighter blue for highlights where a light might hit it. Only the shadow and highlight didn't match the room. When Randall turned the fish, the colors stayed the same.

"Come here," Randall said and yanked the fish free. "It's cold. Like ice. Come feel it."

I shook my head.

"Come on. Quit bein' a faggot. It's a fuckin' fish."

"That ain't right. That ain't supposed to happen like that."

He held it in his palms, lifted it up and sniffed it. "Stinks." Then he stuck out his tongue and licked it. Turned and spat on Mom's carpet. His spit was blue. "Tastes like shit!"

"Put it down, Randall. Come on."

Only a week earlier, I had found Randall doing something that I didn't know any person had the heart to do. Something that gave me that run away feeling. But it was my brother. As much of an asshole as he could be, and as scary as he was starting to become, I told myself he was still my brother and that it wasn't right being scared of him like that. He made me promise not to tell Mom or Dad about it, so I told him I wouldn't, and I never did. It wasn't anything they needed to know about anyway.

He was in the backyard. On the side of the house by the hose. I heard the hiss of the water running, so I went over there to see what he was up to. Could hear him laughing. Not a hard laugh. Not the kind of laugh like when we watched our favorite Harry Hare episode when Harry bonks Cooter Coon over the head with his mallet, driving him into the dirt down to his neck. Tweetie birds appear and circle the raccoon's head, and Harry sprinkles water over him so that a tree grows right out of Cooter's forehead and the birds had a place to live. The laugh was more quiet than that. Like he didn't want nobody to know he was laughing.

"What you doing?" I said, but he didn't need to answer because I saw what he was doing.

179

He looked up and when he saw it was me, just smiled, waved me over with a jerk of his head.

"Remember them cats we saw fuckin' all them months back?"

"Mom says they were just play fighting."

"You hear the noise they was makin'? Them cats were fuckin'. Mom told you that cuz she don't want you jackin' your dick thinkin' about no pussycats."

"Where'd they come from?" I pointed to the kittens he was holding underwater in the plastic bucket we used when Mom and Dad made us wash the car.

"See, the way it works, dumbass, is two cats fuck, the girl cat gets pregnant, then these little cutie pies pop out her back end."

"Well…what're you doing that for, Randall? Let 'em go."

I pushed him and he lifted his hands out of the bucket and backed away. Still smiling. He let me push him out of the way because it was already too late. Kittens were sunk to the bottom of that bucket. Dead. Water was red, and I saw it was because Randall was pushing down so hard on the things that he squashed a couple of them, made them bleed. One had its guts coming out its mouth like it was trying to blow a bubble gum bubble.

I cried. I cried hard and loud and he slapped a hand over my mouth so fast and rough that I cried harder, only it wasn't loud because of his hand blocking the way. Holding me like that, hurting me, he whispered into my ear.

"You tell Mom or Dad about this, and I'll drown you in the bucket next. Understand?"

I nodded and he let go. We went to the playground after that. Buried those kittens in the sand. Real deep so nobody would ever find them. Then we just played like normal. Going down the slides. Swinging on the swings. I didn't feel normal, but I was too scared to act any other way because Randall kept on looking at me like he was daring me to act different.

We never talked about the kittens again.

Randall set the fish on the ground. Watched it flop around. Everything it touched it stained blue. Like whatever ink the artist used to paint the thing was rubbing off, but it didn't show on the fish. It was just as pure blue as it was when Randall first pulled it out of the device.

"You're not gonna come look at it?"

"I can see it from right here."

"Well don't you think it's...I don't know. Cool?"

"No. Something like that ain't supposed to be possible, Randall. It ain't natural. Put it back. And let's get rid of that iPad thing."

"Hell no. Don't you see what this means?" He raised his foot and stomped down on the fish. The blue exploded and splashed onto the walls. All three shades of it. The colors didn't mix on impact. Each one stayed its own shade, dripping off hung pictures and lamps and the broken pieces of Jesuses.

"What'd you do that for?"

"You're the one said to put it back."

"In the...computer thing. Not kill it!"

Randall shook his head. Laughed the way he laughed with the kittens. "It's a cartoon, Boyd. Can't kill a cartoon. It ain't real."

I pointed to the pieces of the fish. Each small chunk still moving. Wiggling. "If it ain't real, then why is it in our living room? And what's all that blue stuff?"

"Cartoon blood, retard!"

I almost asked him how we were gonna explain all the mess to Mom and Dad, but considering I had just watched my brother pull a cartoon fish out of a digital tablet and then stomp on it, getting in trouble with our parents didn't seem all that important.

I snuck a look at the device. Lying on the ground where Randall had left it.

And staring right at me, from the other side of the screen...was Harry Hare. He had a look like he could see me the same as I could see him. A look I had never seen on my favorite cartoon rabbit's face.

"Randall?"

"I see it. I see it, all right." And he dove to the floor. Got the fish blood all over his clothes.

Harry still had his big eyes on me. Sort of started to smile. Seeing him smile like that made me feel a little better about the situation. The whole thing was weird. Impossible. But if Harry Hare could be…real. If he could come into our house, play with us, take us on adventures, then maybe it was okay. Maybe instead of scary, it was a miracle.

Before I had a chance to think about it anymore, Randall shoved his arm through the computer screen again. Up to his elbow. Then his shoulder. He pushed so deep that his left ear and part of his face dipped down into it.

"Grab my feet!"

I did. And then he started kicking. And he was sucked halfway into the screen. It didn't look big enough to fit all of him, but somehow his body squeezed through, and I almost lost my grip on his feet because of the way he was kicking. I pulled as hard as I could, started to cry but never let go.

And then he was free. Like the screen spat him out.

And he wasn't alone.

***

Randall dripped with colors. Like someone had melted a box of crayons and tossed it over him. At first I thought he was hurt because of the red I saw, but his white teeth shone through the liquid rainbow and I saw he was smiling.

Harry Hare wasn't smiling. Wasn't making any face I could read. Just stood there in our living room. Staring at us. His cartoon eyes rolling between me and Randall again and again. The eyes were a baby blue color, two black pinpricks for pupils. His gloved hands reached up and rubbed his long ears, the fur white with light gray for shadow. I knew it was fur because he was a rabbit, but when I stared at him, all I could see was white. No individual hairs. There were jagged shapes around his edges, like the artist that drew him was trying to imply hair or fur.

"Look at him," Randall said. "Isn't he great?"

I nodded. Because he was. I couldn't believe what I was seeing. I wanted to reach out and touch him but then decided I didn't want to feel the cold that Randall had felt on that fish. Didn't want any of that cartoon color to get on me.

Harry backed away from us. He bumped into the couch behind him and gasped. Little light blue droplets of spittle sprayed from his mouth when he did it and splashed over the carpet. The yellow overalls that he always wore smeared a sunshine-bright stain over the upholstery.

"Who are you?" Harry said, his voice exactly the same from the cartoon. "Where are we? Why'd you bring me here, kid?"

I had an urge to run and hug him. The way I always thought I'd act if I went to Disney World and saw all the characters walking around the park. Seeing my favorite cartoon character in the flesh, in my own house, was almost too much for me to handle. But I didn't want him to think I was some kind of baby. Didn't wanna scare him off.

"I'm Boyd. This's my brother Randall. You're in our house."

"I'm in your house." He reached into his pocket and pulled out his flask of carrot juice. Took a long swig, the orange drippings splashing on the floor. He licked his chops and wiped his mouth. "Why's your color look like that? Hurts my eyes."

"Holy shit, this's crazy." Randall stepped forward and tried to touch the rabbit, but Harry slapped his hand away. "It's him. It's really him."

"Yeah, it's me. And there I was. Minding my own business. Waiting on ol' Cooter Coon to come sniffing around my hole like he does. Then I see that one sticking his head out of the clouds. I see him and I'm thinking it's the Artist. We've all heard of the Artist. Our creator, right? And he reaches down and snatches me up like I'm some kind of prize in a claw game."

"I won you in a claw game before," I said excitedly, then realized how stupid that sounded.

183

"Didn't win *me*, kid. Only one Harry Hare on this planet. Wait. That where I am? We on another planet? Because I know *you're* not the Artist."

"And why can't I be the Artist?" Randall asked, trying to wipe the white color from his palm.

"I can just tell." Harry took another long look at both of us, then finally smiled. "Man, you are the ugliest kids I've ever seen. Anybody ever tell you that?"

"Fuck you, rabbit." Randall's eyebrows looked mad the way they shoved down over his eyes, but he was still smiling.

"Name's Harry, kid. But I guess you know that. And I'm not one for sticking to rules and good behavior, but watch the language, will you? That's one rule we can never break."

"Well I got news for you," Randall said. "We're not in your world anymore. I don't know if you can say we're on another planet or not, but we might as well be. And here, in my world, I'm God. I'm the Artist. And you have to listen to what I say. So if I wanna say fuck you, then I say fuck you."

Harry squinted at Randall, then turned to me. "Your brother's making me nervous, kid."

"It's all right. We just can't believe you're here, that's all."

"Yeah, I'm starting to wonder if Backwoods Bear put something in my carrot juice again."

"It's just…you're my favorite. Been watching you since as long as I can remember. Waking up and eating cereal right there in front of the TV on Saturday mornings. Only time Mom'll let us eat in the living room is when you're on."

"On? Whattaya mean when I'm on?"

"Your show. You don't know you're on a show? That kids watch? It's a cartoon."

Harry scratched his head, and when he did that, little needles of white cartoon hair floated down. Randall wouldn't stop smiling, and it was the smile that made me nervous. Made me want to warn Harry and tell him to hop back into the computer so he wouldn't get hurt.

If he was still in his world, the cartoon world, I knew I didn't have to worry. Because cartoons don't die. You can do all sorts of things to them. Blow them up. Shoot them. Stick them in a blender and hit puree, they never died.

Even though the cartoon fish's chunks still moved around like cut up worm pieces, it wasn't putting itself back together. And I could tell by how the pieces moved, how they sort of quivered, that they felt pain. That Randall had hurt the fish, and that maybe the fish had never felt what hurt was before Randall stomped down on it.

"Look," Harry said, and leaned back on the couch. Looking more relaxed. He grinned wide, his big buck teeth sticking out past his chin. "I don't really care where we are, what planet this is, or who the two of you really are. All I know is I haven't had an adventure today. Not one. Was on the verge of one when you ugly boys pulled me up here."

"So what're you sayin'?"

"I'm saying. What kind of trouble can we get into around here?"

Trouble wasn't a word I tended to like hearing. But when it came out of Harry Hare's mouth, I couldn't help but jump up and down.

***

Mean ol' Mrs. Buckingham. Lived across the street from us. She'd been mean since the day I was born. Mom said she wasn't always that way. Said she was sweet once. Had a husband and a daughter. Daughter died when she was in her twenties. Mom never said how, only that it was a shame, that she was taken too early. Then Mr. Buckingham kicked the Buckingham bucket next. Not even a year after his daughter went.

I would have felt bad for the old lady. Maybe if I was alive to meet her daughter and husband. Maybe if I could've seen her before she turned into a wrinkled ol' witch who liked to scream at kids for no good reason other than to make them cry or scare them, I might've felt sorry for her.

There was one time I was walking along the sidewalk by myself. Wasn't doing nothing. Hands in my pockets, just walking along. Whistling. Think I might've even been whistling the theme song to the Harry Hare show. It was that time of year when acorns fall out of trees. When you can't hardly step anywhere without crunching down on them. I was just about at her house, but wasn't thinking about it. Didn't even realize it until I kicked an acorn and it rolled into her yard. That was it. There were already a million of the things in her yard, from her own tree, and I guess she was standing out there watching, just waiting for a kid to do something she didn't like, and she must've saw that acorn roll onto her lawn, must've saw it was me who kicked it.

That hunchbacked hag came charging at me like a cow defending its calf. Jumped out of her house faster than I thought an old woman like her could manage. Got right in my face and got to yelling hard. So hard her whole face turned red and all the veins on her neck stuck out like nightcrawlers. Thought she was gonna fall over and die she was trying so hard to be mean to me. Don't even remember what she said. Just that the longer she yelled, the madder she got, and the madder she got, the more high-pitched her voice became. And she kept spitting on me. Little spit sprinkles flying from her mouth as she screamed and hollered, watering my face like it was a flower in a pot.

I tried to tell her I didn't mean anything by it. Didn't do nothing on purpose to make her mad, but she wasn't hearing any of that. The worst part was that I started crying, no matter how hard I tried not to, and when I ran home, Randall saw me crying and made fun of me for a week over it. Called me WahWah.

That was the only time I ever got close enough to ol' Mrs. Buckingham for her to have a go at me. But I'd seen her jump on just about every kid in the neighborhood for whatever reason she could come up with. If there's no such things as witches—and at this point I figure it's possible that there's such a thing as anything—Mrs. Buckingham was the closest thing to a real one. Even stories around the neighborhood that if she catches a kid snooping around at night, she takes them in her house, boils them alive, then feeds the meat to all her cats. And she's got so many cats it didn't seem like it would take all too long for those felines to eat a kid up. Every scrap.

As far as I knew, she never got the chance to snap at Randall. For all the trouble my brother got into, it didn't seem like he ever got caught. Was a master at getting away with things. It was one of Mrs. Buckingham's cats that had its litter of kittens drowned by my big brother. She never suspected him or said anything about it. Made a big stink about the missing kittens, blamed just about every damn kid but Randall for it. Something about my brother's face that made people trust him, I guess.

So when Harry asked what kind of trouble we could get into, me and Randall both knew what to do. It was payback time. Not just for us, but for every kid she ever yelled at. Every kid she ever made cry.

"So this old lady," Harry said, hunched behind the bushes between me and Randall, "she's that bad, huh?"

"Pure evil," Randall said.

I told Harry everything I knew about her. Told him about my run in with her, the rumors about boiling kids alive. I left out the part about what happened to her kittens. As he listened, his smile got wider and wider and the color started to drip off him like he was sweating paint.

"Well then I think we found our target, kids."

I wasn't sure how we were gonna get close to Mrs. Buckingham's house without her noticing us. Especially with a tall, bright cartoon bunny. I wondered if she'd be too shocked by Harry when she saw him for her to do anything other than scream and call for help. Maybe even have a heart attack right there and join the rest of her family wherever it was they floated off to.

As much as I hated her, I didn't want to hurt her. Just scare her. Make her cry the way she made me and so many others cry.

But before we could even stand up from behind the bush, Harry cracked his knuckles—which made a sound so loud that it echoed over the whole neighborhood—and then dug his cartoon fingers into the ground. In the cartoon show, Harry could dig through cartoon dirt like it was nothing. Since we were in our world and we were dealing with real dirt, I wasn't sure it would work the same way.

But it did. As fast as he drove his fingers into the dirt, he was gone. Leaving a narrow hole behind him. We could watch his progress because he didn't dig deep enough not to disturb everything above him. Our lawn lifted and spread apart where he tunneled beneath it. The sidewalk and street cracked, looked like one long speed bump across it. Car alarms went off. Some water sprayed out of the cracks in the street.

"Should we go in after him?" Randall asked, and tried to fit into the hole. He came back up quick, shook the dirt from his hair. "Not big enough. And too dark, anyway."

I was glad to hear that because the last thing I wanted to do was go crawling through that dark, tight space. Started panicking just thinking about how hard it probably was to breathe down there.

"Whatta we do?" I asked, wiping the sweat from my palms onto my jeans.

Neighbors were already noticing the damaged street and sidewalk, traced it back through our lawn. We hid back behind the bush and stayed low, but I wasn't sure they couldn't see us. Randall giggled like he was having the time of his life.

Then there was a scream. A scream so loud I could swear I felt it in my teeth. Then some loud crashing sounds like there was a live tornado inside of ol' Mrs. Buckingham's house. Which is maybe not a bad way to describe Harry Hare.

Not thinking, when that scream rang out the way it did, I jumped up from behind the bush. The neighbors didn't see me because they were looking toward the witch's house too.

Then the front door creaked open. A tidal wave of cats rushed out and flooded the yard and street. The cats darted every which way, some of them speckled with blood, all screeching and meowing and hissing.

Mrs. Buckingham stumbled out next. Legs wobbly and looking ready to give out any second, but somehow she stayed upright. Her white hair was completely red with blood. More running down her face and dripping from her eyelashes and the tip of her nose and chin. As she stumbled closer, I saw that it wasn't just red on her head. But a brown color. Too solidly brown to be from the real world.

Harry followed her out. When the neighbors first saw him, a few of them gasped, but most didn't make a sound or even move. Could only stare. Probably trying to figure out what it was they were looking at. Trying to make sense of what couldn't be made sense of.

Harry held his mallet in one hand. One end of it painted red. And not cartoon red. But real life red. The shades changing as different shadows and light fell over it, making it sparkle.

Then he lifted the mallet over his head. "You got a mosquito on your head, lady. Don't worry! I'll get it!" And he slammed the mallet into the back of her skull. Caving it in. Bloody brains slapped her lawn, and more blood poured out of her head and face and painted the countless acorns littering her property.

When the blood sprayed Harry in the face and when the old woman dropped to the ground, got to twitching and spasming, he leaned back, his hand on his belly, and howled with laughter.

That's about the time the neighbors started screaming and running.

I hoped that was the end of it. That Harry would come running back our way and we could hide in the house and hope nobody came to our door. There was no way anyone could have known Harry was with us. And when they called the police, I figured the cops would think they were all crazy saying a cartoon bunny murdered the old witch widow.

But it didn't end there. Harry, still laughing, held his mallet up over his head again. Chased every one of those neighbors down. There had to be a good five of them. I couldn't see who they were because my vision went all blurry on the edges and all I could see was Harry, his vibrant color as bright as a television screen in a dark room, as he dashed from person to person, caving in their skulls with his mallet and throwing carrots like daggers, sticking people in the back as they tried to run away.

"Whatta you say we look at the stars together, huh, toots?" he said, then nearly took a woman's head off her neck.

I didn't understand it. Why my favorite character would do a thing like that. He got into plenty of mischievous adventures on his show, but it was always harmless. Then again, the characters he bonked over the head with his mallet would end up with a halo of spinning stars or tweetie birds instead of their brains pouring out of their eye sockets.

Once everyone in sight was dead, Harry stuffed his mallet into his pocket, which slid in easily even though it looked too big to fit. And he pulled his flask of carrot juice out and took a long drink.

"All right!" Harry said. "Your turn. Come and get me! Show me what you ugly people got under your sleeves!" His smile started to fade as he stared at all them bloody people in the street, none of them moving.

I realized he didn't really mean to hurt them. Just did what he always did and thought they'd all have a good laugh. Thought the people would get up and chase him, set traps for him, the kind of thing that always happened on his show.

"What's going on?" he called to us.

"Get over here!" Randall yelled, but was still grinning. When I saw that grin on his face I couldn't believe it. "Hurry up!"

I waved Harry over, wiping tears out of my face with my other hand.

Harry stared at the blood dripping from his overalls, from his gloves, and he whimpered as he ran, leaving long, white tracks from his feet.

We ran into the house and slammed the door. I locked it and leaned against it, couldn't make myself stop crying.

"Wait, wait, wait," Harry said, shaking his head and

pacing. "That wasn't supposed to happen. Why won't they get up? What's all that red stuff coming out of them? And why...why are you crying?"

He put his hand on me and I felt that icy cold Randall was talking about and I flinched away and hid behind my brother.

Harry swallowed hard and dropped to the floor. Used his ears to cover up his face and started to cry himself. His blue tears soaking into the carpet, along with all the other colors splashed all over the place. The fish pieces still wiggled around and scooted about.

"Whatta we do now, Randall?"

"Gotta hide him."

"Where?"

He checked out the window. "Nobody out there still. But he left footprints from the street, lead all the way to our door."

"Can't we clean them up?"

I heard the sirens just as I finished up asking the question.

"No time. Let's get him to Mom and Dad's room. Stick him in the tub for now."

"The tub? What for?"

"So we can wash all that fuckin' blood off him. Now go on!"

I didn't want to touch Harry again, but I grabbed his arm and started to pull him upstairs.

"Pick him up, retard. Can't have them footprints leadin' up the stairs, can we?"

Harry was still covering his face with his ears. Crying awful. I thought he'd be too heavy for me since he was as tall as he was, but I gave it a try anyway, using all that adrenaline pumping through me. He weighed almost nothing. Like carrying a sack of cotton balls.

I wondered, him being so light and all, how he found the strength to hit hard enough to kill a person. I guess cartoon muscles don't work the same way as real ones.

I went slow at first, but when that cold started to work into me, started to chill me to the core and make me shiver,

I hurried up. Once at the top of the stairs, I sprinted to Mom and Dad's, tried to kick in the bathroom door. The way I always see people do it in movies. Chuck Norris and Van Damme and all the other hero types. Always looked so easy, but when my foot collided with that door, it bounced right off, sent a lightning strike of pain up my leg and threw me on my butt. Harry's freezing, bright body landed on top of me and his colors sloshed off and coated me. Got some of it in my mouth and filled it with a taste like roadkill that had been sitting in the sun for a week. Never tasted roadkill, but smelled it before, and I figure the taste is something similar.

I spat it out, almost vomited, but held that back. Didn't need any more mess than we already had. I stood, opened the door with my hand, and gently laid Harry in the tub.

He wasn't crying anymore. His big eyes quivered when he looked at me.

"Am I still your favorite?" he asked. "I didn't mean to hurt anyone. Not really hurt them. Just trying to have a little fun. You know me. You know me, right, kid? You know I like to have fun. That's all."

"Out of the way!" Randall burst into the room, shoved me hard to the side so I stumbled and hit my shoulder against the toilet.

When I turned to yell at him for it, I saw the knife in his hand. The serrated one Mom used to cut bread with.

Harry tried to pull away, but the knife cut through his ankles too fast. Randall didn't even have to saw back and forth. Just set the knife against one ankle and slid it back one good time. And the foot just fell away. Every color on Harry's body sprayed from his ankle stump and painted the tile walls and started to fill the tub.

A scream exploded out of Harry's mouth that felt like needles in my ears. I covered my head and tried to scream to help block the noise, but it didn't do any good. When I pulled my head free of my arms, I saw that Randall had already cut off the second foot.

The long toes on both feet wiggled, and those cartoon hairs kept puffing off of them.

Harry flopped around in the tub, now making a choking sound. The colorful blood spraying from his wounds filled the room with a stink I don't even know how to describe. I can tell you it was bad enough to pull that vomit right out of my stomach.

Randall tried to run by but I reached out and grabbed hold of his pants. He tried to kick free, but my grip was too good, then I wrapped both my arms around his leg and held on tight.

"Lemme go, you little shit."

"Why'd you do that, Randall? *Why?*"

"The tracks, retard. Tried to clean 'em off, but they won't come up. Only other plan I could think of. Now lemme go before it's too late."

When I still held on, he used one of them severed rabbit's feet and slapped me across the head with it. The thing wasn't heavy enough to hurt me, but when that stinky blood splashed over my head and soaked into my hair, I let go. Dunked my head in the toilet to wash it off. The colors made tie dye patterns in the water, never mixing together.

I didn't wanna go with Randall, but staying in there with Harry with that awful screaming was out of the question. So I jumped up and ran after my brother, still had my hands over my ears. I wanted to do something to help the cartoon rabbit—still my favorite character—but I didn't even know where to begin.

I was halfway down the stairs when I saw Randall slipping his own feet into the giant rabbit's feet like big slippers. I didn't know how he could do a thing like that. When he did it, the feet got to hopping around, almost tossed him right back out, but he managed to get control of them, had to brace himself up on the wall for support. The color soaked into his jeans and sort of rode the fabric up to his knees, almost made it look like he had cartoon legs.

"Randall? What the hell're you doing?"

"You just stay right there and shut up. When them police come over here and start askin' questions, you don't say nothin'. They ask you anything, just shake your head and look scared. You got me?"

I didn't answer him. Wouldn't be hard to act scared, I knew that much. And since I wouldn't have even known how to explain anything that had happened since that salesman came to our door and disappeared, keeping quiet was fine by me.

Randall walked from the front door, across the living room, and to the back door. His knees kept jerking up as the feet tried to hop away. Then he threw the door open and ran across the backyard, pulled the feet off, and tossed them over the fence. Ran back in, grabbed the pieces of the wriggling blue fish and tossed them over the fence too.

A knock at the door.

I flinched and got to shaking real bad. Realized Harry was still screaming.

"That fuckin' rabbit needs to shut its goddamn mouth," Randall said. At this point, he was almost completely covered with color. I wasn't sure how he'd explain that to the cops, but with Harry hollering like he was, the color was the least of our worries.

Randall sprinted up the steps. I heard a lot of banging around up there, and then just like that, Harry was quiet. Which made me nervous. Even after everything the rabbit did, I didn't want Randall to hurt him. Not anymore than he already had.

Randall jetted down the stairs, almost tripped, then stopped right next to me.

"They ask about the screamin', it was you. Cuz of the big scary killer that ran through our house after killin' all them folks outside. Got it? You're just a kid and it scared the shit outta you. Say something!"

"You told me not to say nothing. I got it."

"Retard."

Randall answered the door in the middle of the cops knocking on it.

"That way!" Randall said and pointed toward the back door. "He forced his way in here and ran out that way. Out the back door!"

The officers hesitated for a second as they looked Randall up and down, then me, then the house, which was dripping in cartoon color, then finally pulled their guns and ran through the house, following the white tracks Randall had made.

I looked up the stairs, then at Randall. "How'd you get him to stop yelling?"

"Stabbed him. Right through the windpipe. Then I knocked him out. Cold. And then, just in case..." Randall reached into his pocket and pulled out Harry's pink tongue. It writhed like a flat earthworm.

My vision went blurry and I felt myself tipping forward off the steps, and then everything went black on me. Like someone hit my power button.

***

I woke up in my own bed. When I saw the stuffed Harry Hare toy I had won out of that claw game a while back sitting on my dresser, I screamed and sat up. My head was aching something awful, and I had to give myself a few minutes before moving again, waiting for the pounding to stop.

I heard some movement coming from above me. Since all the rooms were on the second floor, I knew it was coming from the attic. Then I heard Randall laughing from up there. It was muffled through the ceiling, but I knew his laugh.

Part of me hoped I'd hear Harry's laugh along with Randall's. Maybe, since he was a cartoon, he would heal fast. Maybe he was whole again and the two of them were up there having fun like a boy and a real life cartoon bunny are supposed to.

I stepped out of my room and almost slipped in all the splashed color in the hall. There was a big puddle of it just under the attic door, the dangling pull cord coated in it.

I didn't like looking at the colors for too long. Didn't hurt my eyes the way Harry said our real world colors hurt his. But it made me feel kind of queasy. It almost looked like someone colored on the floor and walls with a crayon or paintbrush, but it was just...different. It was like my eyes couldn't figure out how to take it in.

I yanked the cord and pulled down the stairs. I wish I would've just ran away then. Instead of climbing those steps and joining my brother. But my curiosity outweighed whatever fear I had, and I walked up those stairs into the attic.

Randall was on his stomach on the attic floor. When I saw him, I thought Harry had gotten loose. Got my brother back for what he did to him. Because at first, it looked like Randall was headless. Then I noticed the device lying on the floor and that he had his head stuck down in it.

He pulled it out, laughing like a million tickling fingers were fluttering at his armpits. When he saw me, he jumped up, ran to me, and hugged me. My brother had never hugged me in his life. And I might've been joyful seeing him so happy if it wasn't for the reasons he gave me.

"See, I started thinkin'," he said. "If we pulled the rabbit out of here, you know, what else could we pull out? Right?"

He still had an arm around my neck, and I shoved it off. "What'd you do?"

"Nothin'! I said I was just thinkin'." He rubbed the back of his head, face went a little red. "Well maybe I did more than think, but it don't matter cuz it didn't work anyway. Guess maybe cuz we got the rabbit out and the computer won't let me change the channel till we put him back."

"Then let's put him back!"

Randall shook his head. "Not done with him yet. But listen. Once I thought about changin' the channel, I was wonderin' what else we could see, you know? Find some kinda porno channel or somethin'. Pull me some sexy porno star out into our world from…I don't know, Fuck World or wherever they would come from."

"What's wrong with you?"

"You would say that. Only a retard faggot like you would say that. Besides, you're too young to understand. But any normal man I know woulda thought the same thing. But it don't have to be just that. We could change the channel to anything we wanted. We could see dinosaurs! Or Jesus! Or whatever we wanted, Boyd! And another thing. We don't always gotta bring 'em out. We could go in."

I wanted to stomp on that computer. Break it into a thousand pieces. But I didn't want to touch it. Didn't want to get anywhere near it. Plus, it was the only way to get Harry back home.

"I was thinkin' about that too. Look how easy it was to fuck that rabbit up. It wasn't nothin'! And you know like I know, Harry Hare's the boss in his world, right? I mean, the show's got his name in it and I took care of him easy!"

"What about all the people he killed? You forget about that?"

"Those people weren't prepared. Didn't know what was comin'. But me? That's different. Think about it, Boyd. We go in with guns. Real guns. Guns from our world that kill permanently. We could drop down into the Cartoon World and run it! We could be the cartoon kings! Wouldn't that be somethin'?"

"Where's Harry?"

"Are you not listenin' to me?"

"I heard you. If you wanna go be king somewhere, nothing I can do to stop you. But I'm staying here. Where I know the rules. Where colors don't make my brain and stomach hurt."

Randall was still covered in the cartoon hues. Didn't look like he'd even attempted to wash himself. A fresh coat of the stuff ran down his hair and face after sticking his head into the screen.

"Where's Harry?" I asked again.

"I shoulda known you'd be no fun. I mean seriously. A kid gets a chance to live in a cartoon, rule it, and he's too scared. Too much of a pussy." He stared at me, head shaking. Then rolled his eyes and pointed across the attic, behind where Dad kept all the Christmas decorations. "Your stupid fuckin' rabbit's over there."

He shoved me in the back when I turned to walk over. Stamped a rainbow handprint on my shirt.

Harry sat in one of Mom's old antique chairs. Arms behind his back, tied up with Christmas lights. His leg stumps rested against the floor, still steadily bleeding. His eyes were half-lidded, a stream of rainbow spilling from his mouth where Randall had cut his tongue out. The hole in his throat dripped, a wheezing sound oozing out of it. His nose was busted and turned sideways, the long whiskers crooked and zigzagged.

He looked up at me when I got close. Moved his mouth like he was trying to talk, but I couldn't understand any of the sounds spilling out.

"I'm sorry," I said. "My brother...he's—"

"I'm what?" Randall grabbed my shoulders with both hands. Squeezed hard. "Crazy?"

"Let me go! *Ow!*"

He tossed me aside and I tripped over a box full of old photo books of when me and Randall were babies. The corner of one of the books jabbed into my side, and I rolled around kicking my legs, trying to catch my breath back.

Randall threw Harry's ears back, then ran his hand across the bunny's bloody face, smearing the colors across it. Harry whimpered and tried to wiggle free, but his cartoon muscles were no use against the tightly wrapped Christmas lights.

He touched Harry's leg stumps. Tickled them and made Harry wiggle harder and cough. "You think cartoon rabbit's feet are good luck like the real ones are? I bet they got even more luck in them than real ones since they're from your world. Thinkin' I'd go grab them later."

He reached into his pocket and pulled out a pair of pliers. Snapped them open and shut a few times, right in Harry's face. Made the rabbit flinch. Harry's big, blue eyes went extra wide.

"Then again, I bet any part of a cartoon bunny's good luck."

He clamped the pliers over one of Harry's buck teeth and yanked it free. It popped off easy, made a wet crunchy sound, and more blood poured out. When Harry tilted his head back and wailed, he sprayed the cartoon blood into Randall's face. Randall only laughed, rubbed the colors in, then moved in for the second tooth.

He rattled them both in his hand like dice, then shoved them both in the space between his upper lip and top teeth. They stuck there, both shaking a little, and he turned and smiled at me.

"That a carrot in your pocket or are you just happy to see me?"

"You gotta stop," I said and stood up, still holding my side. "This ain't right, Randall. You know it ain't. Me and you, we've been watching Harry Hare all our lives. That don't mean nothing to you?"

"Sure it does. Why I'm havin' such a good time. Wouldn't be nearly as fun if it was a different character. Least I don't think it would. Maybe I'll find out later."

"We gotta put him back. Maybe if we put him back, he'll get better. In his own world, maybe—"

"Yeah, yeah. Whatever. Told you I ain't done with him yet."

"You're gonna kill him!"

"And? Still got reruns, don't we?"

Randall, with the teeth still in his mouth, cocked his fist back and hit Harry across the face. Then again and again. Kept on punching until he got so tired he had to take a break. His knuckles dripped.

"Don't hurt to hit him. Like punchin' a pillow. Come here."

I shook my head.

"I said come here. Like it or not, you're gonna help me."

"I'm not doing anything with you. Not anymore. Not ever again!"

Randall lifted his knee to his chest, then stomped down on Harry. Right where his balls were. I didn't know if cartoons had balls or not, but by the way the bunny howled and thrashed around, his leg stumps pumping and drumming on the floor, stamping it with colors, I figured he had them all right.

"Look at that. Maybe I'll rip his cock off next. Stuff it up his ass. Ever wonder what a cartoon rabbit's cock looks like?"

"Randall! Please!"

"I never did till just now," he said through a laugh, then reached out and yanked Harry's ears right off his head. They stretched first, then snapped off, made a sound like a firecracker.

Blood sprayed like twin fountains. So high it painted the ceiling.

Harry made a gurgling sound then. Groaning and coughing, choking on his blood as it sprayed from his neck hole. He didn't wiggle anymore. Just sort of sat there. One eye swelled shut from Randall's fists. The other lazy and half open, staring right at me.

And I knew, looking right back at him, that I had to do something. That I couldn't just stand by and let Randall do this. Not to my favorite character.

There was nothing I could do about the kittens. I had gotten there too late. But I told myself that if I would've gotten there earlier, I would've tried to stop him.

This was that time. If I stood by and watched any longer, it might be too late. And a world, no matter which world it was, without Harry Hare wasn't one worth living in.

Randall tossed the ears away which scooted around like caterpillars, leaving kaleidoscopic trails behind them. He grabbed the crotch of Harry's yellow overalls and tore a hole there. Shoved both hands in and ripped it wider.

I looked away. Didn't want to see what a cartoon rabbit's dingaling looked like.

"Holy shit. I mean…holy shit! Boyd, I'm bein' serious. You gotta see this." He got to laughing harder than he had all day, and Harry's gurgling turned into a whimper.

I crept across the attic, going the long way around so I had to climb over boxes and old junk.

When I finally reached the device, I looked down at the screen and was being looked at right back. By every other character in the Harry Hare Show I could think of.

Cooter Coon and Backwoods Bear and PuttPutt the Platypus and BeetleBrain and Uncle Skunk and every critter from that world. All piled up, shoulder to shoulder, staring up at me. Not a smile on any face. They cringed when Harry screamed. Some crying, shaking their heads.

"You have to help him," I whispered down to them. And I lowered my top half into the screen.

The Cartoon World was freezing cold. Like dunking my head into a pool in winter. The air itself was made of colors, and it was hard to breathe. Like taking a drink and then breathing it in. I started to panic the same way I panicked just thinking about crawling down Harry's rabbit hole in our yard, but I calmed down once I saw all the characters looking up at me. Arms out.

I reached out for them. Cartoon clouds splatting against me like moist marshmallows. Birds flying around my head, their beaks stretching into grimaces as Harry's screams kept exploding from behind me. The screams were louder in the Cartoon World. Like they were being blasted out of giant speakers in the sky.

They looked too far for me to reach, but when I extended my arms out, they sort of stretched like taffy. It didn't hurt for them to stretch like that, and I quickly wondered what else I could do in that world.

I couldn't carry them all up with me. Not because they were too heavy, but because there were just too many of them to hold. So I grabbed the one I thought could help the most. The biggest, most ferocious one I could think of.

The bear's huge paws wrapped around my hands and I pulled. We flew through the air as my body snapped back to its normal size like a rubber band. Backwoods Bear roared and showed all his teeth. Big teeth. His black lips curled back so I could see all of them, and there were so many I couldn't count.

And then, just like that, we were back in my world. In my attic.

A massive paw patted the top of my head.

Then the giant cartoon bear stomped toward my brother and the rabbit who, up until a boy from another world pulled him out and started ripping pieces off, was his arch enemy.

***

I probably should've covered up my eyes. I knew Randall was doing a bad thing. Same way I knew he was doing a bad thing when he drowned those kittens. But he was still my brother. I still tried to convince myself I cared for him, no matter how mean he was.

But something about what he was doing to Harry Hare really got to me. Not only because it was my favorite cartoon character of all time, but because of how much he liked hurting him.

Randall was too busy slapping Harry across the face with something long and pink to notice Backwoods Bear coming up on him from behind. It wasn't until I noticed the waterfall of colors splashing out from Harry's crotch that I realized what that long, pink thing was.

Even though he was hurting bad, feeling what pain felt like for the first time since the Artist first drew him and colored him into existence, when he saw Backwoods Bear standing tall over Randall, a smile stretched across his face. It was hard to tell it was a smile at all with how busted up his face was and all the blood and the missing teeth. I knew it was because of the laugh that sputtered out. Small and quiet at first, then louder. The trademark Harry Hare laugh I always heard when Harry gave his enemies the slip, just when you thought he was gonna get caught this time. Just when you thought it was the end for the poor bunny.

But Harry Hare always came out on top.

"The fuck's so funny, bunny?" Randall said, then slapped him with the pink tube one more time before jamming it into Harry's mouth.

"Now where I'm from," Backwoods said, his voice deep like a roaring truck engine, "it ain't proper to go a wastin' parts of a tasty rabbit like that there. Cuttin' off bits and a tossin' 'em to the floor. You's s'posed to eat the whole thing. So none o' that there tasty rabbit be a goin' to waste."

There was a wet splatting sound after that. Randall gasped. I was behind Backwoods so that I couldn't see what had happened yet, but then the Bear spun around, chuckling in that deep, redneck way he always did in the show. The kind of laugh that tells you the person doing it ain't all that smart.

A-huck, a-huck, a-huck.

His paw was shoved through Randall's back, all the way through so it was sticking out between his chest and stomach. When the bear wiggled his long, cartoon claws, ribbons of guts stretched between them.

Randall was still alive. Staring down at the claws sticking out of him. Raking his fingers over the bloody hole and choking as blood spilled out of his mouth. His feet kicked, but slow and lazy, like he was doggie paddling in mid-air. His eyes looked sad, first looking down at the bear claw, then swinging over to me.

I wanted to feel sad for him. Figured it was the kind of thing a little brother's supposed to do when he's looking at his big brother right before a bear tears him apart. But I just didn't. I didn't choose not to feel sad, it just wasn't there. Wasn't in me.

"What're you gonna do with him?" I asked Backwoods Bear.

"Reckon I'll rip him up right here right now. That is, little mister, if a you ain't a mindin' I do so. Yer house and all. Kinda house you got here, little mister? Why're the colors a makin' my eyes burn for?"

"Wait…" Harry, still tied up, struggled to keep his head up. His words were hard to understand with no tongue and all that blood pouring out of his mouth, and he had to plug his neck hole with one of his fingers. "C-can't…can't kill him yet." He spat a fat wad of rainbow that splashed over the floor. "Not done with him yet."

I walked over. Untied Harry and lifted him in my arms. When I heard the thumping sound coming up the attic steps, I figured Mom and Dad had come home early, but it was Harry's feet. They hopped along toward the device, still bleeding, and tumbled into the screen, disappearing. The pieces of blue fish were right behind them.

Holding Harry in my arms, I didn't mind the cold so much. And as I carried him closer to the computer, all the pieces Randall had torn off, including that long, pink tube, were already diving through the screen, back to their world where there was no such thing as pain or death.

"Are you gonna be all right?" I asked, and realized I was crying.

He smiled at me, his head shaking real bad. Then he touched his bloody forehead against mine.

"You're my favorite ugly kid. Always will be."

I laughed and dropped down to my knees by the device. "You're taking him with you, aren't you? Back to your world?"

"In my world...he won't die. No matter what we do to him. He'll never die. And down in my rabbit hole, kid, I've got lots of toys to play with."

I nodded. "I'm sorry for what happened."

"Not as sorry as your brother's gonna be. Now hurry. I can...feel myself fading. Like the Artist is...wiping me off the page."

I dropped the rabbit into the screen and watched him float down, back in his world. His feet and ears and teeth and everything else spun through the air like a tornado of bunny parts, reattaching themselves to the whole. By the time Harry Hare touched cartoon ground, he was himself again. Every piece. And he grinned up at me, waved with his fluffy, gloved hand. Took a long, deep swig from his carrot juice flask.

"I hate that there rabbit a somethin' fierce," Backwoods Bear said. "But if a someone's a gonna eat him, it's a gonna be me. And besides. Ain't right what this'n was a doin' to him. And he's kin to ya, little mister?"

Randall looked like he was holding on to life by a string. Face white, eyes hardly open at all. Making a sound like air seeping out of a balloon.

"Boyd..." He tried to reach out to me, but could only lift his hand a tiny bit. "H-help me..."

I only looked back at him for a second before looking

back at the bear. "Not anymore he's not."

"A-huck, a-huck, a-huck!" The bear's brown, cartoon body bounced when he laughed. "I reckon not. You have a good'n, little mister. You see the Artist anywhere 'round here, you a tell him ol' Backwoods Bear could use him a wife bear. You tell him that fer me, will ya?"

"I will. I'll tell him."

"Well all right then."

And Backwoods Bear hopped back into the computer screen.

Randall screamed all the way down.

***

I was sitting on the couch in the living room when Mom and Dad got back home.

I spent the rest of the day and all night cleaning up. My biggest worry was all the cartoon color soaked into the carpet or staining the walls, but I didn't find a single drop in the house, or outside in the street. Figured it must have got sucked into the device along with all the other rabbit parts.

Mom noticed her broken Jesus statues right away, which I knew she would. They were too busted up for me to even try and glue back together, so I just put that table back up right and piled up the pieces on top of that.

"Oh, Boyd! My-my Jesuses! What in the world did you boys do?"

"Where's your brother, son?" Dad said, crossing his arms.

I shrugged. Set the device down beside me on the couch. "He ran away."

"What you mean ran away?"

"Said he was sick of me and sick of you and sick of this place. Broke the Jesuses. Then he left. Didn't say where he was going."

I figured they'd hear about what happened to Mrs. Buckingham and the other dead neighbors eventually. I'd just tell them exactly what Randall told me to tell the police.

I was just a scared kid, that's all. Don't know nothing about nothing.

"And I'm guessin' it's your brother who did that to the goddamn yard out front?"

"Guess so. Don't know. Y'all told me to stay home, so I did. Not like I could drive around looking for him or anything."

They sighed and looked at each other for a long time. Then Dad walked off and said he was gonna call the police. File a report, then go out and start trying to look for Randall.

I grabbed the device and set it in my lap. Went back to watching my show.

"What's that?" Mom asked, sitting next to me and hugging me, kissing the side of my head.

"Like a iPad, but a knock off."

"Where'd you get that from?"

"Man came to the door. A Salesman. Said it was free."

"Nothing's free, Boyd. Who was this salesman?"

"Don't know. He wasn't here all that long."

She frowned at me. "You tell your daddy about him before he drives off, okay? I don't like it. Maybe he ought to tell the police about him."

"Okay. I guess so."

"What's that you're watching?"

I showed her and smiled.

"Harry Hare. You still watch that show?"

"My favorite."

She kissed my head again and stood. Looked exhausted. "Well don't stare at that thing too long. It'll hurt your eyes."

"Not as bad as when they look at us."

"What's that?" she said, already halfway into the kitchen.

"Nothing."

I sat back and grinned. Harry grinned back at me.

"Okay. Go ahead," I said. "Coast is clear."

"Whatever you say, Ugly!" Harry hopped into his rabbit hole and crawled until he reached his underground den.

Randall was tied to a chair by a cartoon worm that frowned at him while he tightened his body around him.

He wasn't a cartoon version of my brother. He was the real Randall. The hole in his chest was gone from where Backwoods Bear had punched through him. Carrots were stabbed into his nostrils, and all over his body, made him look like an orange porcupine.

Harry pulled his mallet out of his pocket, winked up at me, then bonked himself on the noggin. Stars appeared and spun around his head, and he wobbled, then fell flat on his back. His gloved hand reached up and plucked one of the stars out of the air, then he hopped back up to his feet.

"Now," the rabbit said, yanking the carrots out of Randall's thighs and swallowing them all whole. Using the star like a razor, he cut the crotch of Randall's jeans open. "I've never wondered what an ugly kid's dingaling looked like until right now. I wonder if it'll wiggle around afterward. What do you think, Earl?"

The worm laughed. "Let's find out."

"Hey, kid," Harry said, looking back up at me. "Might be a good time to close your eyes."

I didn't. I watched the whole thing. And it didn't wiggle at all.

***

A tap on the top of my head woke me up.

I didn't even realize I had fallen asleep until I woke up on the couch, the device lying on my thighs. It didn't get hot like my video games did. Stayed cold.

The screen was on. Randall's screams still poured out of it, and I saw that he had changed locations. Wasn't in Harry's rabbit hole anymore, but was now in the trash heap where Cooter Coon and all his Coon kin lived. He was nailed to a junk car while the Coons took turns shooting at him with their guns. The little one, Cooter Jr, used a slingshot to fling rocks at him.

When the bullets hit, a bleeding hole would open up on him. Then just as quick, it would heal up. I guess pain and suffering didn't exist in their world, but only for their kind.

The place kept him from dying, healed him up quick just like it did for the characters who inhabited it, but I could tell by the look on his face and the way he flinched every time a bullet hit home that he felt every bit of it.

I had been so caught up in looking at my brother on that screen that I forgot about the tap on my head that brought me out of sleep in the first place.

"Enjoying the show, Boyd?"

Wearing the same red outfit, the salesman stood behind the couch. The propeller on his hat still spun, even though they were in the house and all the windows were closed. He held a paddleball in one hand, bouncing it over and over without even looking at it. Smiling that long smile of his.

"Who are you?"

"Nobody. Nobody at all. Sorry about your brother. It wasn't anything that could be avoided. So I don't want you blaming yourself for it."

"I don't. He didn't have to do what he did and now he's paying for it."

"That's right. That's just what it is."

I looked over and realized Mom was sitting in her chair. Awake. Sipping coffee and watching a late night talk show. Probably waiting for Dad to get back. I felt kind of bad that they were gonna waste time looking for Randall when I knew exactly where he was. But it wasn't like they'd believe me anyway.

She didn't notice the salesman. Didn't notice that I was talking to him, either. Just sat there, looking bored and worried at the same time. The coffee cup shook every time she lifted it to her lips to take a sip.

"She can't see me," the salesman said.

"Why not?"

"She doesn't need to."

"What about me? Why can't she see me?"

"She can see you just fine. Snoozing on the couch."

I didn't like that. I wanted her to see me. Even if I looked crazy talking to nobody, I wanted her to be able to see me. And I didn't like that I could see the salesman. There wasn't anything I wanted from him.

"You know why I'm here?"

"You want it back, don't you?"

"I don't want anything. But I did come back for it. Other kids are waiting for their turn. And not just kids. Just about everyone has a favorite channel." He stopped paddling, leaned down and squinted at me. "How about you, Boyd? Is there anything else you'd like to see? Any other characters you'd like to meet? Could be anything. You could be a superhero. A war general. A cowboy. You could feast on all your favorite foods cooked just for you. The possibilities are endless."

I shook my head and handed over the device. There wasn't a channel in the world that was gonna change my mind. I had already seen my favorite character. And I was happy staying in my own world, where I knew the rules.

"You sure?"

"Positive."

"Yeah, I knew you'd say that. But it's my job to ask." He backed away from the couch, the device in one hand, the paddleball in the other. He got to bouncing the ball again, so fast it was just a red blur. "You be a good boy, Boyd. Explore your world. Get out there and live. Too much television will rot your brain."

I nodded and watched him disappear out the front door. I turned to look at Mom and she saw me. I breathed easier now that she could see me again.

"You're awake. Was the TV too loud?"

"No. Just had a weird dream."

"Wanna talk about it?"

"No." I stood and pulled the remote off the arm of her chair and clicked off the TV.

"I was watchin' that, you know."

"I've had enough TV. Will you come with me to my room? Read me a story?"

She smiled. "You haven't wanted me to read you a story since you were four."

Because someone told me reading was for faggots.

"Will you?"

"Of course I will." She set her cup on the end table and stretched when she stood, smiling at me the whole time.

I liked books a whole lot after that. Real books, not the one's for kids. Not the one's with pictures in them. I didn't like them just for the stories or the time I got to spend with Mom.

There were no colors in books. And something about the white pages and black words made me feel safe. We read every night, me and Mom. Sometimes Dad even came in and joined us. We talked about Randall, but after a while even that stopped. I got the feeling, deep down, Mom and Dad were glad he was gone.

And I was the happiest, ugliest kid in my whole world.

I WANT TO DIE
BY SYLVIA SOSKA

The night was silent. A few lazy snowflakes floated down to their fallen comrades which covered the streets in the early winter. The serenity was broken as a young boy erupted from his childhood home and ran down the street.

He could taste the blood in his mouth as he ran out of the house. He could hear his mother and father yelling after him. Or maybe they were just yelling.

There is a price to pay when dealing with damaged psyches, but no one gets a psychological analysis when they make a baby, so parenthood becomes the battleground for self-medication. In this case, a few punches to the head and body in place of words that could have better expressed the feelings that had come rushing to the surface.

Liam ran down the darkened street, through the cold, putting as much distance between his house and himself as possible. Sometimes, if they were fired up enough, his father would run after him and drag him back into the house. It got really bad then.

At that time of year and that time of night, the world could be very lonely and quiet. It could be a harsh world for 'the kid who gets beat up at home' – other students avoided Liam like they could catch what he had. Maybe they were afraid that if they got close to him, their parents would start hitting them too. He felt so alone and there was no end in sight for him.

In the still of the evening, he turned down a familiar street to a road that led to his elementary school playground. No one was on the streets and the school yard was as vacant as afterhours tend to be there.

Liam slowed his pace as he entered the property. Panting, his breath hung in the air as he found a bench to sit down on.

Being alone is a funny thing. Everyone lies to you, tells you that if you really need someone, then someone will be there for you. No one tells you that all the hard things you have to go through, you have to go through alone. Unless there is someone else there to make you miserable.

Silent tears rolled down Liam's face. His head sunk as the hopelessness consumed him. Should he run away? If so, where? He'd told people before and nothing had ever come of it. Does he suffer four more years until he graduates and moves out? Does he hit the gym and get some muscle to defend himself?

"No one cares."

No one cares. What would be the point of it, he thought bitterly. *I have nothing. No one will ever care about me. Nothing will ever get better.*

"I want to die."

The sentence came out easier than it should have, but there was a comfort in saying it out loud. There was a peace in letting go. Giving up on nothing was barely giving up. It made more sense than the other options.

More tears joined his quiet sobs as he lowered his head again. Liam felt the proverbial last fuck he had drifting far away into the eternity of darkness that seemed to surround him. At that moment, Liam wished for death, for an escape more than any other wish his heart could muster.

A chain rattled.

Liam lifted his head. *Was that a chain just now?* He looked at the abandoned schoolyard to see it was no longer such. Less than twenty feet away from him, but still shrouded in darkness, stood a man with a chain in his hand.

Embarrassed, Liam looked away. Had the man seen him crying? His eyes scanned the ground for the dog that belonged to the man, but saw none. *Why would he be holding a chain leash if there is no dog? There has to be a dog.*

Liam looked back towards the man, a better look this time. The figure stood facing him, its posture just slightly off. There was no dog.

As Liam looked at the chain man, a feeling of dread

climbed up his spine. *You asked for death, and here he is. He only comes for the boys and girls that invite him, just like you. He's here now for you.*

The chain rattled.

I don't want to die.

Liam was up and out of the schoolyard faster than he thought he was capable of. He didn't dare look back until he was running down his street towards his house. Behind him was nothing. There was no one. He was once again alone.

They say you should never give a name to demons. That if you recognize their existence, you are welcoming them into your world. Human emotion is a funny thing. It can create and destroy, and in Liam's situation, it called something to end what he couldn't until he realized it wasn't what he truly wanted.

Liam never told anyone about the chain man. As he grew into the man he would become and people shared supernatural experiences, he would stay quiet, and if questioned, he would say that nothing ever happened.

And in a way, he was right. Nothing happened. Even though he had seen the chain man once, many years ago, when he was at his lowest.

FIRST DATE STUFF
BY JEN SOSKA

"Ask me anything," she said teasingly as she sat down next to him.

"First date stuff?" he replied warmly.

"Ask me anything means ask me *anything*," she retorted. "It doesn't have to be first date stuff."

"Umm... do you have any brothers or sisters?"

"That's boring."

"I'm sorry. Um, I can think up something better..." he stumbled.

"I'm just teasing," she cooed. "You're so cute when you get flustered, I love it. Yes, brothers *and* sisters. I come from a big family."

"Where are you from?"

"All over."

She cuddled up closer to him on the couch. She was beautiful. Ivory skin. Crimson lips. Emerald eyes. Dark hair. She made him nervous.

"My turn," she said. "What do you look for in a girl?"

"Can I just say you?" he asked quietly, dropping his gaze.

"Yes. Yes, you can."

She leaned in and kissed him hard. He was taken back by the sudden escalation, but quickly found his rhythm and kissed her back. Her teeth grazed his bottom lip, and she bit him gently. He chuckled softly, then she bit down hard, making him jump.

"Jesus, careful!"

He brought his fingertips to his lips, carefully assessing the damage. Tiny pin pricks of sensation as his lips went numb. He tried to get up, but she easily pushed him onto his back. There was enough feeling left for him to feel her weight as she straddled him. He tried to speak, but only a soft moan escaped his throat.

"Careful," she cooed. "It's okay. I like you."

He tried to move as complete paralysis set in. She watched it take effect with morbid curiosity.

"I want you to meet my family. I know, it's a little soon in your culture, but when I meet someone I care about, I just want to start our lives together. You know what I mean?"

She warmly placed a hand on the side of his face.

"Just try to relax. It'll be better that way."

Her left eye began to tear as an insect leg reached out from the corner of her lids.

He stared in horror. A solitary tear rolled down her cheek as she stared casually at him.

Two more legs emerged, feeling their way around her eye. Slowly, tiny spiders scuttled from her hairline. The spider trapped beneath her eye pulled itself free, followed by a bloody tear drop.

He tried to scream, but it caught in his throat. His blood ran cold.

More and more spiders erupted from underneath her clothing, crawling up her neck.

"They're all so excited to meet you."

She leaned in and kissed him deeply. He could hear his heart pounding in his ears. Something touched his tongue as it moved from her mouth into his, the massive creature forcing its way down his throat.

They crawled all over him, sneaking their way under his clothes, into his open mouth.

Inside of him.

"Welcome to the family," she whispered.

SHANE MCKENZIE is the author of many books, including *Muerte Con Carne*, *Pus Junkies*, *Addicted to the Dead*, *All You Can Eat*, *Mutt*, *Fat Off Sex and Violence*, and lots more. He wrote comics for Zenescope Entertainment in their Oz series, Grimm Fairy Tales series, and Grimm Tales of Terror series. The film *El Gigante*, done by LuchaGore Press and directed by Gigi Saul Guerrero, is based on the first chapter of *Muerte Con Carne*. He lives in Austin, TX with his wife and daughter. He's staring at you right now.

deadite press

"Header" **Edward Lee** - In the dark backwoods, where law enforcement doesn't dare tread, there exists a special type of revenge. Something so awful that it is only whispered about. Something so terrible that few believe it is real. Stewart Cummings is a government agent whose life is going to Hell. His wife is ill and to pay for her medication he turns to bootlegging. But things will get much worse when bodies begin showing up in his sleepy small town. Victims of an act known only as "a Header."

"Entombed II" **Brian Keene**- It has been several months since the disease known as Hamelin's Revenge decimated the world. Civilization has collapsed and the dead far outnumber the living. The survivors seek refuge from the roaming zombie hordes, but one-by-one, those shelters are falling. Twenty-five survivors barricade themselves inside a former military bunker buried deep beneath a luxury hotel. They are safe from the zombies...but are they safe from one another?

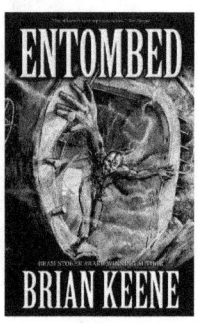

"Zombies and Shit" **Carlton Mellick III** - Twenty people wake to find themselves in a boarded-up building in the middle of the zombie wasteland. They soon discover they have been chosen as contestants on a popular reality show called Zombie Survival. Each contestant is given a backpack of supplies and a unique weapon. Their goal: be the first to make it through the zombie-plagued city to the pick-up zone alive. But because there's only one seat available on the helicopter, the contestants not only have to fight against the hordes of the living dead, they must also fight each other.

"Muerte Con Carne" **Shane McKenzie** - Human flesh tacos, hardcore wrestling, and angry cannibal Mexicans, Welcome to the Border! Felix and Marta came to Mexico to film a documentary on illegal immigration. When Marta suddenly goes missing, Felix must find his lost love in the small border town. A dangerous place housing corrupt cops, borderline maniacs, and something much more worse than drug gangs, something to do with a strange Mexican food cart…

"Like Porno for Psychos" Wrath James White - From a world-ending orgy to home liposuction. From the hidden desires of politicians to a woman with a fetish for lions. This is a place where necrophilia, self-mutilation, and murder are all roads to love. Like Porno for Psychos collects the most extreme erotic horror from the celebrated hardcore horror master. Wrath James White is your guide through sex, death, and the darkest desires of the heart.

"Bigfoot Crank Stomp" Erik Williams - Bigfoot is real and he's addicted to meth! It should have been so easy. Get in, kill everyone, and take all the money and drugs. That was Russell and Mickey's plan. But the drug den they were raiding in the middle of the woods holds a dark secret chained up in the basement. A beast filled with rage and methamphetamine and tonight it will break loose. Nothing can stop Bigfoot's drug-fueled rampage and before the sun rises there is going to be a lot of dead cops and junkies.

"The Dark Ones" Bryan Smith - They are The Dark Ones. The name began as a self-deprecating joke, but it stuck and now it's a source of pride. They're the one who don't fit in. The misfits who drink and smoke too much and stay out all hours of the night. Everyone knows they're trouble. On the outskirts of Ransom, TN is an abandoned, boarded-up house. Something evil happened there long ago. The evil has been contained there ever since, locked down tight in the basement—until the night The Dark Ones set it free . . .

"Genital Grinder" Ryan Harding - *"Think you're hardcore? Think again. If you've handled everything Edward Lee, Wrath James White, and Bryan Smith have thrown at you, then put on your rubber parka, spread some plastic across the floor, and get ready for Ryan Harding, the unsung master of hardcore horror. Abandon all hope, ye who enter here. Harding's work is like an acid bath, and pain has never been so sweet."*
- Brian Keene

AVAILABLE FROM AMAZON.COM

www.ingramcontent.com/pod-product-compliance
Lightning Source LLC
Chambersburg PA
CBHW070114030726
47506CB00002B/743

9781621051893